DIE AUFMÜPFIGE EHEFRAU

DIE DREI EHEFRAUEN
BUCH ZWEI

JESS MICHAELS

Jedes Buch wird nur dank eines riesigen Teams von Personen Wirklichkeit. Danke an Mackenzie, die mir immer hilft, die richtigen Worte in der richtigen Reihenfolge zu finden. Danke an meine Mutter und an Kelsey, die immer bemerken, was wir übersehen. An Teresa für ihre großartigen Titelbilder. An Ana und Nina, die mir helfen, mein Online-Ich am Laufen zu halten.

Und danke an Michael, meinen besten Freund, meinen Komplizen, meinen Business-Guru und die Liebe meines Lebens.

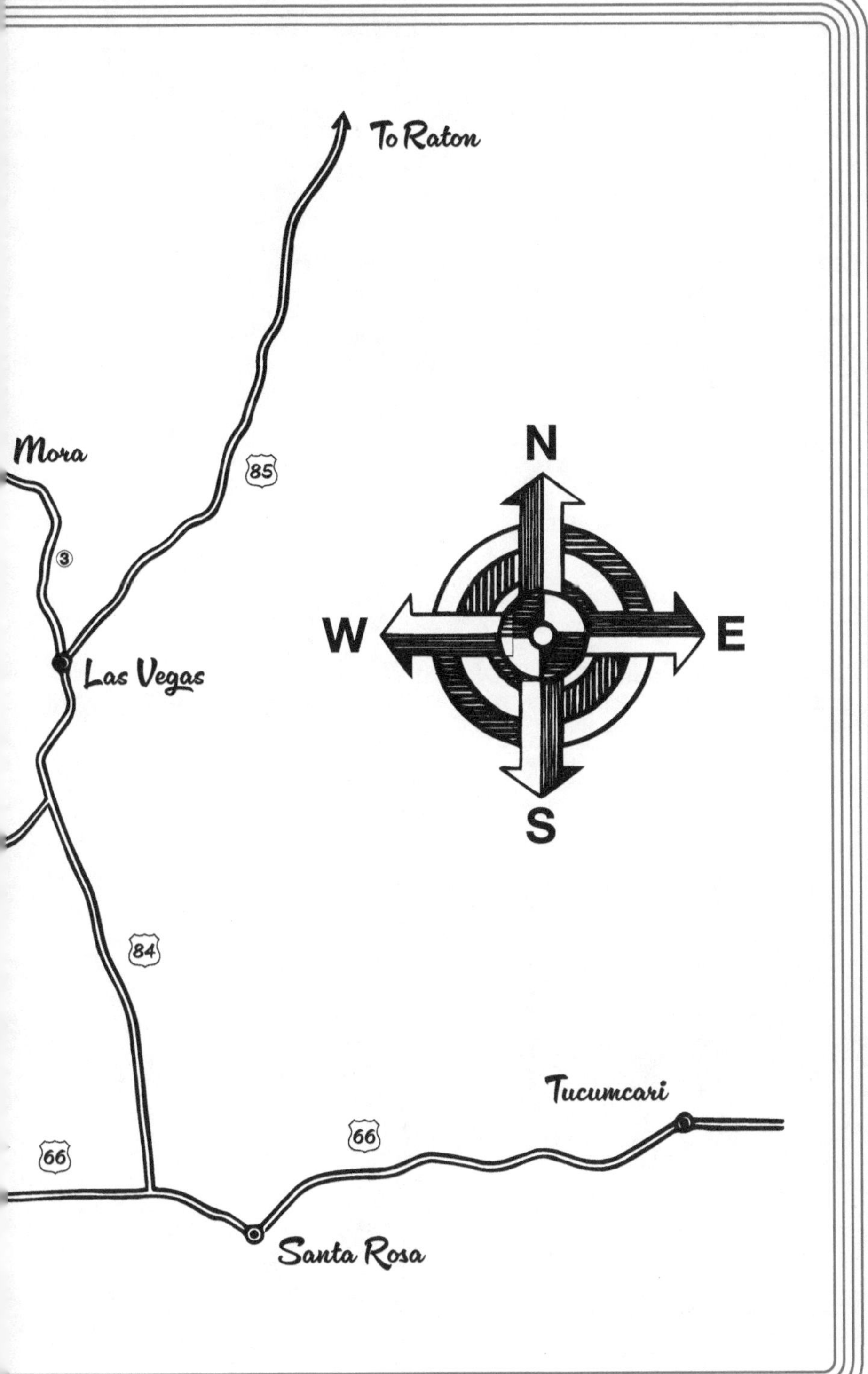

To Raton
Mora
85
3
Las Vegas
N
W
E
S
84
Tucumcari
66
66
Santa Rosa

THE DESCENT

BY FRITZ PETERS

VANITAS VANITATUM
PUBLISHING
LOS ANGELES

VANITAS VANITATUM PUBLISHING
LOS ANGELES, CALIFORNIA
6300 Canoga Avenue, Suite 1330 | Woodland Hills, CA 91367
www.vanitasvanitatum.com

The Fritz Peters Collection
Managing Editor: Alexandra Carbone
Cover Design: Mathieu Carratier
Typesetting: Stewart A. Williams

First Published: New York: E. P. Dutton & Company, 1952

ISBN 978-1-957241-06-7 / 1-957241-07-4
ISBN COLLECTION 978-1-957241-00-5

LCCN: 2023916486

THE

DESCENT

US 85 gradually descends and declines sharply at
LA BAJADA (the descent) HILL—a sheer bluff
capped with black basalt at the end of LA BAJADA
MESA.

—*New Mexico – A Guide to the Colorful State*
(Hastings House, New York)

We are all conceived in close Prison; in our Mothers wombes, we are close Prisoners all; when we are borne, we are borne but to the liberty of the house; Prisoners still, though within larger walls; and then all our life is but a going out to the place of Execution, to death. Now was there ever any man seen to sleep in the Cart, between Newgate, and Tyborne? between the Prison, and the place of Execution, does any man sleep? And we sleep all the way; from the womb to the grave we are never thoroughly awake; but passe on with such dreames, and imaginations as these, I may live as well, as another, and why should I dye, rather than another? but awake, and tell me, sayes this Text, *Quis homo?* who is that other that thou talkest of? *What man is he that liveth, and shall not see death?*

—John Donne
(From Sermon XXVII)
—*To the Lords upon Easter Day at the Communion, the King being dangerously sick at New-Market. March 28, 1619*

NOVEMBER 12, 1951

1

Doris Hart was thirty-four years old, unhappily married, childless, and—as she had told her psychiatrist at her first session—sexually unsatisfied. Her weekly visits to the hairdresser had not altered the quality of her hair which was coarse, and the various styles they tried out on her had done nothing to make her any more beautiful. Having failed to improve her ruddy complexion with the aid of Elizabeth Arden and Helena Rubenstein, she now bought her cosmetics at any ten-cent store.

Since before her marriage to Donald Hart, a bookkeeper in a department store in Albuquerque, New Mexico, she had supported herself by working as a supervisor in the Simpson Memorial Hospital which was located inconveniently on U.S. highway 85, eleven miles north of Bernalillo, a distance of about twenty-eight miles from her home in Albuquerque. She had continued to work after her marriage because she didn't believe that, in what she called "our time," any man should have to support a woman.

On the 12th of November, 1951, she went on duty at the hospital as night supervisor at eight o'clock in the evening. She had stopped to see Dr. Cramwell, her psychiatrist, on the way to work and he had somehow managed to suggest to her that her job might have something to do with the unsatisfactory relationship she had with her husband. She could not, as she took off her coat in the nurses' washroom in the basement of the hospital, remember the conversation very well. She could not even remember who had said what, and thought to herself that perhaps it was her own idea. It had occurred to her earlier in the day that alternating months on night duty—all during her marriage—could constitute a problem. Was it she herself who had (unconsciously?) suggested this to Dr. Cramwell?

She put on her cap, took a look at her face in the mirror, and decided to forget the whole thing. She believed in psychiatry, of course, but it was terribly embarrassing to talk about your sex life (or lack of it) to a perfectly strange man; particularly when he sat there behind his glasses with what always seemed to her to be a withdrawn and all-knowing look on his face.

Nonetheless when she was seated at her desk in the emergency room, she thought about Doctor Cramwell again. What was it that he had said so casually about her job? *Do you like working in a hospital?* Something like that. Now she was able to look at the room, with all its white cabinets, its stocks of plasma, its wheelchairs and rolling beds, without wondering why she shouldn't like her job. Or *was* that what he had meant?

She reminded herself sternly that she was not going to think about Cramwell any more and looked at the duty list. Dr. Fenton of Bernalillo was the duty doctor, and Morales and Brown were on call for any special emergency. Everything was in order, all the emergency-room stocks were up-to-date, there were three empty beds available on Ward 5 and one on 6. The temperature was twenty-four above zero at six-thirty p.m., the road conditions were generally good though scattered snow had been reported in the mountains. There had been no emergency cases in the hospital for eleven days. It looked like a quiet night.

Doris glanced at the wall clock just as the telephone rang. The clock read eight-twelve and the call was a routine report about a sleet storm in west Texas on Highway 66; the storm was proceeding westward although it had not yet reached the border of New Mexico. Since it was over two hundred miles from Albuquerque to the Texas border, and since there were hospitals along the way—not to mention the hospitals in Albuquerque—it was not likely they would get anything from that direction. Anyone driving in a sleet storm after dark would probably have sense enough to stop anyway. As for U.S. 85 between the hospital and Santa Fe, there was not much danger from there. The snow was probably north of Santa Fe. Except for the fact that people could always have accidents—particularly on La Bajada Hill, there was no reason—no special reason—why they should have them tonight.

Doris lighted a cigarette, glanced at the sign on the wall which proclaimed "No Smoking" in large red letters, and settled down to read the book Dr. Cramwell had recommended to her: *Man and Woman, A Study in Primary Human Types* by, oddly enough, Dr. Cramwell himself.

2

AT NINE-SEVENTEEN P.M., DR. FENTON had been in the corridor of the Simpson Memorial Hospital for exactly twenty minutes. Although none of the cases had come in yet, an unprecedented number of nine accident cases—all coming to that hospital—had been reported.

He paced the floor, his ears—they felt to him as if they were standing up like the ears of a rabbit—alerted for the sound of the door opening at the end of the hall. For what seemed the millionth time, he was asking himself why he had ever decided to become a doctor. The human race, and in his heart he told himself that he had come to hate it for its stupidity, was, unquestionably, the lowest form of organism in the entire world. What could possibly be the sense of dragging him out on a cold night to save—or try to save—the lives of a bunch of idiots who drove wildly through the night at fantastic speeds on highways that were designed, in his estimation, for horse-carts and nothing more? Why should these people be saved? Why should anyone lift a finger to help them when the youth of the country (including his own son) were being killed left and right in Korea? Why not kill them here first?

He stopped at the door to the emergency room and stared at the woman sitting calmly at the desk. Something about the heavy placidity of her reddish, ugly face irritated him beyond control. The way she sat there!

"Is everything ready?" he asked brusquely. "Plasma? Sutures? Dressings? What about the nurses? How many have you got on duty? Where's the surgical nurse? What about oxygen? Do I have to think of everything?"

The woman stared at him coldly before she replied. "Everything," she said in a firm, icy tone of voice, "is *always* ready, Doctor Fenton. I haven't been working here for..."

He cut her off with a weary gesture of his hand. "All right, all right, I'll take your word for it. Don't tell me how efficient you are." He started away from the door, sighed, and turned back. "I'm sorry, Mrs. Hart. I'm nervous tonight. It all seems so useless. Shouldn't they begin coming in now?"

Mrs. Hart's face did not exactly melt, but it softened a little. The thing you had to remember about Fenton was that he was hot-headed. If only Doctor Morales was on duty instead. The Spanish-American doctors never seemed to lose their heads in spite of their so-called Latin temperament. She looked at the clock, paused, looked back at the heavy-set, gray-haired man in the doorway, and said: "They should be here any minute. Don't you think it might be a good idea to get one of the other doctors in? If they all come in at once, it might..."

Again he cut her off with a gesture and a sharp look. "No. They'll all be in shock anyway. The only thing we'll be able to do is get them to bed. We aren't going to be doing surgery tonight, after all!"

She shrugged her shoulders and looked away from him. Like all the other doctors, he was going to try and get the cases for himself! Or was that strictly true? In an effort to be fair, she acknowledged that they didn't usually operate right away, and it was true that almost all accident cases were either less serious than they seemed to be, or else so serious that almost nothing could be done for them. And they were always in a state of shock, as Fenton had said. The important thing was to keep them warm, get them to bed, and give them plasma. Besides, Morales or Brown would have to come from Albuquerque and the cases would all be in before they could get here. Instead of asking Fenton, perhaps she should have called one of them on her own initiative.

She looked at the book still lying open on her desk, and read the sentence:

"It must be accepted that the nature of woman is such that the male will always automatically rebel against certain, what might be called, primeval female sexual manifestations, and with this in mind, it may be assumed from the start that psychological problems are an essential—in fact an inescapable—factor in the marriage relationship."

—and then she closed the book. What on earth did that mean? She must remember to ask Dr. Cramwell on Wednesday.

She had only had time to put the book away when she heard the door opening at the end of the hall and got up from her desk.

3

BY MIDNIGHT IT WAS ALL over. Doctor Fenton and the police were gone; Doris was back at her desk; the emergency room was cleaned up, and all the patients were, at least temporarily, all right. One was dead, three were on the critical list. The information reports were reasonably complete on most of them, but they had been unable to get the relatives' names in one case.

Doris looked at the reports again; she was nervous and—she made herself be honest about this—angry. She could not understand why she should feel anger and it made her question herself guiltily. Perhaps, as Dr. Cramwell had said (well, implied!) there was something about this job that had a bad effect on her. She reminded herself sharply that he had not said, or implied, anything of the kind. That had only been her own interpretation of the way he had put a very simple question to her. Somehow, he *made* her feel guilty! Damn Dr. Cramwell!

She leafed through the reports quickly, and then put them to one side of the desk. She did not want to look at them again, she did not want to think about them any more. What kind of a world was it anyway? A world in which, as Fenton had pointed out, not so illogically, man was continually fighting himself while the doctors and nurses broke their backs trying to save them...for what? No wonder Fenton had almost collapsed and left even before Doctor Morales had time to get there. It was surprising enough that he had finally asked her to call Morales. He was really in a bad way.

She decided to go back upstairs and take another look at the patients. She'd seen them all only a short time before, but there was—as she had often told her husband and as she had said defensively to Doctor Cramwell—no good reason not to be too careful (was she feeling guilty about *that* now?); in fact there was no such thing as *too* careful or *too* efficient. As she walked to the elevator, she reminded herself grimly that she still wished that some of the nurses (or the other supervisor, for that matter) could be as careful as she was. The trouble with too many people nowadays was that they didn't *care*.

NOVEMBER 8, 1951

1

On Thursday, November 8th, 1951, the sun rose—according to a man-invented device called *time,* and obedient to the predictions in almanacs, newspapers, and on various calendars—at 6:43 a.m. Of the people who were awake and aware of this phenomenon (and considering the hour there were a good many in the United States) only one among them was intent on what was happening. The man was named Charles Wells. He stood in front of the window of the second floor bathroom of his house in Three Bridges, New York, looking west, acknowledging the rising of the sun on the eastern slope of the valley before it had lighted up the town.

Before the sun had risen, there had been a glow of light over the valley and while it may have disturbed or awakened other inhabitants of the town, there was no outer sign—nothing in the houses and streets—to indicate that the night had ended for people.

Partly because he was an old man, Mr. Wells did not mind waiting and watching, nor did he mind waking early. This morning, although the bathroom was warm and he was well-clothed in woolen pajamas (the last pair his wife had bought for him before her death), his bed-socks, fleece-lined slippers, and heavy bathrobe, he shivered as he looked out upon the frost-covered landscape.

It was curious, he thought, that man should speak of the sun as something that could *rise.* He was appalled at this indication of the self-involvement of mankind; an egoism that permitted the assumption (despite any knowledge to the contrary) that even the sun related its actions to the welfare and needs of the earth. From the point of view of the sun itself, it must be vastly different, his thoughts went on; and he found himself trying to become the sun's eye, "rising" minute by minute, hour by hour, across the entire surface of the planet. Actually, from that height and distance, the sun could neither know nor care about what it was doing (in or to the mind of man). It might perhaps be watching, listlessly and indifferently, the slow revolving earth as it jostled people into wakefulness, brought them light, or—at the same moment—laid the cold hand of darkness upon them. What is given must be, simultaneously, taken; for every ray of light or warmth a corresponding breath of cold and dark existed.

The picture in his mind—the idea that through his own Imagination he could *become,* for however long he was able to sustain the mental effort, the sun—excited him. He began to see himself (in fact all of humanity) as infinitesimal organisms subject to cosmic forces which were neither interested nor concerned with what is called life and exis-tence. As if he were a part of the sun, he looked at the universe and the functioning of the laws of nature, and he began to feel what seemed to be his own nothingness, his true place in the world. He also had a sense of what was happening to the world with the sunrise...why not call it the *earth-turn?*... Earlier, before it had come to Three Bridges (and did it notice this little blotch of a town with its buildings, its streets, and the great four-lane highway to the south?) the sun had illuminated the Atlantic seaboard, the Atlantic Ocean itself. Before that Great Britain had awakened (to its new government and its new restrictions); France had felt its warmth. Earlier still, the Russians, the strugglers in Korea, the Pacific Ocean had felt the impact of the beginning day and the light.

It gave him a sense of infinity and grandeur within himself as he went backwards around the globe that he visualized in his mind. For when his thoughts had carried him (reversing the course of the light) across the Pacific and to the California coast, he had crossed through early into late, through the states of beginning and ending: where there had been night, there was now day, and where there had been day, there was now only darkness and perhaps the eye of the moon. The beginnings and the endings were only for men, and never for the sun itself. Endlessly, the sun radiated light and warmth, while its satellite worlds revolved and revolved, warming themselves like dogs before a fire. But for the worlds the day would end, and for the dog the fire would go out...

His mind-picture flashed westward: soon Detroit and Chicago would respond to the impact of the sun's first rays and perhaps at that identical moment, Moscow or Berlin (he was not very sure of the distances) would fade into the night.

He looked away from the window, drew his bathrobe closer about his shoulders, destroying the pictures of his imagination, coming back to where he stood on his own two feet. His day, and his part in the world—in life—however useless and small, had begun again. Because he was old and because of the temper of his character, he smiled to himself. Not only was it, in the daily sense, one more beginning; but at his time of life each day was bringing him closer to the end of his day on earth. He was conscious of the approach of death—or was it his own faltering step in death's direction? Whichever it was, and in whatever way they would finally meet, it did not matter to him now. It would have mattered a little more before Molly's death. It mattered now only because of Peter. But he had nothing else in the world, nothing to hold him back, nothing to make him want to prolong a life that had already been long.

Without looking back at the view of the land from the window, he shuffled to the door of the bathroom. He would go downstairs and put on the water for the coffee. Peter liked his coffee as soon as he was up, and it was almost seven o'clock. He had heard the clock strike the three-quarter hour just a few minutes before.

Peter Wells heard his father's step on the stairs. He was astonished at the old man's vigor at eighty-two and he felt a twinge of conscience about leaving him. He knew that nothing could stop him from getting into his car that very afternoon and going away. He could see himself as he would be after lunch: behind the wheel of the Oldsmobile with Kelly (he glanced down into the face of his brown, white, and black half-Beagle, half-Bassett Hound, waiting expectantly at the foot of the bed) on the seat beside him, driving out of the town where he had been born. He would pause at the junction with Route 20, look right and left, and then pull out into the right-hand lane. Then and only then would he let the power of the car out.

He smiled at this picture of himself, glad to be going, and then sat up in bed. He must remember, he told himself as he pulled his feet up from under the covers, to fill the car with gasoline. And was there anything else? His bags would only take a few minutes to pack; there was no one in Three Bridges he needed to see or to say goodbye to, apart from his father and Mrs. Jones. Mrs. Jones who would be arriving at seven-thirty to get the old man's breakfast; who would come every day for as long as Charles Wells was alive.

He jumped out of bed and tore off his pajamas, shivering as he seized his underwear from the chair. The old codger was already puttering away in the kitchen—probably making coffee. He'd better get down!

2

THE LIGHT DID NOT PENETRATE through the venetian blinds in the apartment of Mr. and Mrs. Stephen Williams, on East Seventeenth Street, in the borough of Manhattan. But fear of the day awakened Marjorie Williams, and what his mother would have called "journey pride" awakened her husband.

The fear in Marjorie aroused her by knotting itself into a solid pain that she could actually feel in her body. The anticipation of his journey was something that Steve could feel, but there was no pain connected with it. His pain began a few seconds after he was fully awake, and it was a pain that would not, he knew, last. He got up quickly, smiled sardonically at the rumpled bedding on the livingroom couch where he had slept, and then walked into the bathroom. He hoped against hope that his wife was still sleeping; if she had taken a pill the night before, she might not wake up at all! Still he'd have to say goodbye to her, and there was no point in trying to avoid these last few hours. It was already six forty-five, and with luck he could be on his way by eight—perhaps even earlier.

As he lathered his face to shave, Steve's eyes moved rapidly, peering into corners, magnifying the dust and the disorder of the bathroom. It was, to him, exactly like his wife; or rather as she had come to be. He knew, although he had no feeling about it, that in his withdrawal from her (for reasons he called "perfectly human") he had retreated into an area of order and neatness that was in enormous contrast to the sloppiness of her life; and as they had, gradually, during the two years of their marriage, ceased to communicate with each other, her whole way of life had become disorganized. From a woman who had kept her home with some pride, who had enjoyed cooking his meals and who had made an effort to look well, she had—in his mind—disintegrated into what had become for him a symbol of formlessness. He found this unforgivable, although his mind had not been able to deny that it was in direct relation to the weakening of the ties between them that this had taken place.

Before their marriage, and for the first few months after they were actually married, it was he who had been the aggressor, the man in love, the pursuer. But as the rope of marriage had tightened around them in such a way that he was never away from her, he had begun to feel himself hardening inside. This sensation had at first betrayed itself by a slackening of his masculinity; but over a period of months he had gradually ceased to be the one who gave their life its direction.

He finished shaving, rinsed his face, brushed his teeth, combed his hair, and looked at himself almost arrogantly in the mirror. He remembered that his father had once said to him that no human situation is ever entirely the fault of one person. He believed this with his mind, although his heart and even his body resisted the truth—if it was truth—of that statement. The very state of marriage had become intolerable to him and had produced something in his wife that terrified him. Why was it that women had to have *everything* from a man? Why was it necessary to them not only to love and be loved, but to possess and be possessed? And with each area of a man's heart or life that they possessed, the desire to acquire and own more increased. She had become to him the incarnation of insatiability. Not content with the ownership of his body, the sharing of everything he did, she had also to know what he was thinking and why he thought it, everything he was doing when he could not be in her actual physical presence...and why he did it.

He was not completely proud of his reflection as it stared back at him. On the other hand, he did feel a certain integrity, a feeling of cleanliness, as if he—at least—had never relaxed his standards, never despoiled himself in the course of their marriage. He looked away from the mirror and walked out of the bathroom. When he had closed the door quietly, he listened at the door of the bedroom and heard no sound. He prayed again that she would not awaken until the last moment.

In the living room, he dressed quickly, removed the bedding from the couch, folded it, and put it in the closet. Then he went into the kitchen, put on the water for the coffee, opened a can of concentrated orange juice, mixed it in an empty milk bottle, and lighted a cigarette. He hesitated before going back into the living room. He had nothing more to do now except to pack his overnight bag and eat his breakfast. He was ready to go.

3

Marjorie Williams had been awake, lying silent and motionless in the double bed in the bedroom; the bed that had once been a proof of their togetherness and was now merely one more example of the emptiness of her life. Even so, it was the only safe place in the world. It seemed to her that the lack of action plus the warmth of the bed and her own stillness in it would somehow postpone what she knew to be inevitable. When Steve had given up his job a week before because, as he had said: "I cannot explain it, but I have to get away," she had known—in every way that it is possible for a woman to know such a thing—that this day and departure were the only things she had to anticipate. The faint hope which still imposed itself upon her in spite of her desire to be realistic was that at least this was not necessarily the end.

She could not believe it possible that there was not some meaning for him in their marriage. Over and over again, she said to herself desperately: "He loved me once...that I can still love him as I do must prove *something.*" If she did not get up, and by not getting up forced him to come to her, perhaps the departure would be postponed, perhaps he would not go at all. But even as she thought this she knew that it would be that very forcing that would drive him away even more certainly.

She looked at her watch. It was almost half past seven. He had said casually the night before—he was so courteous, so polite, so out of reach—that he would be leaving at about eight o'clock, and her instincts warned her that he was already straining to get away and that it was only a habit of false gallantry or code of behavior that kept him from leaving the apartment without even speaking to her.

The fear struck deeply then. He might do just that! She got up quickly, put a wrapper over her nightgown, and started for the bedroom door. With her hand on the knob she hesitated. He might see her as she went to the bathroom. How did she look? She moved quickly to her dressing table, sat down and ran a comb through her hair, looked at her face, and shook her head. She did not have the energy to make herself up, there was no time; and (she said this to herself as she looked disparagingly at her face in the mirror): "That is what you are. Powder and lipstick won't change it." She shrugged her shoulders as if to throw off some enormous burden, stood up, and walked firmly out of the bedroom. He was not in sight, but she could hear him in the kitchen.

In the bathroom, she too looked around. But it was not the dust or the disorder that she saw. What she saw was the tight, prim arrangement of his toilet articles, waiting to be put into an overnight bag. He lived with what was strictly necessary and the economy represented by his razor, his shaving brush, shaving cream, toothbrushes, tooth powder, seemed in vicious contrast to the bottles of lotions, creams, boxes of powder, soap, toilet water; all the things of hers that spread themselves in a jumble over the shelves. How cold it must be to live in such sterile cleanliness, such concentrated preoccupation with order. She felt a sudden wave of sympathy for this man she had married. Not Stephen Williams, her husband, but this human being who was locked inside the prison of his own integrity. As he sometimes said: "There are certain things people do not do..."

It was perhaps the first time that she had ever seen what now seemed to her the tight little fence of limitations around him. It made her feel better, less guilty, less...to *blame.* She washed her face hurriedly, made it up, touched her hair with her hands and then, with her head erect, walked out of the bathroom. At least, she would try to say goodbye to him on his own terms.

4

MR. AND MRS. HENRY FRANKLIN had always taken a winter vacation. While this had been, originally, Mr. Franklin's idea and Mrs.
Franklin had acceded to it in what she called, privately, a weak moment
early in their marriage, she had come to like it, otherwise she would
certainly have changed it. When she awakened on the morning of
November 8th, just as the sun sent its first pale rays through the open
window of their bedroom overlooking Lake Michigan, she thought
to herself, pleasantly, that the Cadillac was waiting in the garage, the
bags were packed, the travelling clothes laid out. In a few hours they
would be on their way.

She turned her head on the pillow to glance across the narrow space
between her bed and that of her husband. He looked very small when
he was asleep and this gave her a curious sensation of power. He was,
in fact, small, but the act of sleep seemed to reduce his size still further.
She had the feeling that she could have put him in her compact.

She raised her well-developed right arm, reached across the space
between them, and shook his shoulder vigorously. "Henry," she said,
"get up."

From a dream, in which he was pursued and almost overtaken by
some enormous unrecognizable monster, Henry came suddenly and
agonizingly to the feeling of his wife's hand on his shoulder. The terror
at the touch as he opened his eyes was displaced by the security of the

knowledge that it was only Mabel's hand. Before he was fully awake, he had reacted automatically, said "Yes, dear," swung his feet over the side of the bed, and was standing up. Only then did he realize that he was, really, awake. He leaned over and kissed her. "Good morning, dear," he said.

And then he put his slippers on.

At nine o'clock they were ready to go. The elevator boy came for the luggage, they said goodbye to the maid, and Henry, at Mabel's suggestion, telephoned to his office. It was not until they were downstairs that Mabel remembered that she had left the medicine kit packed in the bathroom. It contained: BiSoDol, Aspirin, Anacin, Bufferin, Nembutal, Seconal, Band-Aids, Witch Hazel, Chlorets, Iodine, Unguentine, Noxzema, Skol, Skat, Air-Wick, extra tooth-brushes and toothpaste, dental floss, Ortho-Gynol, and a month's supply of Super Tampax. "Henry," she said. "The medicine kit. In the bathroom."

He went obediently to the elevator.

At nine-seventeen, Central Standard Time, they were in the car, with Mrs. Franklin at the wheel. Given good driving conditions, they had every reason to assume that St. Louis would be their destination that night. The reservations had already been made, and while it was not a great distance, there was no point, as Mabel always said, in travelling too fast. The reason for driving was to see the country. She started the motor and shifted into first. The sound of the motor, the acknowledgment in that sound of its power, security, and strength pleased Mrs. Franklin.

As for Henry, he would have preferred an Austin.

5

WHEN MARY HUME AWAKENED IN the tourist camp in Flagstaff, Arizona, she said to herself: "I think we are absolutely insane." She looked at her husband, still sleeping in the bed beside her, at the cot where her son, Toby, lay curled up in what looked like a tight ball, and then thought of her daughter, Emily, probably still asleep in the next room. What, she asked herself, are two responsible, reasonably adult human beings doing in the month of November on a Goddamned camping trip with two children? It had been going on for two weeks already, and there were two more weeks to go. The thought of the car standing outside the cabin door, splattered with mud and filled with a jumble of luggage, clothing, food, sleeping bags, and dirt made her shudder, and the idea that she would have to get up and start the whole family into motion filled her with horror.

The brushing of teeth, taking of baths, washing of faces, eating of breakfast; the packing, loading and getting into the car and starting off for another day of sightseeing...the whole idea was paralyzing. If she had to look at one more National Monument, one more of Nature's Scenic Wonders...why didn't they just drive off the edge of the Grand Canyon?

In sudden fierce determination she nudged her husband: "Bob! Wake up!"

He rolled over, blinked, yawned, and then smiled at her, stretching his arms and touching the wall behind the bed with his fingertips.

"Good morning, baby," he said happily. "Boy! I had a wonderful sleep!"

She smiled back at him. "Mmmmm. Well it's over now. Remember where you are?"

He frowned at her questioningly and then laughed. "Sure! Flagstaff. And today's the day we go to the Grand Canyon!" The very idea seemed to exhilarate him and he sat up in bed, wide awake. "Gee," he went on, "it's been years since I've been there. Wait until you see it."

"I have seen it," she said. "My father took me to see it when I was ten years old. I never knew what a martyr he was!"

He looked at her doubtfully. "What do you mean?"

She yawned, covering her mouth with her hand. "What do I *mean?* Don't tell me you're enjoying all this?"

"Enjoying it? Of course I am, and so are you."

She got out of the bed and stared at him. He looked very young with the sleep still wrinkling his eyes, but there was a troubled expression on his face as he looked back at her; the look a puzzled child would give to an irate and difficult mother. "Okay then," she said, "I'm going to the john. Get the kids up and get them started. We might as well get to the damned Canyon and get it over with." In spite of the sarcasm in the words, her voice had softened reassuringly.

Nevertheless, he stared at her back as she walked away from him into the bathroom. He was never absolutely sure whether she was kidding him or not, and he wondered if she really was not having a good time after all.

At nine forty-five, Emily, aged ten, got into the car. She held her doll in one hand as she clambered gingerly over the heaps of suitcases, blankets, sleeping bags, and air mattresses into the back of the 1948 Pontiac station wagon. Her brother, Toby, aged eight, was already seated on the right hand side, and he watched her suspiciously. She stopped, on hands and knees, just before she reached the seat. "It's my turn to be on that side today," she said flatly.

Toby shook his head and tightened his mouth. "Nope."

Emily gave a disgusted, frustrated sigh and turned to look at her mother and father in the front seat. "Mummy, Toby's on the…" she began and her mother's voice (although Mary did not look around) interrupted her sharply. "If you children can't work these things out for yourselves, I…"

"But Mummy!" The small high voice seemed to fly through the roof of the car. "He never lets me…"

Mary turned in the seat and stared her daughter down. "I do not want to hear what Toby does or does not do. You're on a vacation and if you can't get along with each other—if you can't cooperate at least to that extent—then we will just go back home and forget the rest of this trip. Now get back on the seat and sit down. Go on!"

The tears started to roll down Emily's cheeks. "You always let him do what he wants because he's younger. It's not fair!"

"Emily!"

As his daughter turned and crawled to the left side of the seat, Robert looked at his wife and then back at the two children. He coughed and when he spoke his voice was tentative: "Well, darling, if it is Emily's turn on the right side, don't you think Toby should move?"

Mary glared angrily at him. "Start the car, Robert, and let's get going. I am not going to go on solving their insane little differences. They're both of them old enough to settle such things by themselves. Now stay out of it. If she'd been ready on time she would have been in the car first and none of this would have happened."

Toby listened to his father and mother, stared at Emily, and smiled to himself. If he thought he could get away with it, he would pinch his sister now, but he'd probably better wait until later.

6

CAROLINE PRATT (SHE WAS NO fool, she'd been around, she knew what life was all about) moved sensuously in the bed in the back seat of her Nash Airflyte, sensed the sunlight coming through the windows of the car, and then remembered, in a hot, ecstatic flash, exactly where she was and what she had been doing. Her teeth were coated with a film—from the drinking—and she could taste garlic. Beyond that, she had absolutely nothing to complain about. She remembered (and she would have laughed with pleasure had she been sure he was awake; what had he said his name was? Tom...Tom Foster) absolutely everything that had happened the night before, and she was glad. She would have liked to tell her father and mother about it in detail just to see the look on their faces. The consternation they would have felt! The very idea of it increased her pleasure in the moment. Her father had given her a car with a double bed in the back for her birthday. What did he think, she wondered, that she was going to do with a double bed, anyway?

She sat up and let the blankets fall from her shoulders, exposing her naked breasts. She looked down at them, locked her arms around them, and shivered with the cold. Only then did she look at the naked figure lying beside her. Garlic or no garlic, sleep or no sleep, she just had to kiss him. She lay down again, pressed herself against his back, kissing his neck and feeling her nipples hardening against his solid flesh. He did not move. Gradually, she began to move her hands over his body, insinuating her fingers between his arm and chest, exploring, re-experiencing. She should be ashamed, she told herself, to feel this way again—after the night before—but she couldn't help it, and what's more she wasn't ashamed at all. It was such poppycock, the way parents and other people brought you up to think you shouldn't enjoy sex. Not only did she enjoy it, she had never been able to get enough of it. She felt as if she could eat him up right now.

The body stirred next to her and then, awaking suddenly, as if someone had fired a gun near his head, the man turned and stared at her. She looked fully and deeply into his eyes, watched the incomprehension tum into memory, the doubt—and yes, fear—recede, and finally he smiled at her, pulled himself up on one elbow, yawned, blinked his eyes, and shook his head. "What a night!" he said, sheepishly.

She did not reply, but continued to look at him, letting the desire burn out through her eyes, willing him to know how she felt and how much she wanted him again. Although he looked away almost furtively, she knew that he had seen and understood.

He yawned again, sat up and ran his hands through his rumpled, curly hair, rubbed his chest, scratched under his right armpit, and then coughed. "Christ," he said. "It's cold!"

She looked down at his body, the line of his hips, the wiry black hair on his chest, and then held her arms out to him. She was trembling with the cold and with her own inner burning. He stared at her for a moment before she saw that wild hunger come into his eyes the way it had the night before, and then his body was against her again. He breathed something incomprehensible into her shoulder and she arched her body up against his, lifting him and straining herself until he felt unbearably and marvelously heavy.

It was just at that moment that the sun came into full fire over the mountain behind them and a large diesel truck roared past them on Route 66, about three hundred feet away from the car.

7

THE ENORMOUS LUNCHROOM NEXT TO the garage was empty except for a man and a woman seated at a table not far from the door. Because it was still so early, Richard Simms was surprised to see them there, and even more startled to hear the man's voice saying, in a harsh, complaining undertone: "You're not so perfect yourself, you know. Always criticizing, always dragging me down. You'd think you had no faults of your own."

The blunt edge of the voice struck at Richard and he felt a sensation of alarm rising along his backbone. He did not look at the couple, and they did not speak again, until he had seated himself at a table at the far end of the room, near a jukebox. Only then was he able to look at them openly and as he did, the woman's eyes caught his glance, and for a moment her nondescript face lighted up in an expression that was at least related to pleasure. Except for the look in her eyes, Richard was aware of nothing about her except her hat: brown and shaped like a mushroom. The color was so close to that of her hair, the hat seemed to be a part of it, and the feather which rose straight in the air to grow directly from her head.

After the flashing look she had given Richard, she turned back to her companion (brother? husband?) and the smile grew on her face as if his criticism had, inexplicably, given her great satisfaction. She nodded in his direction and the feather came dangerously close

] 28 [

to striking the man between the eyes. "Finish your coffee, George," she said.

Obediently, the man's hand grasped his coffee cup, his shoulders slumped, and he bent over as he drank. The woman watched him, nodded approval, drew on her gloves and stood up. With another glance in Richard's direction, she waited, assuming an air of studied patience as her husband (they *must* be husband and wife, Richard decided) felt in his pocket for change, counted it, and laid some coins on the table. He looked up at the woman, pushed his chair back, and came to his feet. He stood for a moment by the table as if he did not know what to do next, and the woman gave him a gentle shove with her hand and another nod of her feather. "Come on, George," she said, pleasantly enough this time, and he followed her meekly to the door.

As he watched them leave, Richard felt the sensation of alarm, which he had momentarily forgotten, tingling in his neck. Why? What was alarming about what he had seen? Irritated with his reaction, he stared at the typewritten menu on the table before him. He did not read the words, he kept seeing the image of the couple...and in a flash he understood something. What he had seen epitomized men and women, marriage, life. It did not matter that it was the woman who had, with the feather in her hat, stabbed the life out of the man facing her—the man could have done it to her with some equally senseless gesture. What mattered to Richard was this unconscious expression of human relations, the need for one or the other of two coupled people to dominate, to lead, to—in a sense—devour. With the feather and the order to finish the coffee, she had deflated the man and he had made no protest, but had followed her out of the place as a child would have followed its mother, or a dog its master.

"Masters and slaves," he said aloud, and then looked up, startled, to find the waitress standing, bored and impatient, by the table. He ordered coffee and toast and watched her walk away from him, across the full length of the room.

He was embarrassed and uncertain about himself now. What he had read into the couple, and what he had concluded about them seemed to him an indication of his own peculiar feelings about people and life. It was all very well to admit that he was nervous and depressed, but the acuteness of his observations, the assurance with which he received (and believed in) his impressions, troubled him. He had, suddenly, no confidence in his judgment; it seemed to him that he made judgments about people as if to prove something to himself or to substantiate the anti-human feeling that pervaded him. He was unable to look at anyone uncritically, and his attitude towards people was savage. The relative truth (and could he go so far as to assume that there was truth in what he thought or felt?) was, he recognized, unimportant to him. What mattered was the lack of affection he felt for his fellow man.

He thought then of the car. He was here, sitting at this table, waiting for his breakfast, and the only feeling of affection he had for anything was for his car. He remembered the way in which he had looked at and touched the car when he had stopped. For that mechanism he had felt real tenderness and gratitude. Something very close to love.

The prickle of alarm increased even as some defiant interior voice told him there was nothing wrong with loving and appreciating an automobile. But another voice, striking deeply at him, asked him if he loved any human being with as much directness, as much honesty... or, it added cynically, at all.

His thoughts were interrupted by the approach of the waitress, bringing his toast and coffee with an air of shuffling disgust. He looked at her with two kinds of horror: despising her first for the appearance she presented, and second because she aroused nothing but antipathy in him. He appraised her coldly, asking himself why it was that this pasty-faced, unclean female should be presented to him at this moment as a representative of the human species. There was a need, burning fearfully inside him, to break through his defenses and protections and reach out to any human being...with any gesture. But to *this?* He smiled timidly and asked her, as pleasantly as he could (controlling the feeling of nausea which she produced inside him), to bring him his check now.

She looked at him with a sneer, and said: "Thirty cents." She seemed to hate him. "I'll pay you now," he said desperately and laid forty-five cents on the table. She looked at him for a moment, coldly, glanced at the change, picked it up, muttered "Thank you," in a blank, hard voice and turned away to clump back across the room.

Watching her back, the ugly buttocks swinging from side to side, he felt the despair mounting inside him. He knew, and he could not possibly deny it, that it was essential to love…yes, to *love*…mankind. And that back, those buttocks, those legs, were human. It seemed impossible, and yet what seemed that much more impossible was that he could hate all of them so much. For his love of the car, and the strangely tender emotions he had felt for the land and the trees and the last colors of the fall as he had driven across the country, were all, finally, an expression of his antipathy for humanity. Are you then so lonely and so frightened as all that? his amused and sarcastic inner voice asked him.

He finished his coffee and one-half of one piece of toast and then got up from the table and left the room. Although he was going back to the safety of the car, he was frightened of that safety now, and he began to understand his feeling of determination and elation as he had driven so fast earlier in the morning, before the sun had risen. It was fear that had been driving him and that would drive him until he could unravel the net that it had cast around him and had found out why it was there. At some point in his life—the memory came from a well inside him, but the association was not clear—he had heard the words "death wish" and they imposed themselves upon him again as he walked to the car. Nature (he looked at the road and shuddered) was dying, now in November, and he wanted to drive up over the next hill to his own death. The expression of the thought in his conscious mind seemed to elate him, but he was suspicious of himself. It was the kind of nervous elation that preceded violence.

He got into his car, feeling an inexplicable terror taking possession of him. There was something good, of that he was sure, in the awareness of his own state of being that he was experiencing, but what produced it, and why did he feel this way? How does such a state arise in anyone?

On the road again, the motor of the car humming under him, he drove carefully at first. The sensation of the presence of death and his own attraction to it came to him from all sides as if it was trying to get at him through the body of the car. Like a passenger sitting in the front seat beside him as he drove, Death turned and looked at him: *There is no protection against me,* it seemed to be saying, *and what—in any case—have you to protect? Haven't you admitted and acknowledged me? Don't you want to die? Weren't you born to die?*

The car gathering speed—as if it had a life and direction of its own—seemed to answer affirmatively for him. Although his affection for it was not diminished, he saw it then as an instrument which was no longer under his control. He watched the speedometer climb past seventy as he started down a long hill and his hand reached out automatically for a cigarette. His other hand—his left hand—rested lightly on the wheel and as his right hand fumbled with the package, the front wheels of the car shuddered on a patch of ice on the road, pulling the car towards the edge where there was no shoulder.

His hands and feet reacted automatically, but he managed not to put on the brake, and he missed the ditch by inches. Trembling, he slowed the car down until the speedometer quivered between forty-five and fifty. "Dammit, dammit!" He cursed aloud and the repeated word let out a flow of fury. Yes, he did hate the world and the people in it, but he didn't hate them that much! Enough to fight them and even to destroy them, but not enough—not enough!—to destroy himself.

He did not light his cigarette until he was at the bottom of the hill, and then he braced himself in his seat, took a firmer hold of the steering wheel, and looked around angrily. Whatever had been occupying the car with him was no longer there—the space was filled with his own fury against himself and what seemed to him his manifestations of idiocy.

"If you want to kill yourself," he thought grimly, "get a gun. But at least know what you're doing."

It was at that moment that he saw the sign saying: "Speed Zone Ahead." He must be nearing Tucumcari. For the first time that morning he remembered, with his heart and not just automatically with his brain, that he would be home in a few hours. And home meant—he frowned—home meant Dorothy, too. He'd have to call her from Tucumcari.

8

Dorothy Simms was awakened by the double ring of the telephone, and she grabbed for the instrument blindly, almost before her eyes were open. She coughed as she lifted the receiver from the hook and then said hoarsely: "Yes?"

"Is this 8-6278?" she heard the operator's voice saying.

"Yes, it is."

"I have a collect call from Mr. Simms in Tucumcari, New Mexico. Will you accept the charges?"

"Of course, operator."

"Hello, Dorothy?" the voice sounded near enough in sound, but tentative and reserved.

"Darling!" she exclaimed. "I'm so glad you called! Where..." she laughed. "Of course, you're in Tucumcari. How are you?"

His voice sounded a little better then. "I'm fine. I should be home in about four hours, I guess."

She laughed again. "But are you really all right, Dick? I got your telegram from wherever-it-was in Oklahoma; you've made wonderful time. Aren't you driving too fast?"

She could see him shaking his head at the other end of the line. "No, but I couldn't sleep very well last night, so I got up early. I'm really fine. What about you? Did I wake you up?"

"Of course you did! And I'm fine, too. I'm so glad to hear your voice."

"Same here. I just wanted to warn you I was almost there."

"Well come along then, but don't drive too fast, Dick, please. The accidents have been terrible lately."

"I know. I read the paper last night."

"All right then. Take care of yourself and..."

He interrupted her urgently—did she detect a note of irritation in his voice? "Don't worry. The road's fine and there's no traffic to speak of. I'll be there as soon as I can."

"Good. I'll be waiting. I'm not going to the office today."

"What? Why not?"

"Because you're coming home, silly."

"Oh." He sighed. "I thought maybe you were...you weren't feeling well."

"No, I'm fine, dear. Now you jump in the car and come on."

"I will." She could see him in her mind again, about to hang up.

"Dick..."

"Yes?"

"I love you very much, darling. I'm so glad you're back."

"Me, too." His voice was very low—there were probably people near.

"Well, goodbye then."

"Goodbye." And then she heard the click of the receiver. The telephone calls, the letters and the telegrams of the past month had had no reality for her, but now, as she sat upright in the bed, her hand still resting on the telephone—as if to retain her communication with him—she felt that he was finally back again. She imagined him getting into the car (how was he dressed? was he cold? did he look tired?) and starting out of Tucumcari along Route 66.

She got out of the bed quickly, ran to the desk in the corner of the room, and took a road map of New Mexico and Arizona from the top drawer. She found Tucumcari, but the mileage was not broken down. It was 172 miles from Amarillo, Texas, to Santa Rosa, then 57 miles to Clines Corners and 53 miles further on U.S. 285 to Santa Fe. Tucumcari seemed, on the map, at least two-thirds of the way between Amarillo and Santa Rosa—say sixty-five miles. 65 and 57 and 53—well, 175 miles in round figures. She looked at her watch: seven-ten a.m. He would probably make it in less than four hours; whatever he had said about being careful, he drove fast by nature. She shook her head. This was only November 8th and he had left New York on the 5th. He must have driven like a madman.

She shivered, partly from cold, and partly from the vision of Dick driving intently down the highway. She crossed the room, lighted the gas heater in the corner, and then walked through the living room into the kitchen. There, she lighted the gas stove, filled the tea kettle with water, measured six tablespoonsful of coffee into the coffee pot (Dick would need a cup of coffee when he arrived) and walked back through the living room and into the bathroom adjoining the bedroom. She was, even though worried, very happy; she had been waiting for this moment for what seemed an eternity. It was agonizing to be so much in love with anyone, and yet she could not have wished it to be any other way. If only he had been in a better frame of mind when he had left for New York. His only comment about the show was that he had sold ten pictures—and then he had added, with an exclamation point, *all to people I knew, of course!*

Well, he'd be back by eleven or so; she would have to wait until then. But even as she said this to herself, her hand rose suddenly to her throat and clasped it as if she was in pain. She was not a worrier! Her nature was against worry, she had never worried about anything or anyone in her life. But it was as if something inside her was reaching vainly out to that man in that black Ford somewhere outside of Tucumcari on that ghastly highway that almost demanded the top speed of every car. Anything can happen on any road at any time and the fact that he had travelled two thousand or more miles safely did not mean that he couldn't be killed or terribly injured in these last few miles. But he was out of reach, so far out of reach that he might as well have been on the planet Mars. Still, she concentrated her own forces of life and frowned, willing herself to extend her telepathic powers out to him. Not that she believed in telepathy or any such nonsense, but surely when one felt as strongly as she did now, surely he must be able to feel her presence, her assurance, her love.

"Don't let anything happen, darling. Don't." She said the words aloud.

9

JIM CURRAN, STANDING IN THE patio behind the guest house on Canyon Road that belonged to Mr. and Mrs. Richard Simms, looked at the edge of the sun as it shone blindingly over the top of the Sangre de Cristo mountains, and then he heard the telephone in the Simms house. He looked at the window of their bedroom, about six feet from where he stood, and wondered what was going on in there. He knew that Richard Simms was away. In fact, he had never even seen Richard Simms, and he didn't know very much about Mrs. Simms for that matter. What he did know was that she had seemed reluctant to rent the house to him, as if she hadn't liked the look on his face; but she was like all the people with money in this God-forsaken town: rentals were slow after the summer season was over and she probably had to have his $65.00 a month to keep her damned budget balanced.

What, he wondered, did she look like right now. In a spirit of curiosity, and with no feeling of interest and not the slightest sexual desire, he thought he would like to see her at this moment. He would like to see her when she got up (she must be up, the phone had stopped ringing at once) with her eyes blinking, without her make-up, naked maybe. The idea of her body gave him no thrill, but he would have liked to see her exposed and frightened and without that polite, efficient and un-cordial smile she always gave him when she happened to see him and had to acknowledge his presence. The stuck-up bitch! And her husband, she said, was a painter. One of those pansy painter boys that littered up the whole damned town, no doubt.

With a faint hope that she might be peering through the blinds of her bedroom window, he zipped down the fly of his pants and watered the trunk of her apple tree. He'd like, just for the hell of it, to pee right on the window.

When he had finished and closed his pants again, he took one more look at the sun, yawned, and walked back through the door of the little house behind the Simms place. He stared at the unmade bed, the dust on the floor, the crumpled newspaper, the bottle and the glass and the general disorder of the room. It was hell for a man to live alone. Not that there was any woman he'd give two cents for, but he ought to have some bitch to clean up the place. A man couldn't be expected to sweep and dust and cook meals for himself.

He turned back to the door, whistled shrilly, and stood in the open doorway until he saw the dog slinking across the lawn in his direction. The brown and white "chili hound," as he called it, hesitated and then ran quickly past him, tail between its legs, into the room. It jumped up on the rumpled bed, shivering, and lay there, looking at him with huge, melancholy, frightened eyes. Just like a woman, the stupid, scared beast.

He crossed the room, cursed the dog under his breath, and looked at the pot of water on the stove. It had been boiling for some time. He took a jar of instant coffee from the shelf above the stove, put it down on kitchen table, looked around for a cup, found there were no clean ones, cursed again, rinsed a cup out, and then put a teaspoonful of the powder into the cup and poured boiling water over it. He didn't even like the smell of the stuff, let alone the taste.

He sat down at the table, lighted a cigarette, poured some milk from a small can into the coffee, and blew on it. It was still too hot to drink. He glared at it and then took his checkbook out of his pocket and opened it. $675.42 was the balance he read. He looked in his wallet and found it empty. Then he reached into his pants pocket, pulled out two crumpled one-dollar bills and some change. When he had counted the change, he shoved it all back into his hip pocket. He'd have to go to the bank. What's more, he probably ought to start looking for some kind of job. His government compensation wouldn't be enough to keep him, particularly since he'd given that Mrs. Simms three months' rent in advance when she'd asked him where he worked and he'd had to tell her he didn't have a job. He had told her about his monthly check, but she hadn't been very much impressed. It was all very well to have been a soldier, but people were already bored with veterans...just one more thing that was wrong with the world.

Feeling suddenly restless, he stood up, drank the coffee—in spite of its heat—in one gulp and walked into the bedroom. He put his hand to his head suddenly, grimaced with pain, and let out a small moaning sound. The dog looked at him and began to tremble again and he struck at it viciously with his right hand, but it was off the bed and under the chair before he could touch it. He'd like to kill that Goddamned dog!

10

CHARLES WELLS FELT AN EXTRAORDINARY affection for his son as they started up the path together, the old man walking a few paces behind Peter. Even Kelly, Peter's dog, seemed to be especially pleased with his master today, running ahead to sniff at something and then bounding back to jump at Peter's legs or lick his hand.

For Charles, knowing that his son was leaving in a few hours, knowing that he might never see him again (he was too conscious of his age, too tired not to feel that his time for death was approaching rapidly), it was as if he had released some emotion in himself that he would normally have held back and not allowed himself to feel. The role of man in the universe was, finally, to leave something of himself in his world: some trace, some result. Looking back on his own life, he knew now that what he was leaving behind was this super-extension of himself, this younger man, whom he now allowed himself to love, silently, as one can only love something that is part of oneself. He did not want to say anything about his feelings, but he had a conviction that Peter knew how he felt, that he was drinking in that affection and getting strength from it. Perhaps that is all anyone can ever do for his children: to let them know—and it was better to do it without words, he thought—that they are loved and that love supports and feeds them.

Peter did sense something of what his father was thinking and feeling. He had impulsively asked the old man to come for a walk with him, knowing he liked to walk, knowing that they could be alone that way as they could never be in the house any more. The house was too filled with the remnants of his mother's presence, the atmosphere of Mrs. Jones, the associations of too much family life for too many years. Here, on the path, under the bare trees, with the frozen ground under their feet, there was nothing between the two of them except their consciousness of each other. But even as he thought this, he knew (and he smiled inwardly at the recognition of what was happening) that he was bringing back his own childhood, walking ahead of his father through the woods towards the top of the hill; going back in time to a period that had been safe and peaceful, untormented.

Peter had always loved his father, but compared to what he had felt between them on this visit, his love for him had been mechanical, automatic, filial. Now, and he felt that it was because his father was letting himself go and giving in to his fatigue, readying himself for his death, he was thankful that he had such a father and he was proud to be his son. The idea that his father might die while he was in California did not disturb him; he did not even find it odd that he should not worry about it. He pictured himself, sitting in some office in Hollywood, receiving a telegram or a telephone call from Mrs. Jones or old Dr. Bradley, telling him either that his father was dying or already dead. He knew, beyond any doubt, that it would happen quietly and easily when it did happen, and he knew that his father was ready. Any other attitude about death would be merely conventional or self-conscious. It was, as his father had said at breakfast that morning, the aim of life to die.

It had not been said in connection with his own death, but as he had looked out of the window at the last of the leaves on the trees outside. "It is going to be a very beautiful day," was the way he had begun the sentence and had then gone on to talk about the rhythm of nature, the eternal circle of life, the way in which man, struggle as he might, could not circumvent any of nature's forces. Probably his father had always felt that way. The only strange thing about it—and that no longer seemed strange—was that he should voice it. He never talked, or at least he never had, about such things. It was as if something in him was releasing itself into eternity. He was already reaching out towards his own end.

Peter stopped at the top of the hill overlooking Route 20 as it started down the first of the great hills towards the Finger Lakes. The landscape, even though most of the trees were already leafless, seemed to him especially breathtaking, and the road, shining in the still early sunlight, wound across it like a serpent fighting its way over and around the natural obstacles of the terrain. A sign, just visible from where he stood, on the right-hand shoulder of the highway, read: "HILL—DANGER. KEEP YOUR CAR UNDER CONTROL."

Peter turned as his father came up to him, laughed, and then pointed to the sign. "I've always thought that was a curious sign, haven't you, Dad?"

His father squinted at it and smiled. "It's a sign of your time, son," he said. "When I first drove over this road, there were no signs, no warnings, no protection...not so very long ago..."

As they walked slowly back down the hill, the old man watched the young man and the dog, sensing the importance of the tie between them. Although he had never asked Peter about it, he understood at that moment, why his son had never married. There was something about his attitude towards life, his feeling about the world that would have made it impossible. He had been like that himself, he hadn't married until he was over forty, and it had been because the world had seemed so full of the promise of new experience for him that he could not bear to settle into a state of living that would, necessarily he had thought, limit his freedom to experience, to grow, to live. He wondered what Peter had done about his personal life, a thing they never discussed. Women, Charles Wells felt sure, must be very attracted by him; the very quality of freedom and individuality that would be most destructive in a marriage was the thing they would covet. Peter seemed to live independently of people, on his own inner resources. Was it he, his father, who had given him that? He hoped so, but as he watched him now, filled with an affection that he would have been ashamed to express openly, he felt that he would be overvaluing his own influence even to assume that he could, as another human being—a father—give that to anyone else in the world. It was something Peter had been born with, something that no one and nothing could destroy or harm.

When they were back at the house, seated together on the couch in the living-room, the dog jumped up between them, licked the old man's cheek in exuberant good spirits, and settled down. Peter sat back, lighted a cigarette, and looked out of the window at the countryside. "I'll miss this country when I'm way out there in that crazy western paradise," he said.

"Is it something you want to do? This movie?"

Peter shrugged. "I've never done a movie script before," he said. "You know me, Dad. Something new. And I don't mind the money, either, even though that is not why I'm going. What it amounts to, I suppose, is that I'm curious about Hollywood. I wonder if it can be as phony as it sounds."

"How long will you be gone?"

"Six months, I guess. At least my contract is for six months." He turned suddenly to his father and his voice became deeper, very serious. "You don't mind my going...just now, do you Dad?"

His father shook his head. "Of course not. Why did you ask?"

"I don't know. It's just that..." he hesitated, inhaled from his cigarette, and then looked away. When he spoke again, his words came slowly and he looked straight ahead. "Don't mind my saying this, but it's as if you...as if you were relinquishing life. I wonder if I *ought* to go. I feel as if I may never see you again."

His father looked at him with curiosity. "That's possible. It's been possible ever since your mother died."

"I know. I know. I just thought that perhaps we should talk about it. I don't mind...*death*...you know what I mean. I think you will die when you're ready. But I'd like to be here, I'd..."

The old man breathed deeply and put his hand on his son's shoulder. "I know what you mean, son. But what you know now and what you have to remember is that my time has to come soon. I have no resistance to death, and you mustn't have any for me."

Peter laughed. "The funny part of it is that we can talk this way about it."

"Funny? Do you mean unconventional?"

"Yes, perhaps I do. But I said 'funny' because we've never talked much about anything. We've never had to. And also, I suppose, because there's something in me that thinks it's a little cold-blooded...as if I *should* be frightened or distressed leaving just now...I don't know."

His father smiled drily. "The civilizing influence is strong. We'll miss each other, but don't *mind.*"

Peter stood up, walked across the room to the window, and stared out "No, I won't. You can depend on that." He turned back to look hard at his father. "I'd better go and finish my packing if I'm going to get away right after lunch."

His father stood up and then walked over to him. He pointed out of the window in the direction of the big hill to the west. "In a few hours, you'll be over that hill, on your way west...on your way to, as you said, something new. Don't look back, Pete, and don't worry about me. Just take care of yourself."

"I will, Dad."

The old man smiled at him. "I think you might make us a drink before lunch today, don't you?"

$$11$$

AT TWO-THIRTY IN THE AFTERNOON on Thursday, November 8th, a Cadillac sedan, containing Mr. and Mrs. Henry Franklin, stopped at a gas station just north of Springfield, Illinois, on U.S. Highway No. 66. Mrs. Franklin blew the horn twice and then stared angrily at the young man who came running around to her side of the car. She let the window down and said: "What color is your gasoline?"

The young man looked extremely puzzled, frowned at her, and said: "Pardon me, Ma'am?"

Mrs. Franklin breathed deeply. "I speak English, young man. What color is your gasoline? Red, yellow, white? Or don't you know?"

Joe Hawthorne, who had been working at the gas station for three years, thought something unmentionable to himself and said: "Well, our high-test is red and the regular's kinda pink-like, I think."

"Do they stain?"

Joe raised his shoulders in a gesture of abandon. "I really don't know, Ma'am."

Mrs. Franklin turned to her husband. "Show him, Henry."

Henry cast a quick look of appeal towards Joe, opened the door on his side of the car, and then crooked his finger in an effort to get him around to his side. "We spilled something on the upholstery," he said apologetically, "and my wife...we wondered if a little gasoline would take it off."

"How about some lighter fluid, sir? I have some inside. That doesn't have any color."

Henry looked at his wife and she nodded vigorously. "That's a good idea," he said to the attendant. "I'll take a can of it." He turned back to his wife. "Don't we need gasoline, dear?"

"Yes. Have him fill up the tank and also look at the oil and water, clean the windshield and the back window, and check the tires. Oh, and while we're here, get a map of Missouri, too." She got out of the car and started towards the ladies' room, and then turned back: "Have the battery checked, Henry, and stay here while he cleans off that spot."

Joe Hawthorne stared at her until she had disappeared through the door of the washroom and then turned around, scratching his head, to look at the husband. "Do you want a one-minute wash job, too?" he asked.

Henry started at the sound of his voice and then said quickly: "No, I don't think so."

Joe walked back to the gas pump. "Hi-test or regular?"

"Oh, hi-test," Henry replied quickly.

The poor jerk. Still, people did what they wanted to do pretty much. He probably liked being bossed around by that old bag.

12

EVEN IN THE EARLY AFTERNOON, the sun on the Pennsylvania Turnpike was sending a reflection into Steve Williams' eyes. He had heard that they had a high accident rate on that road, and he could easily understand why. He'd had to stop twice just to keep from going to sleep out of boredom. Now, with the car, a 1950 Chevrolet, staying firmly at seventy-five miles per hour, he was determined to get to the end of the Turnpike (he thought he'd turn off at New Stanton and avoid Pittsburgh) without making another stop. If he'd been able to leave as early as he had hoped, he would already be near Wheeling instead of where he was.

He had felt driven and pushed all the way, and while it was almost exactly five hundred miles to Wheeling from New York, he hoped he would be able to make Zanesville, Ohio—another eighty-odd miles— before stopping for the night. He did not feel tired, and he could stop for a drink if the sun got too bad; but there was something inside him (and when he thought of Marjorie it made him want to go faster) that was propelling ahead and away from New York.

For the first time in months he was being honest with himself, he wasn't afraid of what he was thinking, and he didn't have to go on leading the kind of double mental life that he had led in New York. He had gone on and on being nice to her, trying not to hurt her (at least not directly), trying not to tell her how much he had begun to hate her, to hate every day that he went on living with her. It had almost come out that morning at breakfast, but he had—thank God!—managed to get out of New York without a major scene, the thing he had dreaded more than anything else. Of course, she had had to cry and make him promise that he would come back; had made him tell her that he did love her, that he was only going away because he had to be alone for a while—after all, he had said very reasonably, very kindly, people do have to be by themselves sometimes.

It was after he had said that that she had looked at him, wiping the tears from her eyes, and asked coldly: "But couldn't you have gotten a leave of absence? Did you have to give up your job?"

"I can't ever go back to that job," he had said. "I've been working in that damned office for five years now. I can't stand the work, the people, anything about it."

She had continued to look at him across the table for what seemed an age before she went on: "Just what is it you're running away from, Steve? You can't run away from yourself forever, you know. And don't think I don't know that you're thinking right now how glad you'll be to get away from me. You're sitting there aching to get away, hoping that you'll never have to set eyes on me again." She had smiled then, a funny, distant smile. "Maybe that's what you're planning to do. Is it? Drive off and disappear forever? The west is a big place. Maybe it will just swallow you up."

"Look, Marjorie, why do you have to go on and on about it? It isn't as if we were both so stupid that we can't recognize that you get tired even of the people you love most sometimes. I'm not going to disappear or be swallowed up!"

"If you insist," she had said evenly. "But why did you have to choose New Mexico? What's out there? You could be alone without going way out there."

He had shrugged his shoulders (he did it again as he thought the scene over in his mind) and said as mildly as possible: "It's a part of the country I've always wanted to see. I've told you that. We've been all over this."

"Yes, we have. We could go there together next summer, Steve. I'd like to see it, too."

It was then that he had almost broken, lost his temper, and had a real fight with her. "But I've told you I have to be alone!" he had cried out, and then checked himself. "Besides, darling, we can still go out there together next summer if you want to."

There hadn't been much after that; there had been nothing else to say, nothing more to do. He'd packed his little bag, put on his hat and coat, and then kissed her goodbye. At that moment, much as he had been anxious to leave, he had felt a twinge of something—guilt, pity for her—he wasn't sure what it had been. But how had she known that he really did want to disappear? It was almost as if she had read his mind!

He straightened himself in the car and stepped on the accelerator a little harder. Whatever was wrong, and for whatever reasons he was "escaping" (he smiled at the word), every mile from New York made him feel better. He realized (it penetrated his consciousness fully now) that he was *alone*...he could do exactly what he wanted to do. He was responsible to no one in the world. It was like being a young man again!

13

Carrie had driven the car into Albuquerque, had made herself as presentable as possible and told Tom to do the same, before she walked into the hotel. He had bought himself a razor, a toothbrush, some toothpaste, and a shirt and tie, with the ten dollars she had given him, and had gone into the men's room in the railroad station to change. She couldn't get him to go into the hotel with her. He said his clothes looked too awful. She was going to buy him some decent clothing, but he said he'd get a pair of pants and a jacket in an Army and Navy store later. He did not want to go in any store with her.

As she brushed her teeth and made up her face, she decided that it was right for a man to have his pride; one of the reasons he had become what amounted to a bum (and he wasn't one by nature, she knew) was that he was unable to allow people to do things for him. People were like that, there wouldn't be any point in trying to change him. She was glad she had picked him up, glad and just a little afraid. She had picked up people before, she had done quite a lot of what was called "sleeping around" but nothing had ever been quite like this. When she thought about it now, it made her feel weak in the pit of her stomach, and there had been some extraordinary extra-quality in the way they had made love. They had been driven to it by something more than just attraction and there had been—in both of them—a fierce loneliness; as if they were reaching out for the last security available to either of them.

When she had finished in the ladies' room, she walked back to the car and found him sitting in the front seat waiting for her. He was not at all bad looking when he was cleaned up, and...she got the same electric thrill every time she looked at him; she almost wished (the wish came from a hard, sordid place in her) that he was still unshaven and unwashed. The very dirtiness of him had contributed in some way to a brutal side of their sleeping together. They stared into each other's eyes (he seemed, for a moment, like a hostile, suspicious animal) as she got into the car, and when she had lighted a cigarette and put the keys back in the ignition, she said: "Would you like to drive?"

"It's all right. It's your car." He didn't look at her.

She hesitated, her own surface hardness was more than met by his, and she felt a form of weakness that she had never felt for any man in her life. "What if it is my car, Tom? Don't you like to drive?"

"Sure."

"All right then. I'd like you to drive." She got out of the car and walked around it, conscious of his eyes on her.

When he had moved into the driver's seat, she got in, slammed the door behind her, and looked at him with satisfaction. Once he'd gotten a clean pair of pants, they could even pass as man and wife. It made her feel warm inside. He was, whatever else he might be, a *man* in the only important sense of that word.

He started the car, backed out of the parking space and then, as he waited until the street was clear ahead of him, said: "What're you trying to do, anyway?"

"What do you mean?"

"Wanting me to drive."

She stared at him for a moment and then crushed her cigarette in the ashtray. She was angry with his tone of voice. "Don't you like to have a good time? I'm not trying to do anything. I like you, that's all."

"Okay with me. Where're we going?"

"To get your pants. There must be some kind of a store along this street."

"Then what?"

"Whatever you'd like to do."

He turned to look at her almost angrily. "What is this anyway? Aren't you going someplace yourself?"

She shook her head. "No. I'm just on a vacation."

He looked away and did not reply.

"Do you like the mountains?" she asked.

"Sure."

"Let's get a steak some place and we'll go and cook it up at Sandia Crest. It's the most beautiful place in the world. I was there last year."

He smiled briefly. "You're the boss."

Her voice lowered, she had a sudden premonition that she did not understand, as if she were being warned against something evil. "You hate people who have money, don't you?"

"I don't exactly hate them," he said. "I think some of the wrong people have money, if that's what you mean."

"What you mean," she persisted, "is that you'd rather have the money than have me have it. Don't you?"

He shook his head, shifted suddenly into first gear, and pulled out into the street. "No. I don't care if you have money. I'd just like to have some myself, that's all."

She opened her purse, took out a wallet, and counted off some bills. "Here's a hundred dollars. I'll give you more but I'll have to cash some traveller's checks first."

She held the money out to him but he shook his head and grinned. "I don't cost that much," he said.

"No," she said angrily, "and I'm not paying you, either. You can pay for both of us. Take it and stop being a fool. I can't help it if my father is buried in oil."

He held out his hand, looked down while she put the folded bills into his palm, and then stuck them in his pocket. "What are you going to do?" he asked. "Drive me to Los Angeles?"

"What do you want to go there for?"

"It's warmer in the winter."

"What difference does that make? If you don't have to sleep on a park bench, the weather won't matter."

"I guess you're right. What's the gimmick?"

"Spend the winter with me."

He shook his head. "That would never work. I'm not the kind of a man who can hang around a woman."

She reached out to him and took his arm. "Why not, Tom? Couldn't you try it?"

He shook his head again. "It won't work, I tell you. You'll get sick of me and..."

"No, wait. Spend a week or so with me. We'll travel around, we'll do anything you want to do. If, at the end of a week—or ten days—you still say it won't work, I'll let you go. What about that?"

He saw a parking space and pulled over to the curb. When he had parked the car, he cut off the motor and then grasped the steering wheel tightly with both his hands and pressed his body back into the seat. "Are you serious?"

"Yes."

"Why?"

"You know why."

"Last night?"

She hesitated. It was something more than that, but she did not know what herself. "Partly. Not just that." She looked away from him at her hands in her lap. "That was...wonderful, darling" (the word slipped out and she glanced quickly at him) "but it isn't just that."

He turned to her abruptly, released the steering wheel, and took her shoulders in his two hands. "Don't say anything you're going to be sorry for," he said. "We had a swell time last night. That's all it is."

Her face reddened and she made herself smile. "All right, if you say so. But...will you do it? Please?"

He released her shoulders and got out of the car. "I'm going to get my pants. I'll be right back."

"Tom," her voice was urgent now. "Tell me that you will."

Although he did not look at her, his voice softened for the first time. "Sure, Carrie."

She watched him turn abruptly from the car, letting the door slam behind him. It was the first time he had called her by name.

$$14$$

If there was anything more maddening than what his mother called "the view," Toby Hume didn't know what it could be. Parents spent all their time getting mad at their children or else telling them to look out of the window and see how beautiful it was. His mother had been absolutely furious when she had seen him reading that comic book just as they arrived at the Grand Canyon—the place where you could first see down into it.

Toby had been surprised at her for being angry because he had heard her say, herself, that she was sick and tired of touring and looking at national monuments. Not that he expected to understand what went on in the minds of his mother or father, but he was tired of always being surprised and almost always doing what seemed to them the wrong thing. If he talked in the car they told him to shut up; if he didn't talk they wanted to know what was wrong with him, and wasn't he having a good time on account of this was a vacation and you were supposed to have a good time. If he had a fight with Emily (and that, after all, *was* having fun) then they got really mad and said they'd go back home right now and not have any more vacation, which didn't make any sense because he wished they would go back home. He hoped, mostly, that it would get so cold that they couldn't camp out any more. When they camped out they went really crazy and he and Emily had to get the wood and carry water, tend the fire, help unload the car, and then all they got was bawled out and shouted at because the wood was too long or too short, or they spilled the water, or the fire was never right for cooking...it was always something. And then five minutes later they'd be talking about how wonderful it was to be sleeping under the stars!

The car stopped and Mary Hume, with a severe look in their direction, ordered the children to get out. They both crawled obediently across the mountain of camping paraphernalia and Toby followed his mother closely until they came to the rim of the Canyon.

"See the river way down there, darling?" she asked him, peering into his face as if to make sure he was properly impressed, and then: "And look at all those marvelous formations—and the colors! Isn't it wonderful?"

This was the fourth place they had stopped and it all looked exactly alike to him. He looked at her in dismay, smiled quickly, and nodded his head. "Who made it?" he asked.

"Toby!"

"What's the matter?"

"Didn't you listen to anything Daddy told you yesterday? He explained all about the Canyon to you and how it was formed by erosion...all about the way the river cut its way into the rocks and... well, really, Toby, I don't know why we bother to tell you anything at all. You never listen."

He looked at her dumbly. "Where are we going to go now?"

She sighed. He *was* only eight years old and riding in the car all day long probably wasn't much fun for him. She hoped, for his sake, that they'd be able to camp out that night and that it wouldn't be too cold. Although she hated camping more than any other human activity that she could think of, she knew the children loved it and that was one responsibility of parents: to do the things their children enjoyed.

"We're going to the Lodge for lunch, and we'll look at the rest of the Canyon on the way."

"Oh."

She knelt down beside her son and looked at him with concern. "What's the matter, Toby? Aren't you really interested, or aren't you having a good time?"

He blinked quickly and looked away from her. "Sure. It's wonderful," he said. "Are we going down into the Canyon on a donkey?"

She shook her head. "No, darling, we won't have time for that."

"Why not?"

"Because we don't have time! We have to leave here this afternoon because we're going to Oak Creek Canyon tomorrow and from there to Jerome—you'll love that, it's a town built on the top of a mountain—and then we're going to New Mexico where you'll see the Indians. There's an Indian dance at one of the Indian villages on Monday."

"But I still don't see why we can't go down into the Canyon on a donkey."

"But it takes *too long,* Toby."

"But I'd rather ride on a donkey than go to those other places."

She stood up and shook her head angrily. "We're not going down into the Canyon, Toby. Now, get back into the car. Sometimes I think you are the most stubborn, arbitrary child! When you're on a trip with people what counts is what everybody wants to do and not just what you want to do. Don't you ever think of that?"

He gave her a look full of hatred and started back for the car. Did *he* ever think of other people! The only thing he had wanted to do on the whole trip was to ride on that donkey!

15

After lunch at a joint called "Daisy's Drive-in" on the Albuquerque highway, Jim Curran took his laundry to the laundromat and decided he might as well wait for it. He had nothing else to do. He didn't feel particularly talkative, and as he watched the man who owned the place, he kept a sour look on his face to keep him from talking. He sat near the machine where his own clothes were whirling around in the soapsuds and wondered if the guy made any money in a business like this. He didn't think he'd like to mess around with other people's dirty clothes all day long, but it was probably as good a way to earn a living as another. Provided there was any real dough in it, of course.

As he sat, the whirring noise of the machines and the continual revolving made him a little sleepy and set up a rhythm inside him, as if he himself were whirling along with the laundry. At the end of the room, beyond the rows of washing machines, there was a much larger machine, apparently a dryer. He turned to look at it after the proprietor had put some wet clothes in it and turned it on, and then he stood up on a sudden impulse and walked over to it. He was conscious of an increase in his habitual restlessness, as if the current of the machines had been communicated to him. As he watched the dryer whirling away and felt its heat, it occurred to him—out of the thin air—that the machine was big enough to put a body into it. Or, his mind went on, better than a body, a live person even. The very idea of a human being inside the machine made him feel—for some reason—calmer.

He waited until the man was near him and then said, casually: "Say, bud, how hot does this thing get?"

The man smiled at him. "About two hundred and seventy-five degrees by the time the clothes are dry. Then that red light," he pointed to a red bulb above and to the left of the large circular door, "goes on and the clothes are dry."

"They must be pretty hot when you take them out, aren't they?"

"Yes, they are. Almost too hot to handle."

Jim looked back at the clothes through the glass door of the dryer and his mind's eye substituted a person: he could see a woman, a tangle of hands, feet, and long hair revolving around and around and getting hotter and hotter all the time. He would have liked to talk about it, and wondered if the proprietor had ever thought of it, but he decided he had better not say anything to him.

"How about drying my clothes in there?" he asked.

The man looked at his watch. "I wouldn't be able to dry them until about four-thirty," he said.

"Well, that's okay. I can pick them up later." He felt a sudden need to get out of the place and away from the machine.

"All right," the man said. "You can get them at about five. I'm sorry I can't do them before that, but a lot of people bring their laundry in in the morning and then want it ready by the time they go home at night. Besides, Thursday is a bad day for some reason. I don't know why Monday is called washday."

"Well, if I don't get back by five," Jim said, "I'll pick them up in the morning. All right?"

"Sure. Any time."

"Thanks."

He got into his car and started it roughly. The nervousness that he had felt, and which had been alleviated for a moment as he watched the dryer, had started up in him again. He had to do something about it, and about that sharp recurring pain in his head. He didn't know what was wrong with him. He'd like to go out and get drunk, or do something violent. He needed to.

On his way back to Canyon Road, he stopped to buy a quart of whiskey and a can of dog food. Even as he put the dog food in the car, he wondered why he kept the Goddamned dog. Of course, it was probably better than living alone, but in a way it only made things worse. The dog was of no use to him, she was afraid of him all the time, and he couldn't even talk to a dog for Christ's sake! Maybe he ought to get rid of her.

Maybe he ought to...he smiled to himself. He had suddenly had an idea.

16

THE SIMMS' HOUSE WAS ABOUT one hundred and fifty feet from Canyon Road, between Delgado Street and the Camino del Monte Sol. It had been given to Richard on his twenty-first birthday, by his mother, Mrs. Carlton Simms, who had migrated to New Mexico in 1921 at the age of forty-seven. She had lived in Philadelphia until her husband's death from a heart attack. With one child and a little over one million dollars, she had decided that Philadelphia was no longer the place for her. She picked Santa Fe partly because she had heard about it from friends and partly because the altitude was supposed to be good for respiratory diseases and Dick had always been afflicted with bronchitis.

She bought the Canyon Road house as soon as she arrived, and she then invested a large sum of money in land and real estate. In 1933, when she gave the house to her son, she owned a total of seventeen houses which were almost continuously rented, and she had gone into the real-estate business for herself. At seventy-seven, she was still active in real estate, but she spent her winters in Tucson, Arizona, and her daughter-in-law, Dorothy, ran the business for her. She was not one to interfere with her son's life, and in spite of her daily contact with Dorothy during the summers, she managed not to question her about Dick, and not to see him too often. They came to Tucson for Christmas with her, but beyond that there were no family traditions or celebrations shared by the three of them. She had her friends and they had theirs. No family was ever ideal, she always said, but she had done her best to maintain a good relationship with her son and his wife. She had turned enough property over to Dick (after all, no painter can make a living!) so that he had an income of about $250.00 a week plus Dorothy's salary and commissions from the business. He would inherit everything when she died.

On the eighth of November, Mrs. Simms—whatever her determination to keep her hands off her son—could not resist telephoning to find out if he had arrived home safely. She had waited until three o'clock before she put the call in, hoping that she might hear from them before then, but there had been no message.

The ringing of the telephone awakened Dick at almost the same moment that the car drove up behind the house and stopped in the parking space reserved for the little guest house that he and Dorothy had built for their own guests and to rent the rest of the year. He had been so deeply asleep that it took him a moment to remember that he was in his own home and not in a tourist cabin somewhere along Route 66. He stared at the telephone for a moment and as Dorothy came into the room, he said: "Let's not answer it. Let it ring."

"It might be something important, Dick."

"If you mean the office," he said, "the hell with it."

She sat down on the bed beside him and put her arm around his shoulders. "I wasn't thinking of the office; I thought it might be your mother."

He buried his head against her shoulder. "She can wait, too. I'll call her later. Besides, doesn't she know that no news is good news?"

"All right," she said, and then drew away from him to look into his face. "God, I'm glad you're back, darling. I'm never going to let you take a trip without me again. At least not in the car. It worries me too much to have you driving alone on these roads. And you drive so fast."

He looked back at her. "Is that a reproach?"

"No, and you know it isn't. How about some food now? Aren't you hungry?"

He nodded. "I'll get dressed."

"Why? You can perfectly well eat in here, and then maybe you'll get some more sleep. You looked absolutely dog-tired when you arrived, and you've only slept for about an hour."

He shook his head. "No, I'll get up. I couldn't sleep any more now anyway, and if I did I wouldn't sleep tonight." He sat on the edge of the bed, ran his hands through his hair, yawned, and then called out: "Was that the new tenant who just drove in?"

"Yes," she called back. "Why?"

"What's he like?"

"That's a long story. I'll tell you while you're eating."

Richard dressed, washed his face, brushed his teeth, and then went into the kitchen. The lunch was on the table. "Haven't you eaten anything yet?"

"Of course not. Did you expect me to let you eat your first meal alone?"

He smiled at her. "No, I guess not." He sat down at the table and without looking at his wife, asked again about the tenant.

"I don't really know much about him," she said, sitting opposite him. "His name is Curran—James Curran—and there's something about his face that I don't like." She paused, her face tightened in thought. "There's something almost...*inhuman* about him...at least that's the word that occurred to me as I talked to him."

"Why did you take him then? It wouldn't matter if the house wasn't rented for a while, would it?"

"No. It wasn't that. But...well, it seemed silly not to take him, and he paid me three months' rent in advance. Besides, I didn't want to turn him down for no reason at all; or just because he looked odd to me."

"Why all the rent?"

She laughed. "It was because I asked him what he did and he said he wasn't doing anything at the moment and then he wrote out a check for three months' rent…as if I'd put his back up by asking him what he did."

"Well, what does he do now? Still nothing?"

She nodded. "He told me he was getting compensation from the government for some war injury. In any case, it's immaterial to me since the rent is paid, and he's a perfectly good tenant. He hasn't given me any trouble."

They were both silent for a few minutes and then she laid down her fork and looked at her husband as he ate.

"Darling," she said, "tell me something, will you?"

He glanced at her briefly and then looked back at his plate. It was the preliminary to a question he had been dreading.

"Yes. What?"

"Are you really glad to be back? Are you feeling all right? There was something about your voice on the telephone this morning…you sounded, I don't know, depressed or something. Is it anything you want to talk about?"

Again he looked at her very briefly and his jaw tightened. "I don't want to talk about it now, Dorothy…but I am glad to be back, I guess." He looked up quickly. "It's nothing to do with you, you know. But the show and all that New York rat-race and I sat there looking at the stuff I'd painted and at the people looking at it…Hell, I don't know. I'd thought the show was going to give me some kind of a boost, but it all looked like so much junk to me. I listened to them talking about 'beauty of line' and 'the extraordinary feeling' and 'the vitality of the color'…it made me sick finally. I've been asking myself ever since what the devil I thought I was doing. It makes me feel like a sick man puking a lot of stuff onto canvas. I began to wonder what painting is…"

"But Dick, you…"

He held up his hand to her. "Wait, let me finish. In a way, I think I'm glad this happened. It was probably high time for me to take a good long look at myself. Here I am, almost forty, self-importantly convinced that I'm an 'artist,' living on my mother's money…" he looked at his wife sardonically, "…just because she turned it over to me doesn't make it anything I've earned for myself…and so what? The whole process seems like a lot of nonsense and stupidity. What have I achieved as a person or as an artist? Pretty little pictures full of decorative charm or something like that. So I sell ten pictures and not one of them was bought except by people I've known for years. They just came to the show and figured they might as well spend a couple of hundred dollars on a painting of mine as some other piece of junk, and they convinced themselves that they were doing a good deed while they were at it." He took a package of cigarettes from his shirt pocket, offered one to his wife, and then lighted hers and his own. "If that's having purpose in life, I'm nuts."

She covered his hand with hers. "But what do you mean by such words as 'purpose' and 'life,' darling? You have as much purpose and as much direction as anyone in the world. You're a fine painter, whatever you may say. You work hard and…"

"And what…?"

She smiled sadly. "I hate to sound…well, *corny*…darling, but after all we're married. We represent something. We have *some* value."

It always came to that with her. He stifled a strong feeling of distaste, angry and uncontrollable. "I know that, dear. You know I know that, but I feel as if I was cheating us by feeling this way and I can't get over it. I'd like to do something to make you proud of me…well, I don't quite mean that. I need to be proud of myself, I guess. It's as if I didn't have any vitality any longer. I don't know what it is, I…" He hated the sound of his own voice, the easy rationalization into an insoluble problem, into something he did not 'know about,' when he knew he meant something far simpler, something he simply did not want to talk about.

He was interrupted by the ringing of the telephone.

"Dollars to doughnuts, it's Mother. I'll get it."

He got up from the table and walked quickly to the extension in the living-room.

From where she sat at the kitchen table, she could hear his voice saying: "Yes. Yes it is. Hello, Mother" but she was distracted by something outside the kitchen window. It was Mr. Curran getting into his car. She stared at his face and shuddered. Silly or no, there was no question but what there was a look of...well, *evil*, about that man. She wished that Dick could see him at that instant.

17

THE HOTEL MAJESTIC IN ST. Louis was famous for its beds and its food. After a very rich and very expensive meal in their suite, Mr. and Mrs. Henry Franklin had gone to see a movie called "Yesterday's Yesterday," and Mr. Franklin had had indigestion during the most important love scene.

When they were back in the hotel at eleven o'clock, Mrs. Franklin gave him four BiSoDol tablets, two aspirin, and made him drink a glass of hot water. She took a small nip of brandy for her acidity and went to bed. Mr. Franklin went to sleep almost at once in spite of the pain and began to dream about a large human-faced serpent coiled inside his belly...the face was vaguely familiar, but he couldn't quite place it. Mrs. Franklin looked malevolently across at his bed. He was really a poor excuse for a husband; it was very hard for her to understand how he happened to be such a good stockbroker.

18

IN ZANESVILLE, OHIO, A COLD wind had descended on the town at about eight-thirty in the evening, almost as if it had come with Stephen Williams as he drove in. He found a tourist camp on the outskirts of town that looked comfortable and warm, took a room even though it cost him six dollars, and then had two drinks, both very stiff. He lay down on the bed after the second drink and woke up around midnight. He hadn't had anything to eat and he was hungry as hell, but he was too stiff with fatigue and with all that driving to do anything about it then. He got up, went to the bathroom, took off his pants, shirt and socks, turned off the heat, and climbed under the covers. He was asleep again in about five minutes.

19

AT ELEVEN O'CLOCK THAT NIGHT, Marjorie Williams got out of bed. She had been crying and she couldn't go to sleep. She walked into the bathroom, looked at the bottle of sleeping pills, and then filled a glass with water. She took the glass and the bottle of pills back into the bedroom, got into bed, and took two of the pills. Then she lay back in the bed, turned off the light, and stared wide-eyed into the night, at the ceiling.

There was no sound in the apartment, and it increased the pain she was feeling; he was gone now, irrevocably. In what way had she failed to give him what he had to have as a man? What had she done that had driven him away from her this way? And for what reason was it her lot to have to suffer through this? How long would it be before she would know if he was ever going to come back? The tears started again, and she turned in the bed and buried her face in the pillow. At least she hoped he was all right.

20

EVEN UNDER THE TREES NEAR the snow-covered top of Sandia Mountain (they had had to put on chains to make it all the way up), you could hear the wind whistling around the car. Caroline Pratt, with her arms around Tom Foster, nestled close into his back, and buried her hands below his belly. He was sound asleep and breathing rhythmically. She felt very happy, very over-stimulated, and she was glad to be awake and experiencing the sensation of their bodies in such close contact.

Tom, in spite of his breathing and the relaxation in his body, was not quite asleep, but he was completely exhausted and his brain was in a fog. He wondered, as his mind sank down into an abyss of near-sleep, just what he was doing in a car with a girl who was, as far as he could tell, a real honest-to-God millionaire. It was a crazy world. He was not completely comfortable in her clutching embrace; he would like to have moved away from her, but at the same time (his mind seemed to be confused) he hoped she wouldn't release him. The warmth of her body, and—he had to admit it—the gentleness of her touch made him feel oddly secure.

21

Robert Hume could not sleep. They had seen everything there was to see at the Grand Canyon, and they had returned to Flagstaff that afternoon. Toby had wanted to go down into the Canyon on a pack trip and he had almost given in, until Mary had gotten mad at him and said he didn't know anything about child discipline. Although he had been glad to see the Canyon again—it always gave him a feeling of peace and real quiet to look down into it—his family had just about spoiled the day for him.

Everything had been capped at dinner when Emily had said: "The only reason we're on this trip is because Daddy used to like to camp and he thinks he still does." He'd been angry with her at the time, but now, in the dark and with his wife breathing silently beside him, it occurred to him that perhaps his daughter had been right, and that they might be hating every moment of the trip. He felt pretty sorry for himself, and he also felt rather like a fool.

22

RICHARD SIMMS LAY IN THE bed next to his wife, rigid and disgusted with himself. Even though he had been away from her for more than a month, he had not wanted to make love to her; he had even thought that he would not be able to, as if he had suddenly become impotent. But he had forced himself to perform, he had been able to do it consciously, and his feeling of disgust was produced largely because now even that—the one thing that had always been spontaneous, natural, and right with them—was something that could be done almost against his will, and because she had expected it.

The guilt and disgust turned gradually, as he seemed to become more and more awake, into anger against her. That she could be so insensitive to have forced him into making love to her when she should have known that he didn't want it, didn't want her then at all...That she should, and this was what made him stiff with anger, always think that sex was a kind of cure-all. He had known at lunch when she had begun to question him that she would, in a supremely egotistical feminine way, drive him into that corner of lovemaking on the assumption (she had always assumed it) that it would make everything all right.

God, what a life!

23

In Three Bridges, New York, Charles Wells had gone to bed early. He had watched the setting of the sun before dinner, and had felt a strange, eerie cold descending about him as the last light had disappeared. The house seemed too big and too empty now that Peter had left.

But it was not only the emptiness and the loneliness that disturbed him. He had told Peter not to worry; he had even told him that he was ready to die, but now his own words came back to him as if he had been making a prediction rather than stating a principle he believed in. He was afraid, somehow. He was afraid of his own willingness to die. It seemed to him as if the urge to live was fading too fast; something in him seemed to be propelling him too quickly towards his own death.

More simply, and he was ashamed to admit this even to himself, he wished his son had not gone away. He did not want to die without him.

24

"**What can I give you** instead of a drink?"

Peter looked at Kelly as he said the words, and the dog, after crouching low on the floor and smiling (he was the only dog Peter had ever seen who could really smile) leaped up on the bed and thumped his tail hard, making a sound like someone beating a carpet. Peter held the glass of whiskey out to him; the dog looked at it suspiciously, looked back at Peter, and then in a spirit of abandon, stuck his nose in, sneezed, gave Peter a reproachful look, jumped off the bed, sneezed again, walked across the room, lay down with his jaw between his front paws, and looked doleful.

Peter swallowed the whiskey in the glass, poured himself another drink, and then said apologetically: "I'm sorry, Kelly. It's all we have in the house tonight." Kelly blinked at him but did not move.

Two hundred and seventy-eight miles. Peter opened the briefcase on the bed beside him and took out a notebook. He wrote down the mileage, put the notebook back in the briefcase, and then put his feet up and leaned against the headboard of the bed. He was tired, but not very tired, and the drink was warm and relaxing. He went over the afternoon in his mind and felt a pang of regret for the country he had left behind him.

It had been cold and very bright as he had driven out of Three Bridges, and Route 20—certainly one of the most wonderful, handsome highways he knew—had seemed to him especially alluring. It was handsome the way people are at certain times; as if it had been washed and dressed for that particular day, almost as if it had prepared itself for him. The first stretch to Cazenovia, where he had often driven with his father, had pulled him along on its four-lane trafficless surface. He wondered how the road would seem when they had finished making it over into the *Thruway* as the Public Works Department called it. He was sorry they had chosen that particular road for that purpose; but at the same time he admitted that he was attracted to these enormous four- and six-lane highways. They had the same appeal, if that was the word, as airplanes and transcontinental trains. Sleek, high-powered, efficient (not that roads, really, could be any of those things but he felt them nevertheless) ... They were an ultimate statement of a certain type of incredible human achievement. The dangerous, and perhaps the wrong thing about them was—in his mind—what they represented.

Where were we going in such a hurry, and *why?* He thought again, seeing the road in his mind's eyes, of the thousands of cars that he had passed, the thousands that had passed him, from both directions. They had swarmed along together in the two-lane stretches, straining to reach the shorter, newer, four-lane stretches, and then ripped ahead. You could tell by watching the cars, without even seeing the drivers, who was in a hurry, who would try to pass.

He took a swallow of his drink, smiled to himself, and wondered if other people felt the same way about roads and cars. He believed that the automobiles had antennae that communicated with you as you drove. He could *feel* them coming up behind him to pass; he could feel their irritation if they were unable to get by him; he could feel the recklessness radiating from some cars, and he trusted these instincts and sensations about a car far more than his actual observation of what they did.

Although he hated trucks and busses because of their enormous size and the way in which they would roar up behind you and force you ahead, force you to go faster than you wanted to go; he knew also that they were the most reliable drivers on the road. The people who had trouble with them were the ones who lost their judgment about them or began to drive wildly themselves, as if to compete with or in some way prove something to, the bus or truck driver.

He told himself to stop philosophizing about the human race and took a road map from the briefcase. Cazenovia, Lafayette, Skaneateles (the lake had looked so wonderful in the cold winter brightness), Seneca Falls, Geneva, Canandaigua, Pavilion, Lancaster...he felt sentimental about all that part of the road. It was the country in which he had been born and to which he always came back. Yet he wondered, idly, whether he would continue coming back for much longer. Three Bridges was not, and could not be, he knew, his real home. He had come back to his father there, and before his mother's death he had come back to both of them; it had been a long series of returning journeys to his origins, but if his father should die while he was out west, would he continue to return? He doubted it. He would have to come back to sell the house, probably, and he could see himself twenty years from now making pilgrimages to the country itself, but the land, much as he loved it, was not the place in which he could imagine himself living for very long. If he ever did settle down, he knew instinctively that it would be in some country he had not yet found.

It was after Lancaster that the road had seemed to change abruptly and he had begun to drive with a determination to get through and out of it. Silver Creek, Fredonia, North East, (Pennsylvania, then) and finally that miserable Erie. There had seemed to him to be at least one hundred miles of Erie. It went on and on and on...rows and rows of architectural monstrosities on both sides of the road. He had felt himself becoming angry with the other cars, angry with the town, angry with the State of Pennsylvania, angry with the members of the human race who could live in such a place. Just because he knew that somehow Ohio would be better, he had driven on in darkness to Ashtabula.

He put down the map, drained his glass, lighted a cigarette, and swung his feet to the floor. He looked at Kelly and smiled, got up and walked over to him. The dog stretched, yawned, and came to his feet. "How about some food?"

Kelly smiled again and then jumped up and licked Peter's hand.

"Okay," Peter said, patting his head. "Let's go see if we can find a restaurant in Ashtabula that has the proper feeling for dogs, shall we?"

Kelly's answer was unmistakably yes.

25

JIM CURRAN HAD SPENT THE afternoon driving around the town of Santa Fe. He had no destination in mind and he had not stopped until he had come into view of a well-rig on the old Pecos road about a mile or so beyond the city limits. He had driven up to it and talked to the two men who operated it for a while. He had enjoyed that reminiscently, as he had once been a well-digger himself, but he'd gotten tired of it as he did of most things, and had gone on to something else.

The drillers were having trouble because they'd agreed on a low price and then found they were working in solid granite, and it was a cinch they would lose money on the job unless they could talk the owner of the land into giving them some more.

As he had talked with them and had watched the enormous iron bit clanking down into the earth, it seemed to Jim that he was watching the earth being raped, and it gave him a feeling of such excitement that he had finally had to walk away from the two men, embarrassed for fear they might notice something.

After dinner in town, during which he hadn't been able to forget the well, he had driven home and had taken enough whiskey to make him sleepy. But his sleep was tormented and intermittent. A hammering in his brain, like the bit of the rig in the earth, kept him in a half-world between consciousness and unconsciousness. There was nothing in his life now: no person, no family, no activity to energize him and keep him going. The injury he had sustained in the war had become more and more the thing on which he pinned his failure since his discharge, and the pain he felt from it from time to time was a constant reminder of what had been done to him.

He had left the Army reluctantly, but there had been nothing he could do about it; he was no longer fit for service. The world, as he saw it, had used him up to the point of uselessness and cast him out of the one thing—the one place which he had felt he belonged—back upon his own resources. For a while it had been all right; as a veteran he had been able to feel important, even respected. But now, with the war in Korea (and he would have liked to be there now) being a veteran of World War II meant nothing. His worth, as far as the world was concerned, was in his monthly check from the government. What he did with his life didn't matter to anyone.

NOVEMBER 9, 1951

1

Richard Simms met his tenant for the first time on the morning of November 9th. The meeting was not accidental. Before going to sleep, he had remembered—for no apparent reason—that Dorothy had said he looked "inhuman" and while he had joked about it when they had mentioned Curran, he knew that Dorothy was not given to rash statements, and made up his mind to call on the man.

It was about ten o'clock when Richard knocked on the door of the guest house; he had waited until then on purpose. Even people who don't work are likely to be up by ten. There was no answer at first, so Richard knocked again—the man must be there, his car was parked outside the house. At the second knock, there was a muffled voice from inside, but Richard could not understand the words, so he waited.

It must have been almost two minutes, and he was about to knock again, when he heard someone rattling the lock inside. The door opened, a slinking, frightened-looking brown and white dog slid out, and then Richard met the angry, red-eyed, unshaven face of James Curran for the first time. He was wearing a pair of gray flannel trousers, a rumpled T-shirt (he'd probably been sleeping in that, Richard thought) and his feet were bare.

"I'm very sorry," Dick said, "I didn't mean to wake you. I'll come back later."

The man did not smile. He simply looked Richard straight in the eye—there was something about his face; not inhuman exactly, but *bad,* shifty-eyed, and...Richard groped for the right word...unbalanced?

"Now that you're here," Curran said gruffly. "What do you want?"

Richard was embarrassed by the unfriendliness and the complete lack of any gesture of courtesy. Dorothy had been a little silly to take such a person as a tenant. "I *am* sorry," he said. "I'm Richard Simms and I've just come back from New York so I thought I'd better come over and meet you. Not only are we neighbors, but I'm your landlord, and I wanted to be sure you were comfortable. I won't stay now, though, and I hope you'll forgive me for disturbing you."

The man finally smiled—faintly—but the suspicious look that he had given Richard as he had opened the door did not disappear from his eyes. When he spoke again there was a half-hearted joviality about his voice that was unconvincing. "It's perfectly okay, Mr. Simms. I ought to be up anyway, but—well, you know how it is—I drank a little too much last night; a fellow gets kind of lonely when he doesn't know people...you know." He held out his hand suddenly and Richard shook it as warmly as he could, but he was so conscious of his own distaste that he felt himself fighting down his tendency to blush and hoped it did not show.

"Of course," he said. "I understand. You must come over and have a drink with us sometime soon. You should meet a few people in town if you're going to stay here." He regretted his words as soon as he had said them, but his natural friendliness and his feeling of guilt about not having wanted to shake the man's hand had forced him to it. "I'll be going on my way," he said, "but I'll see you soon."

"Yeah. Thanks for coming over, Mr. Simms. And don't think this is regular with me. I'm usually up with the sun."

Richard nodded affably and turned away with a gesture of his hand. He realized then that if he hadn't been so intent on seeing the man, he would have known he wasn't up if only because he hadn't let his dog about before. As he approached the door of his own house, he was startled by the sound of Curran's voice calling the dog. Whatever he had thought about his face, there was something vicious in the sound of his voice then, and Richard turned back involuntarily to watch the dog crawling fearfully towards the little house. Curran's eyes met his for an instant, he smiled very briefly, and then Richard entered his own house. He started for the studio, hesitated, and frowned. More by instinct than for any reason, he went to the telephone, dialed the number of Dorothy's office and waited. The line was busy.

He left the telephone and walked through the kitchen to the studio at the end of the house. He had made it out of the old garage, and it had become his favorite room. He drew back the curtain that hung across the big north window. Except for a corner of the house in which Jim Curran was living, he had a reasonably unobstructed view; there were no other houses on that side.

He stood in the window, looking out, and sighed. On awakening he had felt a need to work; the thought that he might be able to paint his own inner confusion onto canvas had risen up like a small ray of hope inside him. He had put it off until now, puttering around the house and the car, seeing that man...he had come into the studio for a moment only, to turn on the heat—but he had postponed the actual getting to work because of a fear that he would only find that he could not do anything. Now, the very impulse had disappeared.

The building outside the window was a physical reminder of the man to whom he had just talked, and it irritated him. He didn't think Curran was "inhuman"; he told himself this again, rebelling against his wife's use of that word, but he was certainly a bad egg, and Richard felt sure they would end up having trouble with him. He wondered if Dorothy had signed a lease with him, and then he moved away from the window. Her number was probably free by this time. He stopped at the door of the studio, and turned back to look at the room. The hell with Curran and the hell with putting it off any longer. He could find out at lunch whether Curran had signed a lease, and it didn't matter anyway. What did matter was for him to get to work and find out whether he could paint or not.

He walked across the room angrily, picked up a stretched white canvas from among the several that were stacked against the wall, and placed it on his easel. He stared at the blank white rectangle and cursed. He wished, ardently, that he had a job, or that he was anything in the world except a painter. This business of having to paint, pulling at him, forcing him all the time, seemed insidious, improper, and in some way almost a *dirty* process. He felt again as he had when he had seen his own pictures hanging on the walls of the New York gallery, and the elation, the joy, the pride, that he had felt when he had painted them had disappeared to be replaced only by shame.

He sat down on the one chair in the room, behind his desk, and looked again at the blankness of the empty canvas on the easel. The purity of it pleased him…what, really, could be behind this impulse to cover it with scratches and scrawls, forms, colors, ideas…whatever you wanted to call them? What kind of sense did they make, finally, and what useful purpose did they serve to anyone, to himself even?

He was, from the point of view of most artists who lived in the southwest, successful. Not very many of them had sold as many pictures for as high prices as he had. He was represented in a good many of the more important museums and he had attained a certain degree of fame and had made some money. He made a wry face and stood up. It had occurred to him rather unexpectedly, and with a deeper shame than he had felt about his pictures, that there was an element of self-pity in his thinking, and the idea made him feel sick at his stomach.

"You're in bad shape, Richard Simms," he said aloud, and went over to look into his open paint box. He was that much more depressed by the hundreds of tubes, the expensive brushes, all the equipment.

2

Henry Franklin liked Kansas City better than St. Louis. He was very much impressed, as he sat silently beside his wife while she drove through the city. He thought the parks were among the most beautiful he had ever seen. He was not, however, really intent upon what he saw. Something had happened to him when he had had such terrible indigestion in the movie in St. Louis the night before. He had then felt—and did still—a strange inner stirring that he could not understand and which seemed to him to be related to the way he had felt when he was very young, fourteen or fifteen, forty years ago.

Whatever it was that was taking place in his...in his what? He thought of the word "soul" but it was a word that frightened him because he had no idea what it meant. *Heart* was perhaps a better word, but it did not seem to express anything beyond a physical organ that pumped blood—or a vague term used to indicate the seat of certain rather terrifying emotions. No, heart and soul were both wrong. He decided that whatever it is that makes a person who and what they are—possibly the "self," if it could be used that way—was doing something queer to him.

He turned to look at his wife; he did not simply glance in her direction, but turned in the seat of the car and stared at her. He stared for such a long time that Mrs. Franklin glanced hurriedly at him—there was a lot of traffic—and said, in what he had long thought of as her "testy" voice: "What are you staring at, Henry? You look ridiculous."

He hesitated, from habit, before answering, and then said in a calm (and to his own amazement) quiet voice: *"You,* Mabel."

She laughed. "What do you mean, 'you, Mabel'?" Her voice was derisive and she imitated him very accurately.

"Just what I said," he went on in the same collected manner. "I'm looking at *you.* It's almost as if I'd never seen you before in my life."

Mrs. Franklin snorted. "This is an idiotic conversation, Henry. I don't know what you're talking about. As if you'd never seen me before...what on earth do you mean?"

Henry smiled, and he was aware that what he had called a "stirring" in himself had mysteriously changed into elation. "You are very fat, Mabel. I always thought you were big. You're not. You're just terribly fat."

Mrs. Franklin put on the brakes so hard that the car behind her almost hit the Cadillac. She looked around and then pulled over to the side of the road. When she had stopped the car, she turned to face her husband. "Henry Franklin, you are going to tell me right now what's the matter with you. I think you're probably ill. I've never heard anything so silly in my life, so...well...you sound as if your mind had failed you. What *is* the matter?"

The smile stayed on his face and he looked at her directly and piercingly. She had never seen such a look in his eyes before and her own gaze faltered and she looked away from him. Something *had* happened to him; he *was* sick.

"What I meant, Mabel, was that you are very fat. After all, that's what I said. You *are* fat."

Mabel, and she was as astonished as Henry, started to cry.

Her husband watched her. "And when you cry," he said, "you're ugly."

3

AT SEVEN O'CLOCK ON FRIDAY, November 9th, Steve Williams was eating his dinner in a lunchroom in Vincennes, Indiana. He was in an extremely bad humor. He had bought a Chevrolet because he had had so much trouble with his old Ford, particularly with the fuel pump, and what had happened? In some place called Loogootee, Indiana, his fuel pump had conked out and he had only made three hundred and fifty miles that day. He could have gone on further, but his eyes were tired, and there had been so much traffic on the road as he'd come into Vincennes that he had decided to stop for dinner at least. He would make up his mind after he had finished eating. He was tempted by the idea of a few drinks and a comfortable bed.

He ate his blue-plate special (ham with some raisins floating around in a paste-colored sauce, peas and carrots, mashed potatoes, a roll with margarine, a cup of coffee) automatically and without the slightest pleasure. Why shouldn't he stop here for the night? What was his hurry? He didn't even know what he was going to, really, except that he did have a physical destination. He'd never even seen Santa Fe, didn't know what he would find when he got there, or what he would do after his arrival.

The idea that he was not in any hurry had an immediate effect on him. He leaned back in his chair, signaled to the waitress, and when she came over to the table, asked her for another cup of coffee. He lighted a cigarette, and felt a sudden luxuriousness arising in him. He would go to a movie, send a postcard to his mother and one to Marjorie. Oddly, although he had hardly thought about his wife all day, now that he did think of her, picturing her in his mind as probably moping alone in the apartment, his feeling was generous and friendly. After all, he was *fond* of her, he'd even been pretty much in love with her at one time. It was strange how—when you got far enough away from someone—you could see them in a very different light.

When the girl had cleared the table and brought his coffee, he got up, walked over to the cashier's desk, and picked out two postal cards. Back at the table, he took a pencil from the pocket of his coat and started to write. The first card he addressed to Mrs. Robert H. Williams, in Trenton, New Jersey. "Dear Mom," he wrote, "Got away on schedule and am having a fine trip. Don't worry about me. Love, S."

He hesitated, with the pencil between his teeth, before he wrote to his wife. After licking the point of the pencil carefully, he wrote the address and then dated the card. "Dear Margie: Everything okay. Hope you are all right. I'll write a letter soon. Don't worry about me and take care of yourself. Love, Steve." He examined it critically. He would have liked to put something more affectionate on the card, but decided against it. As it was, she'd probably think "take care of yourself" meant that he was still crazy about her. Women really were a pain in the neck.

He drank his coffee, paid his bill, bought stamps at the counter, and then walked out into the street. Why not stay at the hotel? Well, why not? The idea that he could, on the spur of the moment, and without having to ask anyone's opinion or permission, stay or not stay at a hotel in Vincennes, Indiana, gave him a good deal of pleasure. He walked slowly across the street, through the swinging glass doors, and into the lobby. The woman at the desk, playing solitaire in a kind of lonely fury, looked up at him as he approached her, but did not speak until he was at the desk. She then smiled (as if someone had turned a switch on inside her) looked directly into his eyes, and said: "Good evening."

"Good evening," he said expansively. "Do you have a room for tonight?"

Her eyes narrowed and the smile disappeared. "How many?"

"Just for me. A single."

"I don't have one with a bath."

Although he had not wanted a room with a bath—in fact he hadn't even thought about it—Steve looked slightly disappointed. "Well, I guess that'll be all right," he said, with an air of regret. "Where can I leave my car?"

"There's a parking lot right around *there,*" she pointed (with a great bending of her arm) through the lobby and around the corner, "and I'll send the boy out for your luggage." She shoved the register at him and he read the notice on the card: "Guests without luggage are requested to pay in advance." As he signed it he raised his eyebrows. Was it that kind of a hotel? He felt a faint stirring of excitement in his belly. He hadn't had a woman for a long time, and the idea of an illicit rendezvous with a strange female, in an unknown hotel and an unknown town, gave him a thrill. Maybe the boy could fix him up.

The boy turned out to be a man about sixty years old. He walked around to the parking lot, pointed to an empty space for the car and took Steve's small suitcase. Then he led him back into the hotel, through the lobby and up one flight of stairs. On the first floor, they passed the men's room and stopped at room No. 21. The man opened the door, turned on the light, put the bag on the luggage rack at the foot of the bed, and then turned to Steve. "Will there be anything else, sir?"

Their eyes met for the first time, and Steve fumbled in his pocket, felt a quarter, and handed it to him. He looked away and said, with an elaborate gesture of his hand and an air of assumed boredom: "Say, how're the women in this town?"

The man looked at the quarter in the palm of his hand, smiled, and said: "It's like every place else." Then he looked back at the quarter.

Steve had his hand in his pocket once more, but there was something in the man's eyes that made him change his mind and the feeling of desire turned into a flat cold lump inside him. He wished he hadn't come into the hotel, hadn't spoken to this greasy little man. He wished he'd never even come to Vincennes, Indiana.

"I guess that'll be all," he said bluntly and put his hand on the door knob.

The man leered at him and started out through the door. "Well, if there's anything you want, just call on the telephone," he said, and Steve closed the door firmly in his face.

Alone, he looked at the sordid little room, the naked light bulb in the center of the ceiling, the bed cover with a hole in it. It all made him feel rotten. He waited until he was sure the man had had time to get down the stairs and then he walked out into the hall, leaving his key in the door. He walked to the men's room, closed the door behind him and locked the bolt. When he was standing over the toilet, he looked at the wall directly in front of him: at an obscene drawing, and read, below it, one of the filthiest—and at the same time most exciting—verses he had ever read anywhere. The desire that had been in him only a few minutes before suddenly leaped into a furious, hot flame again, and he unzipped his trousers with a trembling hand.

He felt a lot better when he got back to his room.

4

"Steve Darling:

"The apartment is very lonely without you and I keep wondering how soon I will hear something from you. I'm sorry if I behaved badly when you left, or if I made you feel that I did not understand the reasons for your leaving. I suppose I don't really understand them, but I don't think that matters too much now. Having been alone these last days (it seems like a very long time already) I think I am beginning to realize that I have not been the best wife in the world to you.

"I don't know, Steve, how much I can change or if I will be able to be a better companion in the future, but I do know that I can't bear the idea of having you stay away too long. I love you very much, darling, and will do all I can to make you happy, but please don't stay away from me any longer than you have to—and have a good trip. I try to imagine you, driving alone all the way out there, and it makes me feel lonelier to think about it.

"I'll mail this letter to General Delivery, Santa Fe, and I hope it will be there when you arrive. All I really want is for you to be happy, and to have the chance to try and make life a good thing for both of us.

"With all my love,
"Marjorie."

She read the letter over, sighed to herself, and then tore it up. It was useless, she knew, to write him that way. What he had run away from was the very thing she was putting in the letter, her love. It seemed unfair and unjust that loving someone could almost seem a crime, and try as she might, she could not fathom his reasons for resisting her affection and devotion to him.

She took out another piece of paper and started to write again:

"Dear Steve:

"Just a note to greet you on your arrival in Santa Fe, and to let you know that I'm thinking about you. I hope the trip wasn't too hard and that you didn't drive too fast. Have a good rest while you're out there, and write to me if you feel like it.

"The apartment seems empty and lonely without you, but I'm fine, and hope you are, too.

"My love, always,
"Marjorie."

Maybe that was better, but it seemed to be impossible to write even a note without saying something that would probably anger him. She addressed an envelope, folded the letter, and put it in. The one hope she had was that perhaps he was not finding it too rewarding or too easy, being alone all the time. He was like a little boy in many ways, and even if he resented her, he needed her at the same time.

5

THE STORM IN THE MOUNTAINS on the evening of November 9th had come up without warning. Caroline Pratt, sitting almost contentedly in the front seat of her car next to Tom Foster—who drove very well, she had decided—did not mind the snow. It had first begun to fall just after dark as they were on their way down State Route 76 from Truchas and Trampas. She had been irritated and surprised, earlier in the day, to find that Tom knew the country well; better than she did, even. They had left Sandia Crest early in the morning, had had a cup of coffee in Bernalillo, a real breakfast in Santa Fe, and had then driven into the Truchas mountains by what Tom called the back way: Las Vegas, Mora, Rio Pueblo, Penasco.

From the original savage excitement and brutality, their relationship had suddenly been transformed into something for which she was completely unprepared. In his admission that he was familiar with the country, and the manner in which he had taken over—driving all day long, not talking very much, except to point out a particular view or place with which he seemed to have some sentimental association—he had changed radically. She had resented it at first, although she kept herself from saying anything about it, and when she asked herself from where her resentment had come, she realized that it was because he had unexpectedly acquired a past. From the stranger, the unknown man about whom she had known nothing, whom she had decided to pick up mostly because she had become lonely driving alone, he had changed into a man with feelings, associations, past relationships, a *life*. Now, as the snow increased and the visibility became continuously poorer, she found herself admitting fear of that past, fear that she would not be able to compete with it, that he would tire of her even more quickly than he himself had tried to tell her. From the casual remarks he made: "We came up here in 1942," or "This place is a place we used to be crazy about," she knew there had been other people, other women...

She looked at him in the faint light from the dashboard and breathed more quickly. She would have, had it been even so little as one day earlier, reached out to him in an effort to arouse him sexually, but she knew by instinct that he would not respond now, that he wanted something else. He was living back in some dream that had never been fulfilled, and it was the dream she feared. It was the dream of which she was—and the recognition forced her into a corner—jealous.

Sitting next to him, unable to reach him, not knowing how to bring him back to the present, Caroline felt what she could only describe to herself as terror, although the word was perhaps too strong...or was it? As if to justify herself, she counted over what she had as a person that might hold him, but there was very little to add up, very little she could offer to him. Money, things, yes; but herself? She did not think of herself as attractive, she hated her name, even. The one thing he had wanted from her, the possession of her body, was already his as completely as it could ever be, but he did not want it now, would not want it continuously. She began to feel trapped and desperate; the intangible thread of sex between them seemed to her far too weak to hold the burden of her needs. She was frightened of what she really wanted, frightened of what she was sure would be his rejection of her. Already, he must be measuring her against whatever other women had been in his life and finding her lacking a great deal.

With his eyes steadily on the road, Tom had let himself go back into his own past all day long. He was aware, in his body more than in his mind, of the subtle change that had come over both of them—it had begun when they had gone to sleep on Sandia the night before—and he was curiously sad. He would have liked to be driving over these roads alone, or with someone else, but not with Carrie. He felt a little sorry for her: she had been very quiet, very meek, as if she had known there was something going on in him that she should not interrupt, and he had wished for a moment that he could tell her what it was the mountains made him feel; but the suggestion, in his own mind, that any form of tenderness should or could enter their relationship, made him resist her with his full force. He was not going to get involved with her or with any girl—money or no money.

They ate, in a silent and lonely manner, in Espanola, without even having a drink before dinner. The storm had been confined to the mountains, apparently, as there was no snow on the Taos highway, and they decided they would drive on to Taos and spend the night there. They both agreed (although it was difficult for them to look each other directly in the eyes) that they didn't want to sleep in the car again.

When they did get to Taos, it was after ten, and although Tom would have liked to get them two single rooms, he was afraid of her reaction if he did, so he registered as Mr. and Mrs. Charles Foster of Dallas, Texas, and got them a large room with a double bed.

It was not until they were in the room that she said, in a tentative and gentle way (it seemed to him that she was really afraid of him, then): "It's been a nice day, Tom. Thank you."

He looked at her, touched in spite of himself by the words "thank you," and then turned away. "I've always liked the mountains," he said. "It was good to see them again."

There was no impetus, no starting point in their words and they relapsed into silence. When they were in the bed, he turned his back on her and she stayed close to him, with her arm thrown lightly over his arm and chest. On a sudden impulse, an impulse that went against everything he had been thinking about her all day long, he turned around, kissed her cheek, and then kissed her on the mouth. She held him very lightly for a moment, all the need and the desperation finding a center in his body, and then she said, haltingly, and very much afraid of what he would answer: "Tom...I think..." she tried to see him in the dark before she went on: "...please don't be angry with me if I say this. I think...Well...I love you."

He did not reply, and his body stiffened against her. She took a deep breath and then said rapidly. "It doesn't change anything. I'll let you go, but I had to say it. I've never felt like this about anyone before. I can't help saying it."

He released himself from the grip of her hands and put his arms around her, holding her close to him. His feeling of pity for her had intensified into something very strong, something that was more than pity alone, something that he could not fight. "It's all right, Carrie," he said.

Their inevitable love-making, forced upon them by the close contact of their bodies, was very different then and when it was over, they stayed close together in the bed. They both had the feeling, as they went to sleep, that they were children again.

6

Emily Hume did sit on the right side of the car on November 9th. She sat there all day long and what was most surprising about it was that Toby never objected once, in fact he was irritatingly amiable all day long.

She had read all the comic books over, looked at all the views obediently as they had driven through Oak Creek Canyon, Sedona, Jerome, and finally into Prescott. When her mother had told her that some bunch of red hills in or near Sedona looked exactly like a Spanish castle, she had agreed so readily (even Toby had only sighed a little) that both Robert and Mary Hume had begun to eye their children suspiciously, as if they were sick.

When they were at dinner in a Chinese restaurant in Prescott, Emily decided that although it had been a very boring day (even more boring than usual) it was probably worth it. The parents were very solicitous, wanted to know if they both felt all right, if there was anything special they wanted to eat, and since it was still early even suggested they might go to a movie.

The only movie showing in Prescott turned out to be, as Emily read on the poster outside the theatre, a "Thrillpacked story of basic human emotions" and they did not go. The parents were so concerned about them that Toby slept with his father that night and Emily slept with her mother.

7

RICHARD SIMMS HAD BEEN ABLE to work. He had even worked on two canvases that day. There had been a strange sensation of an old fury working inside him even as he knew in his mind that he would probably destroy the pictures before he finished them. He had not felt any real fire burning inside him as he worked, but there had been something very strong, formed from habit and sheer technical skill that had made him feel better. He had worked like a good craftsman all day and the knowledge of his own ability had given him pleasure. It was not until after dinner that night that he had begun to feel the letdown. He had gone back into the studio while Dorothy was clearing off the table, and had taken a quick look at both pictures. He had known at once, with a sinking feeling, that there was nothing in them. The colors were all right, the forms were perfectly pleasant to look at—inoffensive at least—but the pictures, as pictures and as art, said nothing to him. There was no idea, no inspiration (much as he hated that word), no communication of any sort in either of them. He felt nothing about them except that they were no good.

He put a determined smile on his face when he came back into the house from the studio. It was less to hide anything from his wife, than because there was nothing—and he knew this in his heart—that anyone else could do about what he was going through. His relation to his work was the most completely solitary and intimate thing in his life and the area in him from whence it sprang was closed to everyone in the world except through the final result: the paintings themselves. It was the only way in which he exposed that part of himself which was hidden, otherwise, from everyone, Dorothy included. But he knew that Dorothy knew that the smile was a command not to mention his work.

As he came into the living room to find her seated before the fireplace with brandy and coffee, he knew as she looked up at him that she *knew,* too; but in the over-quick way in which she smiled and poured his coffee, he knew that she would not say anything. He watched her as she poured the coffee, a lock of her brown hair falling down over her cheek, and it was at that moment that he understood something (he had, somehow, known it before, but this was the first time it came to the forefront of his consciousness) about what was wrong. He had isolated it into his painting, into his feelings of failure, had blamed himself for some incomprehensible trouble and depression; what he knew in that unexpected flash of understanding was that he had been looking in the wrong place. The dissatisfaction, the guilt, the lack of purpose, centered in his life and not in his work.

Looking down on her, his body tensed from what was going on in his mind, the aura of femininity about her, the knowledge that she was bearing his troubles and confusion with an enormous womanly strength, made him almost hate her. But it was not only Dorothy against whom he was rebelling then. The world of women, particularly of his mother and his wife, that had surrounded him and led him and taken care of him all of his life...that was what he had begun, unconsciously, to hate. He had been supported, protected, and cared for like a pre-adolescent child for as long as he could remember; and for that he had perjured himself in every way: catering to his mother, letting his life be led for him, even to the point where, having once transferred his life to Dorothy (escaping from one strong woman to another equally strong) he had become a proper husband, making love on schedule, doing as he was told.

His painting, and at that moment he also knew that he was essentially a good painter—he knew that as the only ray of light in his life—had been his only escape; the little private world which they had been unable to control, direct, or manage. But even that had not come out unscathed in thirty-nine years. When they had both found that they could not intrude on that world, they had nevertheless almost managed to make it their own by talking of him as a good painter, a fine artist, a talented and brilliant man...as if they, finally, had also made that possible.

It occurred to him, very briefly, that he could stop painting forever; it would be one way—the only way—to at least rob them of that. He was a man all right, he thought sardonically to himself, but a man in outer form only. He had been, successfully and very delicately, emasculated. What was really bad about it was that it could not have happened without his own connivance and help.

He sat down, trembling a little from what he had been thinking, and poured the brandy with a shaking hand. The realization and the admission were almost too much for him. He felt that he had just taken an irrevocable step towards a world that he neither understood nor wanted. He could not go back on himself now.

8

As they sat together over their coffee and brandy, Dorothy Simms felt a spasm of fear passing through her. Richard had come in from the studio, where he had apparently gone to look at the work he had done that day—if he had done any, he hadn't said anything to her about it—and had sat down, poured the brandy with a trembling hand, and said nothing. What she had felt from him, and from the look on his face, seemed to her threatening as well as frightening. His self-dissatisfaction, self-doubt, the questions he was asking himself, were all things that were—as inevitably as the tide pulls the sea out from the shore—things that were taking him away from her.

She had looked up, smiled, and then asked (knowing as she asked him) how his work had gone. He had looked back at her with an odd smile, had not spoken for a few minutes—minutes during which the silence seemed heavy and weighted—and had then said: "All right, I guess." From the manner in which he had pronounced the words, she knew that he did not want to talk about it, that she had made a mistake to bring it up. "That's good, darling," she had said amiably. "I know that as soon as you get back to work, you'll feel better about everything."

He had only smiled at her reply, and had then said suddenly: "Say, by the way, did you sign a lease with Curran?" She had nodded quickly, glad to have the subject changed. "Yes, for six months."

"Too bad. I went over to see him this morning, and he *is* a..." he hesitated, "...well, a queer duck. I don't like him."

Because of the way in which he had said it, Dorothy felt defensive and a little angry with what she took as criticism. "I don't see why that is so important," she said. "He can't get us into any trouble, and the rent is paid for three months, which is a blessing."

The same smile again. "I didn't think we needed it that badly."

She repressed an impulse to counter sarcastically to this remark, and said, as simply as she could. "I don't really think Mr. Curran is that important, Dick. Certainly nothing for us to argue about."

"You're right. Sorry."

She reached out to him across the table. "Look, darling, what are we really talking about? Your voice sounds angry and critical and...I don't know. Is it something I've done? What's the matter?"

He looked at her steadily, still withdrawn and impassive. "I don't think there's anything the matter, and I don't think we're really talking about something else. Let's not make a thing out of it."

She shook her head and looked away from him. "All right. I guess it's my turn to be sorry, then. But..." she looked into his face again, "you seem almost hostile tonight. Did you have a bad day?"

His face could not control the anger he seemed to be feeling then. "Yes, I did have a bad day. I often have bad days. Must we talk about it right now?"

"No, of course not, Dick. Not if you don't want to."

He stood up, walked across the room, and then walked back to stand before her. "Look, Dorothy, it is not a question of whether I want to or not. I don't ever talk about my work when I'm in the middle of it. And you've been married to me long enough to know that..."

"Dick!"

He looked down at the hurt expression in her eyes.

"And don't look so hurt! My God, it's bad enough without that!"

She smiled sadly and continued to look at him. "That's what I mean,

Dick. What's bad enough? This is something more than your work. I know that much."

He raised both his hands and then let them drop to his sides. "All right, so you know it's something more than my work. What do you think it is, if you insist on making something out of it."

She shook her head again. "I don't know what it is, Dick. I wish I did. But it does seem to me that if we could talk it out, we'd both feel better. Isn't that reasonable?"

He nodded his head. "Yes, Dorothy, very reasonable indeed. Like everything else with you, it all makes good logical sense. But you're the one who thinks something is wrong, what do you think it is? Just exactly what is it that you want to talk about?"

"About whatever is the matter with you. And something certainly is."

He laughed. "It certainly is, and every time I'm questioned about it makes it that much easier, I suppose. *Must* I be cross-questioned about everything?"

She put the coffee cups on the tray, picked up the tray, and stood up. "No, Dick, of course not. Let's forget it. I'm sorry I brought it up." She was as distant as he had been all evening.

He watched her as she held the tray in her hands, seemed about to say something, then shrugged his shoulders and turned his back on her and went to stand facing the window. She walked away from his stern back into the kitchen, rinsed out the cups, put them in the dish dryer on the sink, and then came back to the living room. She looked at him, stifled the desire to go over to him and put her arms around him, and said, in the same reserved, chilly voice: "I think I'll go to bed now, Dick."

He turned, glanced at her very briefly, and said: I'll be along in a little while."

She waited then for some time, without any thought of sleep, until she heard him coming into the bedroom. He undressed in the dark, and when he came to bed, he slipped in quietly, although he must have known (she was sure of that) that she was not asleep. He lay rigidly by her for a few minutes and then she put her hands out to touch him. "Whatever is wrong, darling, I'm so glad to have you back again. I missed you so much while you were away." She hesitated, drew a deep breath, and then went on. "The important thing is that you're here, and that we're all right in ourselves; that we remember that we're together and that we love each other."

He did not say anything for a while, and did not respond to her touch. When she had withdrawn her hands, he said, "I guess you're right. Let's try and get some sleep, shall we?"

9

IN THE MORNING, WHEN RICHARD Simms had awakened him by knocking at his door, Jim Curran had felt almost nothing except vague anger at being disturbed, but as the day went on, his dreams of the night before, the anger he felt with the world in general (and the envy and rancor he felt in relation to such people as the Simms, for instance) began to build up in him. He had stayed home all morning, and most of the afternoon, despondent and lethargic, and it was not until late in the day that he decided he had to go out. He wanted a drink, and he was tired of drinking alone; he wanted to be in the company of people, even though he felt nothing but antipathy towards them—antipathy and resentment.

He dressed, much as if he was putting on a protective cover against the world; took a quick drink of straight whiskey and started for the door. As he did so, the dog (she had been hiding under the bed most of the day) started across the room after him and he urged her out as he stood in the doorway. She crept slowly past him, terrified that he might strike her on her way out, and then bolted out the door. He smiled grimly in her direction, walked to the car, and then looked around at her. She was waiting near the car, watching him, and he remembered something he had thought of the day before. He remembered that he had had an idea as he had left the laundromat.

He opened the door of his Plymouth, called softly to the dog, and when she was very near him, leaned down over her. She cowered, trembling, on the ground below him, and he patted her head. With a look of enormous gratitude, the dog jumped up into the car and sat, waiting expectantly, on the front seat. Jim closed the door behind her, walked around the car, got in on the driver's side, closed that door, and started the motor. He would have to go downtown first to get a couple of things (might as well pick up his laundry, too) and he would have to wait until after dark anyway.

When he had driven out to the laundromat and picked up the laundry, it was already dark. He stopped in town, went to the drugstore, decided to have a sandwich there, thought of having another drink, and decided against that. He was too intent upon what he was going to do later. He bought a roll of one-inch adhesive tape when he had eaten, went back to the car, patted the dog again as he got in, and then drove back up past his house on Canyon Road out towards the site where they had been digging the well the day before. It wasn't necessarily an ideal spot, but there were very few houses around there, and the well-diggers would have stopped working by that time.

When he arrived at the well-site, he looked up at the rig, deserted, alone, and silent. He would have liked to start it up himself, but even if he had had the key to the ignition (the motor was from some old car), it would be risky. There was one house somewhat nearer than he had remembered; he could see the lights from where he stood. Even if he couldn't start it up, he derived a curious satisfaction from looking at the well-rig, imagining it hammering its way into the earth, pounding and pounding. It calmed and fascinated him in much the same way that the washing machines and particularly the dryer had made him feel.

He was interrupted in his reverie by the dog coming up to him. As usual, and in spite of his gentleness with her in the car, she slunk towards him and as he watched her he was excited by the recollection of his purpose—he had forgotten it for a moment—in coming to this place.

He smiled at the dog, reached his hand out carefully, and stroked her head. Overjoyed at this attention, the dog came closer and Jim picked her up. He walked to the car (holding the dog under his left arm) took the adhesive tape and a pair of pliers from the glove compartment, and walked back to a tree not far from the well-rig. Still holding the dog under his arm, he squatted on the ground, opened the container of tape, unrolled a long piece of it which he held in his mouth, and then he placed the dog in a sitting position with her back against the tree. He strapped the tape around her body, fastening her to the tree; stopped to unwind more tape with which he secured her more tightly. Then he held her muzzle closed with one hand and taped her jaws together.

He sat back and examined his handiwork in the moonlight. With a smile on his face and a feeling of ecstasy boiling up inside him, he picked up the pliers and reached for the dog.

10

Marion Mercer was fifty-five and she knew she looked it. She had been living alone ever since that bastard, Armando, had left her, and she hated it. She knew that he had never really cared for her, and now, with her fourth drink in her hand, she admitted that all she wanted was to have him back just so that she could at least have someone in the house with her. She had built the house for him, and now here she was sitting in it alone. She was always alone these days.

She thought idly of doing something about dinner, but the only thing she really wanted was another drink—when she'd finished this one, of course. As she lifted her glass to her lips, she heard a weird and horrible cry from somewhere—or at least she thought she did. She was pretty drunk. Even so, she went to the door, put her hand on it, and listened intently. There was no sound. She probably hadn't heard anything after all.

She drained the glass, walked unsteadily into the kitchen, poured herself another drink, carried it back into the living room, and then she heard it again. Or did she? For some time after that she kept thinking that she was hearing a strange, eerie, almost bloodcurdling moan...it was like nothing she had ever heard before. She did not investigate it—after all what could she have done about whatever it was (sounded like some animal in the distance) if she had found it—decided she would not be bothered cooking anything, and had two more drinks before she went to bed. By that time she knew that it must have been her imagination. There wasn't a sound outside; and if it hadn't been something in her mind, it had at least stopped.

11

When Peter Wells reached Terre Haute, Indiana, he was curiously depressed, and although it was already dark and he was tired, he decided to go through the city and stay somewhere beyond it. About two miles past the last houses of the town, he saw a neon sign for a court, with the words "Vacancy" quivering at him in bright blue, and he pulled off the road. It looked all right to him; almost anything would have looked all right.

When he had registered, paid, given Kelly a run, and taken his bags into the small, dingy room, he sat down in the one chair and stared glumly around. It was a place (and he had picked it unconsciously) that suited and deepened his mood of depression and fatigue, and it seemed to him that it was just as well. He might, by the increase of his state of mind, find out what was at the bottom of it. He made a weak gesture towards Kelly—reaching out his hand and snapping his fingers—but the dog did not respond other than by looking at him sadly and thumping his tail in a melancholy way. He had, and he sighed as he realized the affinity between himself and the dog, communicated his own mood to Kelly, too.

There was no reason—his mind began on this train of thought as if to build up a defense for itself before it was attacked—for him to feel this way. He was making the trip to California for an obviously good reason. He wanted to go to California, he wanted to write a movie script, he would be glad of the experience and the money...and then his line of thought broke. Why did he want to go to California? Why did he want to write a movie? Why would he be glad of the experience? In fact, was he pleased about any of it? He shook his head, stood up and walked over to the bed where he had left his bag. He opened it, took out the bottle of whiskey, poured himself a drink, and then sat down again. After the first sip—the taste of which he hated—(why hadn't he at least asked for some ice?), he set the glass down, lighted a cigarette, and stared at the room again.

What he had wanted to do was to stay with his father. The idea that he was telling this to himself because he was afraid his father would actually die while he was away crossed his mind, and he rejected it. He was sure that his present feelings had nothing to do with his father's possible death, but there was something behind them that was more obscure—more sinister—than that. He wanted to be with his father—and that knowledge shot through him in a freezing flash of reality—because he was lonely. His father was what he had in his life now, nothing more. His father and his dog.

Ever since his discharge from the Army, he had led the barren life of a successful writer. Barren? The word had set itself automatically into his thoughts and he smiled as he realized how accurate it was. He knew now (it was all coming very quickly) that he had managed, with his success, with the enormous number of people he had come to know in New York, and the steady grind at work he liked, to convince himself that he was leading a happy and constructive life. It had never before penetrated his consciousness that it was anything else—it had never seemed barren, living in it—but it was empty now; now that he was somewhere in the middle of the United States, away from everything that had formed his life for the last five years.

What was he really doing in Indiana, on his way to Hollywood, where he would acquire more friends, more money, perhaps more fame? Like a rising sickness, he knew then that he did not want any of those things...But why? Why not? The question was answered with a delayed explosion of realization...an answer he was getting too late. His loneliness was such that he wished with all his heart that he had stayed within the aura of safety, protection, and—above all—unaloneness, that he had felt with his father during those few days in Three Bridges.

Was it sentimentality or self-pity that formed the next thoughts in his mind? His father loved him—it had taken him almost all of his forty-odd years to find that out—and he needed, terribly, the security his father provided. Except for that, his life was not shared with anyone.

His mind went back to what his father had said about death and nature, and he knew then that death was only all right if life had been prior to it, fulfilled. In order to die well, properly, as his father would, one had first to have lived well. His own life—he did not think about it then in terms of "love"—was unnatural because it was not shared. In the same way that man had been created, physically, not to live alone, life was a process which required sharing with other people. To be liked, loved, admired, praised, envied...none of these things were enough.

He poured himself another drink, and let the feeling of loneliness possess him, and then he began to laugh. Loneliness was just another trap, another obstacle between himself and the truth underlying his state of being. The truth was, and the abrupt discovery of it made him feel...what? ...*merry* was the best word...that he wanted to know where he was going, in the car as well as in life itself. Man's destination—and his father had conveyed this to him—was not on earth. The passing presence of knowledge had never let him understand this before. In a second, in a squalid tourist cabin, the understanding had become a part of him. He remembered, vaguely, irritatingly, something that had put this in better words than he could. He rose from his chair with an instinctive animal-like movement, stepped over to the bed, and pulled a notebook from the open suitcase. After leafing through it, he stopped on one page, smiled, and read the quotation to himself:

"We endure the decay of fortune, of bodie, of soul, of honour, to possesse lower pictures; pictures that are not originals, not made by that hand of God, Nature; but artificial beauties: and for that bodie we give a soul; and for that drug which might have been bought where they bought it, for a shilling, we give an estate. The image of God is more worth than all substances; and we give it for colours, for dreams, for shadows."

He closed the book and shook his head. Human progress was not so very fast, after all. John Donne had written that in 1625. But, as if his hand had reached out across those centuries, back into the past, where it had been momentarily clasped, he felt happy. He did not, his mind seemed very slow, know what it was he felt, but he smiled at Kelly, who jumped up and ran over to him, and then he stood up. Why hadn't he telephoned his father before?

12

Mrs. Jones knew her place. Although she had worked for the Wells family for more than fifteen years, had seen Mrs. Wells die, and had seen Peter go into the Army and come back, she did not feel that she had any right to voice her personal feelings or opinions about the family. But, on November 9th, when old Mr. Wells decided to stay in bed, she would have liked to give vent to a few statements.

It was all very well for the old man to say that it was nothing more than a slight cold, but a cold—when you are past eighty—is not necessarily a laughing matter, and for that man to stay in bed all day!

When she brought his tray to his bedside, Charles Wells saw the determined, disapproving look in her eyes, recognizing it as a curious manifestation of concern and sympathy. It was as if she disapproved of God for permitting him to be so weak as to stay in bed.

For himself, it was an increase in his lack of resistance to death. The cold was very slight, and it did not trouble him. He was not troubled, really, at all, but he was interested in his great fatigue...he had never been so tired in his life, and before he went to sleep that night, he wondered whether he would have the energy to wake up the next morning.

NOVEMBER 10, 1951

1

THE LICENSE PLATES ON THE automobiles registered in the State of New Mexico bear the legend: "The Land of Enchantment," and as Dorothy Simms went out to her car on Saturday morning, just before nine o'clock, she stared at the plate on her husband's Ford, parked next to her Mercury. Enchantment, she thought to herself, is a curious word, with more than one meaning. To enchant could be a dubious thing, and the very land of New Mexico, arid and forbidding at times, was enchanting in too many senses of the word.

She sat for a while in the front seat of the car, before starting it, and two levels of her mind seemed to be working against each other. On the one hand, she was irritated at having to go to the office on Saturday morning because someone wanted to look at a house—someone who, like so many people at this time of the year, would not want to buy a house but would probably enjoy being driven around the city—and on another, deeper level of her mind she was thinking about her husband. For the first time since their marriage, she wished that he was something other than an artist. There was an aim, or was it, more accurately, a reward?, that seemed necessary to artists—a nebulous, indefinable need for satisfaction—that she was unable to understand. It seemed to her that Dick was reaching out for something to fulfill a violence in himself, and in the reaching, some integral part of him left the everyday world to explore, search, struggle, for...for what?

How far from nature can man stray, finally, and what are the rewards of creative art...for the artist? It had, she knew, nothing to do with whether he sold pictures or not, or even whether he showed them. But the whole process, from her point of view, appeared to be a violent, destructive thing...when he could, once more, shatter the wall inside himself and express that shattering on canvas, he would be all right. But how could anyone enjoy or need that? What was it that drove people to art in the first place?

She had originally accepted that he was an artist in much the same matter-of-fact way that she would have accepted it had he been a plumber. But a plumber did not arrive at a place where he could no longer install a toilet, lay a pipe, or repair a faucet. She could not understand why a painter could not paint. If he said he couldn't, for whatever incomprehensible reasons, she knew he was telling the truth. But the reasons, she felt instinctively certain of this, were not rooted in art. The obstacles, or blocks, were tied up with some corresponding block in his life. She could feel him probing, analyzing, rejecting...and she knew that he was beating his way around the problem in an ever-decreasing spiral of self-torture that would, eventually, reach the center and break through. Then, and not before, he would get it out of his system. But she did not know how much longer she would be able to go on *not* helping him, which was what he seemed to need from her; nor could she accept—with ease or grace—his surliness, his ill-humor, and the fact that she was powerless.

What her mind continued to return to was that there was (as much because of his protestations to the contrary, as for any other reason) something fundamentally wrong in their life together. She did not *mind* (and she told herself that she did not hold it against him) that he had only made love to her perfunctorily, once, since his return from New York, but it did not seem natural to her. It deprived them both of an area of expression that was, under some circumstances at least, the most important thing in their marriage. The things they had been able to say with their hands, their bodies, and their feelings—the things that did not belong in words—were now left unexpressed, as if they were no longer there to be expressed, and it frightened her. When she reached out to him—as she had the night before—and felt only the stiffening of his body, the rejection of herself, she was alarmed. She had even touched him later, in his sleep, and he had moved abruptly away, to sleep on the edge of the bed. She had felt that he would have preferred to sleep alone, and that he had not done so for fear of hurting her.

She started the car and backed out of the parking space into the driveway. She knew that she could not talk about it to him now, that the formulation of the situation in words would only make it that much more difficult for both of them. She would have to wait until he spoke about it himself or solved it in some other way.

As she turned the car and headed towards the road, she glanced in the direction of the guest house and saw—or thought she saw—the leering face of that Mr. Curran looking out at her through the curtained window facing the drive. She looked away and drove out into the road. For some idiotic reason, he too had become a problem in her life. He was constantly getting involved in their conversation, and while she had had her own fears and doubts about him—as a tenant mostly—Dick's reaction to him had been so serious, he had talked so much about him, that she began to feel there was something sinister about the man.

She felt, suddenly, lonely…and isolated from life. She seemed to have nothing of her own any more. She was losing contact with her husband—which was all that really mattered to her—and she was working at something which she did not like, fundamentally, and for a woman who was perhaps only her enemy. Not that she didn't like Mrs. Simms, but in all honesty, when Mrs. Simms died (and not before) Dick would belong to her at last.

2

Stephen Williams' happiness at his escape from his wife and his life in New York had turned into something sour and heavy inside him. He had driven all day long—from Vincennes, Indiana, to a small town in Oklahoma, called Vinita—and the entire day's drive had been just so much heavy labor to him. His sense of freedom and independence had disappeared completely, and the thought of the future, which had seemed boundless and excitingly free only the day before, now presented itself to him as something to be dreaded and feared. Where was he really going? And did he want all this freedom after all? The slight feelings of guilt that he had felt about Marjorie from time to time had now magnified themselves into something enormous and dreadful.

When he reached New Mexico, he would be alone there, he would not know anyone. It occurred to him that he did not have to go there at all; he could go anywhere he wanted; but at the same moment, he also knew that he really had no place to go and that it would not matter if he changed his destination. What he had been escaping was something that was inescapable in any case; it lay in his chest, laughing at his petty attempts to get away from it. It flashed through his mind, just before he went to sleep, that he could go back, but a surge of anger and pride rose up to forbid that course. He would never allow Marjorie to forgive him—he knew just how she would do it, too, with that ever-loving, ever-right, female manner of hers.

Life did seem to be a trap that night, and there was nothing to alleviate it except the horrible promise of another long and tiring drive in strange and hostile country the next day; across roads that led to nothing, towards a destination which he now only feared.

3

From Kansas City, Missouri, Henry Franklin had driven the Cadillac. He drove faster and better than his wife, a fact that she noted with mixed feelings of confusion and bitterness, and something which—while he was also aware of it—he was careful not to mention. He felt magnanimous towards Mabel; his only real emotion about her was, he knew at last, pity. And, whatever their marriage had been up to now, he felt genuinely sorry for her. She could not help what she had been, and she could not now help her confusion, consternation, and bitterness. She was, in his eyes, a woman who had been suddenly and impossibly robbed of her child or perhaps just of her most precious possession. After the scene in the car the afternoon before, they had gone to a motel outside the city (instead of the hotel where Mabel had made reservations) and she had made no more than a feeble protest. It was her acquiescence, as much as that crashing force inside him that seemed—still—miraculous; that made him feel so strong. He had no desire to take further revenge on his wife. Her capitulation had been curiously complete, and as they drove in silence (faster than she liked to drive) he looked at her from time to time with genuine concern. Something in her had been destroyed, and while he was glad of this, his feeling was similar to that which one might have at seeing some very ugly landmark suddenly destroyed by an earthquake. He missed the presence of the thing he had hated, as if a grievance had been removed too quickly.

When they stopped at Dodge City, Kansas, that night, he treated her with solicitude and tenderness, and as if this was even more difficult to bear than his cruelty (for he now thought of it as cruelty) of the day before, Mabel cried for the second time in two days. She did not protest at having to share a double bed with him that night, and when they were in bed together, she stayed close to his small body, as if asking for protection for the first time in her life.

4

Tom and Carrie had slept late, and had awakened in Taos with an increase of the child-like, puzzled, and innocent feelings they had both had on going to sleep the night before. Tom, in the moments before he was fully awake, before his resistance to the woman in bed with him had had time to take full effect, felt a combination of shyness and tenderness that bewildered him briefly, and finally—as his mind became more alert—made him angry. The furious sexual beginning through which they had passed seemed to him over, and it was with a false, habitual, cynical smile that he pressed his body against hers. His feelings of the night before, his submission to her use of the word *love,* his acceptance of her, embarrassed him. The night, in much the same way as alcohol might have done it, had betrayed him into the beginnings of something he did not want to face in the daylight.

He began to make love to her automatically, angrily, even cruelly, as if by exhausting himself physically, by being brutal, he could destroy what he felt had taken place between them. But when it was over, he felt even more uncomfortable than he had beforehand. The bitterness that had gone into his love-making, that had been directed against her— against what she had made of them—had, instead, turned itself on him.

She had not spoken to him, had not even opened her eyes, had only submitted to him passively. What he saw in her face afterwards was like a reflection of what was going on inside himself, which he neither understood nor wanted to know about. He took a shower, washing himself vigorously, as if the very scrubbing would wash away his suspect feelings. He frowned his way sullenly through breakfast, disinterested and almost unaware of the girl sitting opposite him at the table, and it was not until she said—as she spoke, her fear of him seemed to have increased—"What would you like to do today, Tom?" that he took his eyes off himself and looked at her.

The strange and unfamiliar mixture of emotions expanded in his chest as he looked at and thought about her, and the one feeling, a feeling of pity for this young, rich girl, blotted out his confusion. She had everything. Everything he would have wanted, and he knew— even if he did not understand how or why it was so—how fantastically empty her life was. Her tone of voice, the humility and fear he had felt in it, was that of a beggar. She had stooped so low—so low as to pick up a hitch-hiker (practically a bum), himself—because (and he did not think this, but knew it from some previously buried instinct that had been exposed since he had met her) of her own enormous sense of insecurity, of not belonging. She was in love with him because she would have been afraid to be in love with anyone else, anyone...*better.*

He smiled for the first time that morning, resisted the very strong impulse to take her hand in his, and said (angry with his shyness, with the difficulty he had in forming the words): "What would *you* like to do, Carrie?"

She blinked hard and felt the tears coming into her eyes. "I'd thought..." she paused and blinked again, holding her tears back—she would not cry!—and then went on slowly: "I'd thought we might go down to Santa Fe and look around. Maybe we'll find a place there we'd like to stay a while." She bit her lip, and shook her head quickly: "But we can do anything you'd like, Tom."

He did touch her hand then, very briefly. "I'd like to go to Santa Fe," was all he said.

The peril of the morning was over when he spoke. The night before, when she had made that awkward declaration of love, even she had not realized what a frightening commitment she was making to him, nor what she was asking of him. That he had not struck her, or hurt her in some other way, was already something for which she was grateful. She was, in an animal-like, blind way, ready to accept anything from him. Somewhere in her mind, she recognized this as folly—madness, even—but there was nothing she could do but accept it.

5

At Emily's suggestion, Robert and Mary Hume had agreed to make a wide circle from Prescott into New Mexico, and instead of re-tracing their road back to U.S. 66 at Flagstaff, they took Routes 89, 60 and Arizona 77 to a place called Show Low (a name that delighted both the children) and then continued on 77 as far as Holbrook where they decided to spend the night.

Emily, who had made an enormous collection of maps on the trip (she preferred Shell and Conoco maps to any others) had been amazed and delighted at her parents' prompt acquiescence to her idea of going through Phoenix. It had not occurred to her (she had mentioned it gloomily, without hope, and with the feeling that she would probably precipitate an argument) that they would even consider the idea. That they did was only proof that anything was possible, that even parents could be miraculously and unexpectedly amenable.

Toby, secretly pleased at the change in plans, maintained a sullen attitude the entire morning. If he had thought of it, they would never have done it. Of that he was sure. He got over his assumed boredom in Phoenix late in the morning, for two reasons: he was tired of seeming gloomy when he did not really feel it, and he had seen, by the time they were through Phoenix, license plates from every state in the United States as well as Quebec and one car which he thought was from France because it had a big white oval plate at the back of the car with an "F" on it. And also because it was a kind of car he had never seen before.

Mary Hume had agreed to the change in route without enthusiasm. She was worried about her husband. Emily's statement about being on a camping trip only because her father thought he wanted to be a camper again, had expressed her own feelings too accurately, and she was ashamed of the frivolous and sarcastic way in which she had talked about the trip to Robert; the things she had said about national monuments. He had suggested, meekly, when they left Prescott that morning, that it would probably be a good idea if they did not do any more camping but stayed in tourist camps for the rest of the trip. His manner had suggested something further, something she had only sensed but knew to be true. It was as if he had said that he would drive them back to Cincinnati and home right away; he had given up, in advance, any possible further personal pleasure in the trip. He had even given up the idea that it would or could be fun for any of them any more. She had agreed, reluctantly and without understanding her reluctance, not to camp out any more. It was not until she had been in the car all day long, as they approached Holbrook, that she began to understand her misgivings: she had failed her husband in a way that troubled her deeply.

When the children were in bed (the cabin in Holbrook had two rooms with a double bed in each, and despite her theory that they should never sleep in the same bed, she put them in one room that night) she closed the door on them and asked Robert to pour a night-cap for herself and for him. When he had poured the drinks, he sat down on the bed, kicked off his shoes, smiled at her, and leaned back against the pillows. But even the attempt at an attitude of relaxation and pleasure was not convincing. It was part of the same quiet, nearly depressed, mood in which he had been all day long. She could feel him holding himself away from her, surrounding himself with an immunity to people, like a wounded animal. He was, in spite of the smile, the faintly over-cheerful look on his face, nursing a private disillusion, and she could not think of anything to say to him that would make it all right.

If this protective mood had not been too strong to prevent her talking directly to him she would have said simply enough that she was sorry about her attitude (which had, after all, been partly humorous and sardonic, and not intentionally disillusioning) ...that she was sorry, principally, because it was she who had—and she had not realized it until now—influenced the children, and made them, by being funny and a little too witty about the trip, into allies with herself against their father. What she had done, and she wanted to take his hand, look into his face and ask him forgiveness for it, was to make him seem ridiculous in the eyes of his own children. Emily would never have said what she did without knowing in advance that her mother would laugh. What now seemed completely unforgiveable to Mary was that she *had* laughed.

They drank their drinks silently, Mary washed out the glasses and they went to bed. It was only her own belief in her instincts that prevented her from talking to him about it in spite of his protective resistance; but she knew it was too soon, she would have to break through the distance between them in some other way before she could put it into words.

They undressed, and Robert waited for her to get into the bed before he turned off the light. When she felt him getting into the bed next to her, she left her arm stretched out across his side of the bed intentionally, and his body descended on it and then moved away from the contact. She moved her arm, let him lie down, and then moved close to him, kissed the back of his neck, and laid her left arm over his shoulder. His body stiffened, as if he was expecting her to say something he did not want to hear, and he held his head stiffly off the pillow.

"Something I forget to tell you, darling," she whispered, "is how much I love you."

"I know," he said, and turned in the bed to take her in his arms and kiss her. But the words were not quite right, and his kiss was perfunctory. He did not, however, move away; he allowed her a little more space...a little more room than he had opened to her during the day. As tangibly as if she could hold it in her two hands, she could feel the shape of his melancholy. She used the word self-consciously to herself, as if there was something wrong with it, and yet it was the right word. Melancholy, she knew, was contained in the small things of life; not necessarily in anything big.

6

At seven-fifteen a.m. on the morning of November 10th, Marion Mercer was awakened by the ringing of the telephone. It was a wrong number. When she had hung up the receiver, she went into the kitchen, made herself a cup of Nescafé, damned herself for the two or three drinks too many she had had the night before—why was it that when she drank alone she almost always had a hangover?—and then went to the bathroom. It wasn't until she was sitting dejectedly, looking out of her bathroom window (one thing she had been able to do more or less in spite of Armando was to have the bathroom face the mountains so that she could sit there and look out) that she remembered the curious howling she had heard the night before. The fact that she remembered it made it seem more real to her than it had seemed when she had actually heard it. Now, it remained—with the wearing away of the alcohol—the only sharp, clear-cut memory of the night.

She dismissed it from her mind. It was impossible to account for every sound one heard in so isolated a spot, and she did not want to think about it anyway. Something else she did not want to think about was what had become of her own life. She had come out here from New York after her divorce and had fallen in love with a man younger than herself, a man who had been (she now knew only too well) interested in finding an easy berth for himself. At that time, New Mexico, the mountains, the space, had all seemed romantic; the perfect setting. It was the proper background for the kind of romance that would be frowned on in a more settled and civilized community. Now, with Armando gone—gone with a woman both younger and richer than herself—what was left to her was only the solitude and the loneliness of the place. She had just enough money—in spite of Roosevelt and the New Deal—from her income so that she did not have to work, and was a complete misfit in any of the social life of the community. She could not, with any ease or pleasure, belong to the part of the population which devoted itself energetically to garden clubs, associations dedicated to the preservation of Spanish art, Indian art, or to the improvement of the life of the Indians. She had no interest in such things or in the people who organized them. As for the heavydrinking, so-called fast-living set, they had no use for a middle-aged, unhappy, single woman who drank too much.

She stared out of the window at the mountains, the same mountains that she had (or at least so she had thought at one time) loved so much when she had first come out here. Now, they served the same purpose for her as the daily newspaper might for someone else: they kept her from having constipation and that was about all. She never looked at them except from this window.

At eight o'clock, with the assurance that she had a well-regulated digestive tract for at least one more day, she had another cup of coffee and started to make her bed. The faint sound of a motor and the heavy thumping of the wellrig told her the well-diggers had begun their day and she thought to herself that it was a good thing she didn't have to stay at home all day long. They had been drilling for two weeks on the land just south of her acreage and the monotonous pounding of the drill into the side of the mountain every morning was irritating beyond belief. She had just finished picking up the living room when she heard the knock at the door.

She always felt her heart beat faster when anyone came to her door.

She lived far enough out of town so that anyone coming to her house had to have made a special effort to get there; she never had "casual" callers. Automatically, she placed her hand on her breast as if to reduce the rate of her heartbeat, and then she went to the door. It was one of the well-diggers; she recognized him from the day they had (there were two of them) come over early one morning to ask for drinking water. He gave her an appraising look as she opened the door, and then took off his hat.

"I hope I'm not bothering you," he said, "it's kind of early, I know…"

"It's perfectly all right," she said briskly. "What is it?"

He seemed embarrassed and—curiously—frightened as he continued to look at her. "I don't rightly know how to tell you," he said. "It's about a dog."

"A dog? Well, what about him?"

He looked at his feet and twisted the brim of his hat in his hands. "It's pretty terrible, lady. Maybe you'd better come and look for yourself."

"I don't know what you're talking about," she said. He made her feel prickly inside the way he stood there. "And I have lots of things to do this morning. I can't come anywhere right now. Anyway, what is it? What about what dog?"

"I thought maybe it was your dog," he said apologetically.

"But I don't have a dog! Besides, I don't understand what it is you want!"

He was suddenly relieved. "Well, I'm glad it isn't yours, but if you know a vet or somebody, I think maybe you ought to call him if you would."

She looked at him suspiciously. She was no longer angry with him, but was beginning to feel frightened herself. "What's the matter with the dog?"

Again he shifted his feet and twisted his hat. "I can't…I…well, it's tied to a tree. Not tied, but taped, and it's…"

She felt the fear begin to run rapidly through her veins. "*Taped* to a tree?"

He nodded. "Yep, and its muzzle is all taped up, too. Somebody was...was...torturing it, I guess. No animal could have done it...the tape and all..."

She felt as if she had received a violent blow and for a moment she thought she was going to throw up right in front of the man. She *had* heard those cries, then! Her face turned very white and she said, as efficiently as she could: "Just a minute, I'll put on a coat."

At ten o'clock, Marion's phone rang again. She did not answer. She had been sick and she couldn't talk to anyone. The only thing that relieved the horror of what she was feeling was that she had been able, before she got sick, to get back to the house and to take her revolver out to the men. It was after she had heard the crackling report of the gun that she had vomited. But she could not erase the picture of that little Mexican cur and its bloody paws...not one single nail was left in any of its four feet.

7

ON SATURDAY MORNING, THE 10TH of November, Jim Curran awoke with a curious sense of well-being. He remembered the facts of the night before, going over them slowly in his mind, and his eyes looked around the room carefully, as if to make sure the dog was really no longer there. Although his mind told him he should not have left the dog taped to the tree; that he should not have done it in that place (there was one house not very far away and the dog's cries had been very loud); and that the well-diggers would unquestionably see the dog and, in all probability, remember it from the visit he had made to the site, he did not really care. What he remembered vividly was that while he had been working on the dog, listening to the cries, watching the little spurts of blood from its paws, something had been calmed inside him for the first time in his life. He had found a special peace—what someone else might have called ecstasy.

He acknowledged that it had been as painful for him as for the dog, but the very pain had drawn something out of him and released it; in a tortured way he had been happy during that brief period and he had been utterly exhausted and spent afterwards. It was what he had always wanted when he had been in bed with a woman, and the sexual experience had invariably fallen short of his expectations. There had been a moment with the dog when he had actually had an orgasm: he had been completely fulfilled.

As the day wore on, his sense of fulfillment and peace began to give way to restlessness and dissatisfaction. The experience with the dog was not enough; he felt that what he had done to her was only the first step in the direction of a goal towards which he was being pulled relentlessly. His mind, nervously, told him that what he had done was, probably, criminal...something for which he could be arrested and put in jail, but he was certain that nothing would happen. His conviction was not based on any logic, but it was nonetheless convincing. The fact that he had—again *probably*—murdered the dog was of no special interest to him; he was concerned, primarily, with what he would do next; how would he be able to achieve the same satisfaction again? In spite of the sexual release and the sense of well-being which had resulted from the one experience, he knew that a repetition would not be enough.

Murder. The word lodged itself in his mind, sticking there to torment him. The fact that people went to war was sufficient proof that the act of murder was not unnatural to human beings; that it was considered a crime when it was not organized on a wholesale scale did not mean that it was—in the eyes of God, for instance—a crime. It was criminal only because it was so considered by society. If he could (and was there any reason to doubt his own ability?) commit a crime without any tangible motive, he would be perfectly safe. The motive, the reason, was always the giveaway.

The more he thought about it, the more he realized that he wanted to kill someone. Not for any particular reason, but because he knew in his heart that it was the proper next step. The only thing he had to be sure of was that he knew exactly how to do it in such a way that it could not be traced to him.

By nightfall, it seemed to him that he had solved most of the problems involved in a so-called "perfect murder." The most important thing was not to be emotionally involved with the victim; and to know exactly what he had to do and follow it through. The choice of victim was of no particular importance; it could be anyone, but preferably a woman. Following his instincts, he bought an axe just before the hardware store closed. His choice of weapon was not based on anything other than his feeling that an axe was the weapon which suited him best and would give him the most satisfaction.

Sitting in his car, with the axe in his hand, he had a feeling of enormous stimulation and excitement; he might even do it that very night. But a few minutes' reflection made him decide against that. The anticipation was, of itself, not unsatisfactory; also, it might be wise to think it over for a while longer. The idea that he could spend the evening and the following day picking and stalking, as it were, his victim, gave him a special, intense pleasure. He went to La Fonda where he had three drinks at the bar before having his dinner there. Seated alone at a table in the crowded dining-room, he looked at and listened to the people at the other tables. It might just be one of them: any one of these smiling, animated, busy people might fall under the stroke of his axe the next day. It gave him a sensation of great power to know that the decision was entirely in his hands.

8

Pushed by an idiotic, senseless determination, Peter Wells arrived at Eldorado Springs, Missouri, at seven o'clock on the evening of Saturday, November 10th. He had seen himself all day long in the same way that he might have seen a stranger, and without understanding what he saw. He had felt so separated from himself that he had seemed to be two people. In spite of the fact that he was tired, he had managed to drive—what with bad weather, inferior roads, and traffic—only four hundred and fifty miles. He felt as if he had been fighting all day long.

It was not until he had actually stopped the car and found himself a place to stay for the night, that he had a feeling of horror with the way in which he had been driving all day long. He saw himself more clearly now—as he had been during the day—pushed mercilessly and inexorably on, for no reason. He did not mind what he had done as something *done.* He was a good driver and he had stopped when he was too tired, but he was alarmed at the lack of sense behind what he had been doing. To allow himself, for incomprehensible reasons, to plow forward all day when he was not even in a hurry...

As he said this to himself, accusingly, he also denied it. He did have a reason—a need—which certainly existed, whether he understood its full sense or not. He felt as if California was not to be the end of his journey; that he was racing forward to a destination that had been selected for him. He was responding more and more to a force that was stronger than himself, and although he would not have admitted it to another person, he was convinced there was purpose in what he was doing.

He had sent a telegram to his father from St. Louis, earlier in the day, and he decided to call him again that night. Why? Even that he could not answer. He had talked to him only the night before, he knew he was all right, there was no urgent reason to call him again. Eating his dinner, he laughed at himself, wondering why it was necessary for him to have a good, practical reason for everything he did. Why should he have to ask himself why he was going to call his father, as if it was unseemly to respond to the impulse? But this, too, seemed part of the unconscious force to which he was reacting, as if talking to his father was all part of a plan which had been laid out for him ahead of time. Except for his natural skepticism, he would have thought he was in the grip of some mystical force that he was unable to resist.

He put the call in at eight o'clock (nine o'clock in Three Bridges) only to find that the circuits were busy. At nine o'clock they were still busy and he cancelled the call. Although he knew that it was impossible to control circuits and telephones, he was depressed by his failure to get the call through. It was as if he had failed, through some fault of his own, to make a communication with his father. He resolved to try again in the morning, and went to bed, but as he was going to sleep, he was awakened by a sudden impulse to turn back towards New York the next morning. He felt it so strongly that he sat up in bed for a moment and then lay back slowly. He was over-tired, he was thinking like a fool...He was not really *thinking* at all. Out of the confusion and restlessness in his heart, questions began to form. He was being pulled in two directions, and the blindness with which he had let himself be carried forward since the beginning of this trip seemed only a means of not responding to either direction. He wanted something, but he did not know what it was; he felt as if he was running rapidly towards an answer before he had clarified the question in his mind. What did he want and where was he going?

He snapped his fingers at Kelly, who had elected to sleep on the floor for some reason, and the dog jumped up on the bed, made some grunting noises, stuck his nose into the covers and smelled deeply; then, after some preliminary circling, settled down near Peter's stomach with a deep sigh of pleasure. The warm presence of the animal, *his* dog, made him feel better. He had a companion; he was *not* alone. He went to sleep with his hand on Kelly's head.

9

ON **N**OVEMBER 10TH, **C**HARLES **W**ELLS stayed in bed for the second day. The cold, creeping insidiously through his body, had penetrated into his bones; his joints and even his teeth ached with it. He had been unexpectedly cheered by the call from his son the night before, and had felt his cold diminishing miraculously after he had talked to him, but the relief had been temporary.

Lying in his bed, without enough energy to read or listen to the radio, he had gone over the last few days that Peter had spent with him before he left. It seemed to him curiously meaningful that they had talked so much, just before Peter's departure, about death. He was not conscious of any desire to die, or any reason why he should; still, they had talked of it as if they both expected it to happen, and now this cold—or was it more than a cold finally?—had come along immediately afterwards to force him to his bed. Something told him that his going to bed, his lack of resistance, was significant. The bed itself represented a place in which to die, as if he had crawled into a corner all his own, in which it would be safe to expire easily and comfortably.

He determined to get up the next morning. However natural death might be, and however logical the things he had said about it, he began to feel that there was something morbid in his preoccupation with it. He seemed to have forgotten that the essence of the human spirit is to fight death up to the very last moment. His attitude was wrong, abnormal. Nonsense. He might very well live to be one hundred or more. He might, yes; but the very thought of it tired him further. All he really wanted to do was to sleep and sleep and sleep.

NOVEMBER 11, 1951

1

The storm seemed to be making up its mind. On Sunday morning, the 11th of November, it paused, considering where and how to throw out its immense power, and then struck playfully at the map of the United States. It blew a cold wind against the windows of the buildings on Seventeenth Street in New York City, and Marjorie Williams stirred restlessly. Her consciousness, like a low flame, flickered at her, telling her that she was cold and lonely.

It transformed itself into snow: steady, gentle and benevolent, and fell quietly in the mountains of Northern New Mexico.

It iced the windshield of Stephen Williams' car as it stood outside a tourist cabin in Vinita, Oklahoma.

In the form of wind, it ripped down over the Kansas plains to awaken Mr. and Mrs. Henry Franklin in Dodge City. Mrs. Franklin got up and closed the window.

It fought the sunrise at Gallup, New Mexico, and gave in temporarily, satisfied to leave a few flakes of snow—as a warning.

By dawn, the sun looked down, God-like, upon the storm, and played back in its turn; pushing gently here and there, forbidding its progress with an enormous warm laziness, checking it more by whim than by design. Its warmth oozed protectively through the first clouds near the border of Missouri and Kansas and dispersed them, and it picked out the car in which Peter Wells had already driven almost fifty miles.

It snowed heavily in Three Bridges, New York, and Charles Wells—true to his determination of the night before—was up, looking out of his window at the landscape, already deep with snow. He seemed to see a map of the country stretching beyond him, and on it he visualized Peter, somewhere on a road in Missouri, crawling inch by inch across the map, ahead of the sun which would not yet have reached the Mississippi. For a moment, he believed so strongly in the sun that the snow dissolved before his eyes, and he willed the sun to shine on Peter. He was not afraid for him—not even if there was bad weather out there—but he wanted him to have the sun always. Standing at the window, he coughed—so hard that his whole body shook with it—and the force which had taken him to the window ebbed out of him quickly. He trembled in the cold, was acutely conscious of the stiffness in his bones, and turned wearily back towards his bed.

At Holbrook, Arizona, Toby Hume was the first of the family to awaken; he blinked his eyes, got out of bed, and tiptoed to the window to look through an edge of the drawn blind. He rubbed his hands together and shivered with pleasure at the sight of the snow.

In Santa Fe, Dorothy Simms stared across the sleeping body of her husband, at the faint gray space that was the window. Was it snowing? It didn't matter, but wouldn't the day ever come. She had had almost no sleep.

In the house next door, Jim Curran cursed the snow, but even his anger with it—it was a problem he had not counted on—could not diminish his knowledge that today was the day for him.

Tom Foster and Caroline Pratt moved a little closer to each other in the bed in the motel on Cerrillos Road. A faint light had already entered through the window, but neither of them wanted the night to end.

Marion Mercer awakened from a nightmare in which a dog, bleeding copiously, had been trying to jump from the floor to her bed. It took her several minutes to realize that she was alone and safe.

2

DOROTHY SIMMS ARRIVED AT THE post office just before noon, and could not find any place to park. She muttered under her breath at the mobs of churchgoers whose cars had eaten up all the road space; and she frowned at the groups in front of the post office, the cathedral, and up Palace Avenue near the Presbyterian Church. The ritual of Sunday morning seemed to her to have become an enormous, organized club meeting; people came to church in order to see their friends, enemies and acquaintances; to make an appearance and to be able to report on who was or was not there, what they were wearing, or how they looked. Devotion did not seem to be conspicuously involved in any of it.

Irritated with the crowded streets, the milling people, and the whole atmosphere of Sunday morning—the slush from the light snowfall was no help—she drove her car to the gas station at the corner of the Plaza, asked them to fill it with gas, and went to the post office for the mail. Crossing the street on foot, her irritation increased. There were as many out-of-town licenses on the cars as local ones. All the visitors from Texas and Oklahoma who had come to ski had helped to transform the town (which she had always loved because of its lack of tourists, its isolation, its sense of being a place where one was not quite—always—in the mainstream of organized American life) into any town in any state. The same hats, dresses, shoes, coats, attitudes, gestures, and remarks existed here on this Sunday morning as those she would have found in any undistinguished middle-western town.

Her feelings of hostility grew as she began to reflect on her private anger of the morning. Dick, more self-absorbed and gloomier than usual, had started in again on Jim Curran. What had happened to his dog? She had pointed out, testily enough, that she was sick and tired of hearing about Mr. Curran, that she did not know or care about his dog, that she was sorry she had ever rented the place to him, and for God's sake couldn't he please forget about his tenant for a while? Underneath the words she said to him in a voice too violent for the subject, lay a bed of insecurity and fear. The distance between them had increased hourly since his return from New York, until she now felt there was no way of bridging the channel that separated them, and flowed steadily between them like a river.

She had criticized and blamed herself for what was going on in her husband to the point where she had lost both patience and judgment. It was all very well to love someone, to stand aside and try to bear, in silence, the extra burden imposed by their self-immolation in suffering, but a time came when two people—joined in their life not only by marriage, but by the togetherness of years and experience—had to come to grips with a situation that was becoming increasingly intolerable all the time.

At breakfast that morning, she had looked at his face with a feeling very close to pure anger. On his features she saw the sullen, self-involved, self-pitying look that is standard in boys of thirteen, and she had almost succumbed to a driving impulse to strike out at her husband's immaturity. But even that impulse was immediately frustrated; she did not even feel she could reach him with a blow. His reaction to her tone of voice and her expressed anger about Curran had been to retreat still further behind his mask; to look at her with a melancholy, martyristic mask.

She took the mail from the letter box: two letters only. One from Dick's mother, and addressed firmly to Mr. Richard Simms, and the other from a real estate agency in Albuquerque. She stuffed Dick's letter into her purse and ripped the flap of the other one. Could she come down to Albuquerque on Monday, the 12th, to discuss the sale of some ranch? Her irritation flared up again, and then subsided. They wanted her to be there at two o'clock; she could easily use it as an excuse to stay away all day; to get there by two, she would have to leave at lunchtime. She might just as well leave in the morning, have lunch there, do some shopping, go to the meeting, and even stay out for dinner. It would do them both good to get away from each other for a day; and it might be fine for him to be alone.

Back at the gas station, she opened her purse to pay for the gas and saw the letter from Dick's mother again. She hoped—and felt fairly sure she was right—that Mrs. Simms was writing to ask Dick to come to see her in Tucson. If so, she would support that suggestion, too. She was sufficiently angry with him now to want to find out whether he would even miss her. He would probably want to go.

She drove out of the gas station, honked her horn impatiently and stupidly at the line of cars blocking the Plaza and Palace Avenue, and then backed rapidly around, and roared up Washington Street in first gear.

3

Carrie and Tom had decided to stay at a motel on Cerrillos Road, just south of town. On Sunday morning, they drove into town for a late breakfast, parked the car in the parking lot behind La Fonda, had a big breakfast in the hotel (where no one seemed to mind Tom's denim pants), and decided to look around the town. They were both in good spirits, and for different reasons, were both shy about showing it to each other. There was a feeling of contentment in their being together that was, again for different reasons, so foreign to what they had ever allowed themselves to ask or expect, that the quietness they maintained was a self-imposed and studied attempt to make it last by not speaking too loudly or otherwise risking a possible break in their mood.

They walked slowly around the Plaza, peered into the windows of the Governor's Palace, crossed Washington Street just as a blue Mercury backed, almost hitting them, and turned to race up the street. Tom smiled, shrugged his shoulders, made some remark about a woman driver, and then took Carrie's arm in his. She smiled to herself, thanking him silently for the gesture. As they stood in front of a bookshop near the post office, looking idly in the window, Tom turned to her:

"Do you like Indians?" he asked.

She looked puzzled. "I don't know anything about them."

"Would you like to go to an Indian dance tomorrow?"

"An Indian dance?"

"Yes."

She hesitated. "How do you know they will have one?" She had been very bored at one Indian dance once, the only time she had ever gone; but that was not the cause of her hesitation. Any activity that was outside of themselves, anything they did that involved other people, that kept them from being alone, was a threat to her still-tentative, precious happiness.

He felt the reluctance in her voice. "It's some sort of feast day at Jemez and Tesuque pueblos tomorrow," he said. "Would you rather not go?"

She took a deep breath; if he wanted to go, she would have to agree to go with him. "I'd like to do whatever you'd like, Tom. It might be fun."

"Have you ever been to one?"

"Yes. Once. Last year."

"Didn't like it?"

She nodded, embarrassed. "I didn't see what it was all about."

They started to walk again, still arm in arm, back in the direction of the parking lot. "It's worth trying twice," he said. "I think the dance at Jemez should be a good one."

She nodded again. "You really know quite a lot about this country, don't you?"

He shook his head. "Not a lot, no. But I spent a summer out here a couple of years ago and I've always wanted to come back again. There's something special about it, I think."

She took a deep breath, stopped and looked at him. "May I ask you a question, Tom?"

He looked at her, half-serious, half-amused. "Sure. What?"

"Who did you come out here with?"

He started to walk again, pulling her along with him. "A girl. Why?"

"I just wondered."

He did not say anything more until he had paid the parking lot attendant and they were in the car. "Does it bother you?" he asked as he started the motor.

She shook her head vigorously. "No, but I don't really know anything about you. I don't know what you do or anything." She glanced at him hastily. "Not that I care...at least it wouldn't make any difference. But I suppose I can't help being curious."

He let the motor idle, his hands gripping the steering wheel. "We'll talk about it sometime," he said, "but I don't want to go into all that now. All right?"

She nodded again, trying to persuade herself that she did not mind, but without success. She was afraid, there was no question about it, of what went on in his mind, of what he really felt, of what he had done and wanted to do. What had that girl been like? Had he liked her better? Would she be adequate?

4

THE WIND AND THE SWIRLING patches of snow did not disappear until the Hume family had reached Grants, New Mexico. There, as suddenly as if they had come out from behind a curtain of threatening mist, they found themselves in an arid landscape, illuminated by the heavy, warm sunshine, without a cloud ahead of them.

The children were both furious because neither Robert nor Mary would stop to see "The World's Biggest and Deadliest Reptile," "The Snake that Killed Grace Wiley," or the other place where the sign read: "Squaw Weaving Now—Giant Malts—Cactus Candy—Poisonous Reptiles." They stopped for lunch at what looked like the only respectable hamburger joint in the town. As usual, when asked what they would eat, both children replied: "Hamburgers."

Mary shook her head at them. "How can you possibly go on eating nothing but hamburgers?"

Toby bowed his head, Emily sighed, and neither of them replied. Mary looked at her husband, who glanced quickly at the menu. "I don't think it matters too much," he said. "Why not let them have what they want? There's something here called a Royal Hamburger with tomatoes and coleslaw. That ought to be all right."

Mary put down the menu and looked at the children again. "Will you promise to eat all the salad?"

They nodded, wrinkling their noses at the idea of tomatoes, and

Toby said: "Aren't we well? Don't we look healthy?"

Robert smiled across at them. "No nonsense from either you, and no back talk. No salad, no hamburgers. Understand?"

They nodded again, taken aback by the firmness in their father's voice, and he ordered the lunch. He was feeling better today, and the sudden change in the weather had made him happy. He wished, briefly, that he was coming in to New Mexico from the east where the contrast in landscape was more dramatic than coming in from Arizona. But even so, there was something different about this land. It seemed to him to have something to do with the way the light penetrated into and sharpened the outlines of the country simultaneously; so that it was lighted from within and without. Nowhere else in the world that he knew was the sun so much a part of life, of one's daily existence. If he was not tied down by his job in Cincinnati, he knew that this was the one place in the world he would really like to live.

He ate his lunch hurriedly, and then glanced out of the corner of his eyes at his wife and two children. Whether it was the sudden release of feeling he had felt because of the land and the sun, or whether it was for some other reason, he felt a kind of emotional spasm as he watched them. The trip, all the way, had seemed to become increasingly laborious, more of a trial than a holiday; something which he had—only the day before—vowed he would never undertake again. It had been no pleasure, he had thought then, for any of them; but now—he turned his head away so that they would not be able to see his face—all of that had dropped away. The current of warmth flowing through him transformed the entire experience. The tribulations, arguments, disappointments, and unpleasantnesses faded from his mind, and he retained only the feeling of his own family as a unit, in a joint experience. The complicated and inextricable ties that bound him to all three of them were things, and he took another quick look at them, that could never be unwound or dissolved, that would go on through similar vicissitudes for all the years of his life to come.

Had he been a more expressive man by nature, he might—at that curiously illuminated moment in a lunchroom in Grants, New Mexico—have said a prayer, burst into tears, or laughed with joy. Because he was who and what he was, his only outward manifestation of the feelings in his heart was to take Mary's hand and hold it.

She turned to him, surprised and unprepared. The look on his face told her all she needed to know; she did not even want to know what had happened to cause it. She was, for the first time in several weeks, what she most wanted to be: the wife of a happy man.

5

ALTHOUGH THE SNOW HAD NOT been heavy between Dodge City and Raton, New Mexico, there had been enough on the road to make driving seem hazardous. Both Henry and Mabel Franklin had been silent and tense all day long, and like a relapse into an illness after a sudden, unexpected drive towards recovery, Henry Franklin's exhilaration and self-confidence had gradually weakened during the day as he drove the big car just fast enough to make it seem a little daring. His rebellion against his wife, which had taken them both by surprise, had begun to seem unnatural and dangerous to him; an act committed without any preparation in relation to the possible consequences.

The responsibilities and decisions which he had automatically and unexpectedly had to take on as a result of his explosion against her had grown into an enormous weight, and he foresaw himself forever burdened with decisive, small details affecting their lives. He was frightened. The habit of dependence on his wife rose up inside him—a smirking reminder of the past—and he wondered what it could have been that had caused his attempt to destroy that habit.

As he continued to force himself to maintain a speed on the road that he knew was dangerous, he felt shaky about his capacities as a man and about his future with his wife; a future that stretched out ahead of him, grim and unending. There was no question, in his mind, of making a break with her, but he was confronted with two impossible alternatives: to continue to direct their lives (an appalling idea), or to let their relationship slide back into its old form. The very idea of this latter possibility made him squirm with guilt and offended pride. He felt that he had, by giving in unconsciously to that irresistible impulse of the moment, put himself into a net from which he could never escape.

Mabel, in a deep, eternal, feminine sense, knew all of this. She felt what was going on in her husband, and her reaction to it was divided. In part, she rejoiced at the weakening in him, but there was also something in her that had been shocked and wounded and this made her cautious. She had lost confidence in her own ability to take back the direction of their lives. The suddenness and the unexpected violence of his revolt against her; the suppressed hatred and contempt which it had expressed, had all left a mark that she could not erase easily. She was not at all sure that she could ever feel secure about him again, or that his willingness to follow her lead in the future would be dependable; she was not even convinced that she could regain her former position in the family.

In neither of them did these things pass as thoughts; they were sensations and feelings which puzzled and confused them to the extent that they labored and fought against them silently and blindly. When they reached Raton, on the afternoon of November 11th, Henry decided— so vehemently that it was only a further betrayal of his growing weakness—that they would go on to Santa Fe that day. Mabel, about to protest, kept her silence by instinct. Something told her, something far surer than her consciousness, that he would trap himself more completely than she could; a protest would only strengthen him. She was right. Her acquiescence and agreement was far more troubling to him than any protest could have been.

She held her breath on several occasions as they rounded the sharp curves on the snowy Raton Pass, and then breathed a sigh of relief when she saw the clear road stretching south towards Las Vegas and

Santa Fe. The snow had been very light below the pass, judging from the look of the plains.

As they started across the wide, flat land below the mountains, she watched her husband at the wheel and felt, as she had not felt in many years, a slight stirring of genuine affection for him: a feeling that called to mind what she had felt for him when they had first known each other, and she reminded herself that she must be fair with him. With an effort, which cost her less than she expected, she said in a pleasant voice: "You're really a very good driver, Henry."

He looked at her suddenly, surprised and taken aback by the tone of her voice and the unexpected compliment. To his further surprise, he heard himself saying, as he blushed faintly: "Thank you, dear." It was the first time he had used any term of endearment to her since Kansas City.

6

When Jim Curran had awakened and seen the snow on Sunday morning, he had been vaguely angry with himself because he had failed to foresee the possibility of snow and the difficulties it might present to him. But when, by noon, it had melted almost completely—enough so that he could dismiss it from his mind as a possible danger—he had begun to feel more and more the sensation of a wheel spinning around inside himself. It was so much as if he really had a wheel in his chest, that he found himself touching the spot between his ribs every now and then, in an effort to slow it down, or perhaps only to make sure that he was still the same person as he had been before that particular morning.

He had the foresight to buy three bottles of whiskey the day before, and had started to drink early, but even the alcohol did not have the proper effect on him. It slowed the wheel for a while, but by four o'clock in the afternoon he was still able to tell himself lucidly that he was not nearly as drunk as he should be. He knew—and at that exact minute he also knew that he had come across a final truth the day before—that he would have to carry through his plan.

By seven-thirty in the evening—he had forced himself to eat a sandwich at six o'clock—the wheel was spinning furiously, and he gave in to it. He went into the washroom of the hotel (he had just noted the time, noting also that he was walking steadily and thinking clearly) and looked at himself in the mirror. He was not, he decided, a bad-looking guy. He didn't look like a drunk, his suit was pressed, his shirt was clean, his tie elegantly knotted. He was very presentable indeed; he could get anything he wanted. He *knew* it.

When he had finished in the washroom, he went out into the street. It was not, at least not to him, very cold. He was in a special exhilarated state (his mind kept reminding him of that) and he knew that it was colder than he thought, but not cold to his blood. He also knew that something—that wheel—was burning up the liquor faster than he could consume it. In a feeling of ecstatic sorrow—his need had become fantastic—he thought of a woman's body, naked and defenseless before him. *Now,* perhaps now, at last, he could even get it sexually. He did not know—for a moment—that he had to have blood, but he wanted his body to burst, even to be destroyed...anything to stop the spinning.

He had no trouble finding her. He saw the girl—fate had placed her there, for *him!*—before he had walked thirty feet. He didn't know if she was a prostitute, but he did know that she was for him. He was behind her in a flash, had put his arm through hers, had said something. She stopped dead in her tracks, looked at him (and as she did he saw that she must be over thirty, knew from her face that she knew everything she needed to know, knew again for himself that she was the woman for him), and after a moment's hesitation, smiled.

They did not speak at first. He led her to his car, and it was not until he had unlocked the car and opened the door that she gave him a suspicious and inquiring look. He reacted quickly, put his hand in his pocket and pulled out a twenty-dollar bill. She smiled, moved her shoulders and got into the car, still without speaking. He closed the door behind her, walked around the car, got in on the driver's side after motioning to her to pull the lock up and open the door for him.

It was then that Julia Garcia had her first good look at the man who had so suddenly, and so forcefully, taken her arm. She had been frightened of him at first, and then the fear had turned into something else. She had seen something in his eyes—loneliness mostly—and she was sorry for him. The one thing that had worried her was whether or not he had any money. After having seen the twenty-dollar bill, she felt reassured. Looking at him in the dim light from the street lamp, she was strangely and incomprehensibly attracted to him; what she did not understand was that she was responding to an enormous need, and that her own response—very quick, almost overpoweringly strong—was to the somewhat subtle sensation of being wanted, needed, that much.

Under the impact of her stare, he turned to her after he had put the key in the ignition and bent over until his face was next to hers. "You know," he said—he seemed to be drunk and sober at the same time—"I love you."

She knew that he was telling the truth. His desire for her was so enormous that it filled the car; it was more than any physical need, it was bigger than anything she had ever encountered. She kissed him then, in a kind of fury—with more than just passion—and disregarded the very faint warning tick in her mind. She felt so pulled towards him that she thought she should get the money in advance. Rarely, when she had been picked up, had she wanted to sleep with the man, but now she felt not only that she wanted him—in what was almost an obscene way—but that she was betraying her own code by her response.

They drove to a spot on Canyon Road, where he parked the car, asking her to wait for a minute while he went inside. He got out of the car and then he looked at her—a look filled with passion and tenderness: "You *will* wait for me, won't you?"

The tone of his voice was irresistible. "Yes, of course," she said, feeling self-conscious because of her Spanish accent. "Where are we going?"

"I'll tell you in a minute. But wait."

She waited, watching him disappear into the darkness towards a house at a considerable distance from the road. What, exactly, was she doing? Her need to possess him had been so magnified by the kiss that she didn't really care. This would be good. She hoped they could make love in some place other than inside a house; but it was cold outside, and the thought of the ground—it must be frozen now—made her shudder. Maybe in the car?

He reappeared unexpectedly, running out of the darkness, carrying a blanket and a bottle; got into the car and sat next to her for a moment (he had put the bottle and blanket on the back seat), panting and staring at the dashboard. "Do you want a drink?" he asked.

She nodded her head and he reached back over the seat and brought out the bottle, which he uncorked and handed to her. She took a short swig of whiskey, made a face, and handed it to him. He drank long— and it occurred to her that perhaps he shouldn't drive, although she sensed that the drink did not affect him—and put the bottle away again. Then he turned to her and touched her breast. She covered his hand with hers and pressed it against herself, and he started the car, turning the ignition key with his left hand and finally withdrawing his right hand very slowly to shift the gears.

He drove slowly and carefully, turned up the Camino del Monte Sol and then out the Old Pecos Road. He stopped the car not very far from a structure which she recognized as a well-rig, sat back, lighted a cigarette, handed it to her, and sighed. "I want you," he said, sitting motionless next to her. Without waiting for any reply, he reached over the back of the seat for the whiskey. "Have another drink," he said.

She took the bottle from him and drank listlessly. She would have done anything he told her.

There was something trance-like in their behavior from then on. After kissing her (he acted as if he was performing a ritual), he got out of the car, laid the blanket on the ground, and then took her hand as she got out. He took off his coat (he didn't feel the cold at all), laid it on the blanket and then sat on the blanket himself, pulling her down to him. When she was beside him, he forced her down on her back—everything he did was simultaneously forceful and gentle—and began a kind of absorbed love-making, running his hands over her body, kissing her, unbuttoning buttons.

She pulled herself up suddenly, and he frowned at her.

"What's the matter?" he asked hoarsely.

"It's cold," she said.

He shook his head fiercely. "No. No, it isn't."

"Give me the money, then."

The frown deepened on his face. "Now?"

She nodded.

He reached into his pocket for his wallet, drew out the twenty-dollar bill, and handed it to her. "You little bitch," he said roughly, and pushed her back down on the blanket. She had no time to do anything with the money, but held it tightly clutched in her hand.

He did not undress her any more than was actually necessary to make the final physical contact, and then, with a furious, determined and cruel intensity, he began to make love to her.

When it was over—and it was over for both of them simultaneously (he had let out a wild moan)—he lifted himself above her, stared at her face—the moon was fairly bright—and started to cry. She moved her head back and forth on the blanket—she was frightened now—and then he stopped as suddenly as he had begun. He got up, fixed his clothes, went to the car, and brought the bottle back to where she still lay on the blanket. He took a long drink and then handed the bottle over to her.

Before she took the bottle from him, she straightened her skirt and tucked the twenty-dollar bill inside her dress. He watched her, disgusted, and shook the bottle at her. "Take a drink. Go on, take a drink."

She took the bottle from him and drank in a stupefied way, as if she could not do otherwise. She felt his eyes staring through her as she drank, and the fear began to gain control over her. There was something in his face, now that his desire was spent, that chilled her, making her afraid to move. She handed the bottle back, sat up on the blanket, buttoned her dress, and wrapped her coat around her shoulders. Because his eyes were still burning through her, she turned away from them, looked at the well-rig, and said: "Can we go back, maybe?"

It was over. Despite the conviction and the need he had felt earlier, he had hoped, somewhere in his heart that he would not have to go any further than he had already. But as he looked at her, listened to the plaintive, frightened note in her voice, watched the tenseness in the soft, slovenly, female body, he knew it was inevitable. He did not reply to her question but went back to the car, put the whiskey in it, and took something else out—something she could not see in spite of the moonlight—and then returned in her direction, holding it behind his back. She watched him, and the fear boiled up inside her. She was rooted to where she sat; nothing could have made her move, and what she saw in his face terrified her. Making an enormous effort, she forced her head to turn from the look in his face and it was then that she heard his quick step in her direction. She turned back in time to see the axe lifted high above his head. She screamed, but it was already too late. It was the last thing Julia Garcia ever saw.

When the body lay, spurting blood and still quivering on the blanket below him, he bent over, tore the front of her dress open, pulled out the twenty-dollar bill, stared at it and then, dropping the axe, ripped it into pieces.

It was at that moment that he remembered the dog. He looked at the tree, took a few steps towards it and then stopped. The tree was completely bare now.

7

In spite of the constriction in his chest, Richard Simms had managed to maintain (desperately, and without examining his reasons for so doing) an attitude of severe courtesy towards his wife all Sunday morning. He had been greatly relieved when she went downtown for the mail late in the morning, but as soon as she had left, he had begun to feel apprehensive about her return. The causes of his inability to talk to her, his huge self-dissatisfaction, his inability to work, were things he no longer even pondered. He felt walled in more tightly all the time, until he could feel it in his body, as if he had been strapped too tightly in a strait jacket. He no longer argued to himself that it was something that had nothing to do with Dorothy; he did not know—or care—what it had to do with. What concerned him was finding some means of escape from his feelings.

His life seemed, as he looked back on it, to have been totally useless, ineffective, pointless. The small reputation he had acquired as a painter was now only an indication of his worthlessness as a human being. He did not believe that he had any real stature as an artist; all his work of the past loomed up, mercilessly, as something he had put over on the public, the dealers, the critics, his friends. He had never actually believed—or so he felt—that he had any true talent as a painter, and he had, in his mind, perpetrated an enormous hoax on himself by succumbing to the plaudits of people who were not artists themselves and did not know anything about painting anyway.

Feeling this way, the presence of Dorothy, who watched him, worried about him, tried to talk to him, wanted to help him, strained him to a breaking point. The rigid self-control which he was forced to exercise to keep from lashing out at her was more than he could sustain indefinitely. If she started in on him again when she got back from the post office, he did not know if he would be able to keep himself under control any longer.

His worst fears were confirmed when she returned. She bristled as she came into the house, walked up to him, and gave him the letter from his mother. He opened it, without looking at her, read it and then handed it to her. When she had read it (he could feel the hostility in her as she read) she smiled ironically, and said: "Well, are you going to go?" He felt, in her tone of voice, a vituperative criticism of his mother for having asked him to come to see her. Was it so damned unnatural for an old woman to want to see her only child and to want to see him alone? He suspected, and it angered him further, that Dorothy had decided for some obscure reason that his mother had a malevolent hold on him. Controlling the anger he felt, he said, as quietly as possible: "I don't know. Is there any reason why I have to decide immediately?"

She shrugged her shoulders. "None at all."

For a second he hated her. "Was there any other mail?" he asked.

She nodded, and what seemed to him a smug smile came on to her face. "Yes. I had a letter from Albuquerque. I have to go down tomorrow on some real-estate deal."

"What time are you going?" He could not completely hide the relief he felt at the prospect of her absence, possibly for a full day. At least she would not be home for lunch.

"I thought I'd go down in the morning and do some shopping. I might even stay down for dinner." She had said these words quietly enough, but she turned suddenly, unable to repress the bitterness in her voice. "It will probably do you good to have me out of your way for a while."

His heart began to beat faster. "What do you mean?"

She laughed. "What do I mean? Oh, Dick, how can you go on behaving this way? Do you think I like this any better than you do? What are we going to do? Go on avoiding each other, go on not talking to each other, go on being polite? Are you still going to try to maintain that there is nothing wrong between us? Are *you* having a good time? Do you think I can't tell from your tone of voice, your whole attitude, that you'll be relieved when I leave tomorrow?"

"I think you're making a mountain out of a mole-hill, Dorothy," he said in very measured tones.

She sighed. "Oh, sure. Everything is just fine. Let's face it, Dick. I don't know what you're hiding from yourself, let alone from me, but you are in an impossible state—it's intolerable for me, and presumably for you—and I am not at all sure that I can stand it any longer. If you can't—for whatever reasons—discuss it with me, perhaps it would be a good idea for you to go and visit your mother. Maybe you could talk to her."

"What do you mean by that?"

"What do you think I mean? How can I explain it any more clearly? And, for that matter, what have *I* to explain?"

"Everything seems to be very clear in your mind," he said, and the anger finally began to break through the wall of his self-control. "Why don't you give me a lecture on what is wrong with me and with life? You sound as if you knew all the answers."

She turned to him, and he could see that she had been stung by the sarcasm in his words. "Perhaps I do know a thing or two that has not occurred to you," she said. "If you'd face whatever is making you feel so full of self-pity and..."

"*Self-pity?*"

"What would you call it?"

He rose from the chair where he had been sitting. "There may be an element of self-pity in all this," he said, "but for you to assume that it is nothing but that—after the amount of conversation you have insisted upon having about it...well..."

She laughed again. "I know. I know. You—and don't tell me this isn't a fantastic manifestation of your ego-involvement—are troubled about the world and your place in it, and that perhaps you aren't the fine, upstanding human being you've always thought you were. Instead of mooning around like an adolescent, why don't you do something about it? Let's assume for a moment that you are right in your self-criticism. Let's assume you're terrible, in every way. Maybe you are not a good painter after all. What are you going to do about that, if it is true? Throw everything away and start all over again? Who do you think you are to take yourself so seriously, actually? Are you so sure I'm wrong? Are you so sure that you are not just sorry for yourself?"

"So that's what you think?"

She sat down wearily. "Yes, that's what I think, and you may now tell me what an ungrateful and terrible wife I am; that I have no understanding of my husband's creative problems. It can't really be anyone's fault except mine, can it, Dick?"

"Have I ever said anything like that to you?"

She shook her head. "No, Dick. Not once. But I know what you are, what and how you think. I don't know why, and I probably never will know, but I think that for my sake you're going to have to get this out of your system, talk to someone about it, and it might as well be your mother."

This time he laughed. "You really hate my mother, don't you?"

"No, Dick, I don't and you know it. But I am a little bored at times by her money, her house, her business...the great Mrs. Simms of Philadelphia!"

"What would you have me do about that?"

She stood up again and shook her head. "My feelings about your mother are not the point, Dick, and you know it. I'm going out. I don't want to talk about this any longer. I don't even know if there is anything to be done about it; perhaps it has been going on too long now."

She started for the door, and he followed her and put his hand on her shoulder. "Don't say that, Dorothy."

"What am I supposed to say?"

He hesitated, bit his lip and withdrew his hand. "Where are you going?"

"I don't know. I'm just going to get away for a while. There's plenty of food in the icebox. I'll be back sometime this afternoon."

"Well, if you have to go...if you feel that..."

"Stop it!" Her voice tore at him. "Stop telling me that I *have* to do anything. There's nothing wrong with me!"

She opened the door, walked out, and slammed it behind her. In spite of the guilt and confusion he felt, he was glad to have her go.

8

By late afternoon, Stephen Williams was over the worst part of U.S. 66, particularly the bad stretch between Tulsa and Oklahoma City. But luck—and Steve believed in luck—was not with him. When he had passed through Shamrock, Texas, the road was much better, but the weather, in its turn, took a hand. Beginning with a light snowfall, which gradually turned to sleet, the storm that had threatened him all day long took shape against him. Driving with a determination based more on his anger with the storm than on any desire to arrive at a particular place, he decided to go as far as he could.

Somewhere between Shamrock and a little town called Groom, the railroad runs parallel to the road for a distance of several miles, and he was—for the only time that day—exhilarated by the sight of a streamlined train, one of the Rockets, ahead of him, going in the same direction. In spite of the sleet and the increasing danger of ice on the road, he pushed forward. When he came abreast of the last car of the train, he smiled at it grimly and started to inch along past it. Both the road and the railroad were going uphill now and his pleasure was lessened as he realized that he would have no difficulty in passing the train; it was going—at this point—about forty miles an hour. Even so, he was pleased as he looked at the faces of the people in the windows; some of them were watching him, and in spite of the lack of speed, a competition was set up between his car and the train.

It took him longer than he had expected. The car was beginning to skid, the sleet was heavier all the time. He passed the engine, with less of a thrill than he had anticipated, and then left the train behind. The faint sensation of triumph turned gradually into a feeling of defeat as the train—he could still see it out of the corner of his eye—picked up speed and turned away from the road on level country.

Before him, for as far as he could see, lay the barren, desolate land of Texas—wide and treeless—and he began to feel lost in the middle of this forbidding landscape. He was, in a way he had not anticipated and certainly had not wanted, more alone with himself now than he could ever remember having been. The feeling that he was driving into the unknown, into space, was sharpened and intensified until he began to be afraid.

He thought back to the days before he had left New York, and what had then seemed an impossible situation now seemed almost pleasant by contrast. Whatever difficulties Marjorie had created, however trying she had been to live with, however much he had wanted to escape her, she had been—at the same time—a companion; someone to whom he had, although unwillingly, come home every night. He pictured her, alone in the apartment, separated from him by two thousand miles, and the resentment, anger, (even the pleasure he had felt at being away from her) were all dissipated. They were both alone now. However bad their marriage might have seemed to him, he had never before envisioned what it would be like to be so far and so completely away from her.

It occurred to him that he could telephone her, but his first reaction to this thought was to suppress it at once. His pride, everything that had made him decide to leave her, rose up to fight the possibility of giving in to what was nothing more than a moment of loneliness. Still, the thought remained, and the more it troubled him, the less proud he became. He had not written to her, after that one post card he had sent from Vincennes, Indiana, and he was sure that she would be worried about him. It would not represent any weakening of his original decision if he did call her, he reasoned. After all, he did not *want* to worry her; she couldn't help loving him as she did, even if her expression of it was sometimes intolerable. And here, in this bleak, unfriendly, stormy land, the idea that he was loved by someone, was a warming thing. He would call her. He would call her when he got to Amarillo, where he was determined to get that night.

When he did arrive in Amarillo, his resolution faltered again. What would she think if he called? Would it mean—to her—that he missed her, that he was sorry he had left? He did not want to give her the impression that he was having anything but a fine time. He decided to postpone making the call until he had had his dinner and a drink or two; he would know better later. He found a court near the center of town, and when he got out of the car, was surprised to find how cold it was. When he had registered, he went into the clean, warm, lonely room with the double bed and was inevitably reminded of their apartment in New York. It seemed awful to be alone; it would be better to be with anyone, even Marjorie, than to be alone all the time, and aloneness was all that faced him. He decided to find a telephone even before he had a drink.

He put the telephone call in from the office of the camp, and was told that the circuits were busy. He waited impatiently near the telephone booth, and when the telephone rang again, he answered it quickly. This time he was told that there was no answer at that number in New York.

"Are you sure you didn't ring the wrong number, operator?"

She repeated the number to him and asked if she should try it again in twenty minutes.

A dull anger mounted inside him. Here he had had the picture of her, sitting at home waiting for him, and had never had the sense to think that she was probably out having herself a good time while he was alone and far away from her. "No," he said peremptorily, "cancel the call."

It would be a long time before he would call her again!

9

THE EYE, THE FACULTY OF observation which led Peter Wells to a career as a writer, for instance, had certain advantages and disadvantages which were not always easily calculated in advance. In the course of a very few days, that eye, like an obstruction between himself and his own life—a part of himself which observed but did not participate—had penetrated deeply enough into his relationship with his father so that he had understood more about them than ever before; it had also, however, weakened his responses by seeing them almost too clearly. That he could have judged his father's possible death with such clarity seemed odious to him. That he had then, successively, been depressed about his own life, his career, and discovered that there was an underlying fear that his father really would die and deprive him of a protection he felt he needed now more than ever, was illuminating, but like all illumination, a little blinding.

The very intelligence, perception, and receptivity which aided him in his work, betrayed him as a living person, as if those qualities—rather than adding to his life as a human being—became of themselves, substitutes for life. Seeing had become a curtain between himself and what he felt, communicated to, or experienced with other people. In all the relationships he had had with people—relationships involving any degree of intimacy—the faculty of observation had finally become more important to him than anything else. Now, like something coming to a long overdue boiling point, his feelings and his needs in life were reaching out for something more, demanding more than mental or intellectual fulfillment. It seemed to him (but this was the commenting eye again) that, like a child whose emotional life has been arrested for inexplicable reasons, he had suddenly discovered that he was loved; had discovered it in his heart for the first time. And his reaction to the discovery had been to retreat from it. He was embarrassed to find that now, at his age, he needed and wanted the love and protection of—for want of another source—his father. It was too late for them to achieve something which belonged properly in his childhood.

As he thought these things, putting his feelings meticulously into words, labelling them, he was saddened by the strength of the habits which forced him into it. Was it impossible for him to have any direct, natural responses to what he felt? Was he going to go through with this Hollywood project to satisfy the habits he had formed over so many years? Was his feeling that he was impelled towards some special destination—he still felt incapable of not going on, as if he were being pulled towards something important—so strong that it would not allow him to turn back?

All day Sunday on the road, and in spite of his absorbed self-analysis, he had been unable not to watch the travellers on the road. Where were all these people going? What were they doing, driving, driving, driving? The relation of people—Americans—to their automobiles (the way he felt about his own car, the manner in which it seemed to endow him with special importance as a person, as if it were an extension of himself, a necessary adjunct to his ego) intrigued him. It seemed to him—and again he felt a sense of discovery—that it was a material representation of enormous magnitude: the cult of the machine— the automobile—had replaced faith. The road, leading endlessly and relentlessly on, a pathway to the unknown, the unexperienced, the future, was capable of leading him anywhere. If there was a heaven for

Americans, it would be on such a road, at the top of a rise; something that would be reached in a car.

All his life, Peter Wells had assumed and believed, except for moments during the war when everything had seemed questionable and unreasonable, that human life was primarily an orderly, planned process, resulting from belief in principles, free will, and consciousness of self. The last few days, his feelings about his father, his doubts about himself and his direction in life, his observations, had reversed this conception—too quickly—and led him into a new, disordered, unpredictable world.

The knowledge, accumulated through several years of observation, had reached a sudden climax inside him, producing a confused variety of tentatively convincing conclusions. The purpose of living—for people—seemed to be an unfathomed mystery now: where he had once seen direction, aim, consciousness, usefulness, he saw compulsion: reaction in place of action. His own indecision (and what now appeared to be aimlessness) had revealed a general lack of decision or purpose in the world around him.

The problem, much as he tried to rationalize and explain it on an intellectual level, did not confine itself to that level. He was frightened of what he thought, and of the feelings which produced his thoughts. He felt robbed; the world in which he had lived, complacently and perhaps arrogantly, had disappeared. No longer was he able to sit to one side of life and watch it, making observations and passing judgments, noting them carefully in his writing, producing novels that were nothing more than critiques of a way of life made by someone who had, instinctively, assumed himself capable of so doing, as if he was, by nature (and not by experience), immune or superior to other people, to life itself.

He stopped, just at dusk, in Garden City, Kansas. The weather, which had improved from the day before, had taken a turn for the worse again; the cold rain which had started an hour earlier had turned into an icy drizzle and the surface of the road had begun to freeze over. He was glad, at least, that his own feelings of compulsion had quieted down sufficiently so that he had sense enough to stop. He had driven just over four hundred miles—a perfectly satisfactory day's run; although why a certain number of miles should be cause for satisfaction was something he asked himself sardonically.

There was only one cabin left in the tourist camp where he had stopped and it was not until after he had registered that the woman, a hard, severe disgruntled look in her eye, saw Kelly.

"You didn't say you had a dog," she said.

He smiled at her. "No one has ever objected to him," he said quietly. "He's very well behaved, he doesn't bark, I'm sure he won't disturb anyone."

She looked at him suspiciously, making him feel that he had behaved in some criminal way by not announcing Kelly immediately. "We don't take dogs here," she said.

He sighed and looked out through the window at the cold rain, the road, and Kelly's head watching them through the window of the car. He was tired, he did not want to argue, but he did not want to go on. He turned back to her. "I'll be glad to pay something extra for him," he said.

She looked at him again, then out of the window at the dog in the car, and smiled. "Well," she said slowly, "if he's well-behaved...I suppose a dollar will be all right."

He handed the money to her and walked out of the office. It was the first time on the trip that there had been any question about Kelly, and he took it as an attack upon himself. If it had not been for the road and the weather he would have gone on...he decided to let well enough alone.

The incident, however, did serve to turn his attention to Kelly. He had practically forgotten him, except at lunchtime, all day long.

He gave the dog a run in the bitter wind outside the cabin, watching him with a feeling of having been hurt, and then they went inside. He put water down for Kelly and poured himself a drink and then watched the dog gratefully. He felt guilty at having neglected him, but he also felt—in a spirit of self-criticism—that his affection for the dog was another indication of what might be called his own lifelessness. His affections and his interests in life had boiled down to a very few things: his father, his dog, his career, and nothing more. He was not a part of any main current of life; he had no wife, no lover, no essential friendships. He felt that he had lost, suddenly, whatever it was that had, up to now, carried him serenely along through his existence. The assurance and self-confidence (or had they been just self-interest?) were gone. How could they be replaced, and with what?

10

THE FEVER BOILED UP INSIDE him from time to time, receding just enough at moments so that Charles Wells was dimly aware of people—at least of a man and a woman—talking near him. Although the difference between reality and unreality was practically indistinguishable, in moments of what seemed to be clarity—and he tried to hang on to them as he felt himself going under again—he remembered where he was, who he was, and mostly that it was very important for him to get in touch with Peter. For reasons which he could not understand, and which troubled and angered him alternately, he was unable to communicate this need, or else Mrs. Jones (was it Mrs. Jones, then?) could not understand him.

Late in the evening, when the fever had abated temporarily, he heard the telephone ringing, and his memory was completely clear for a few minutes. That would be Peter calling, of course. But it was not, or at least Mrs. Jones said it was not Peter, just the doctor. He had a horrible feeling of helplessness. If he had answered the telephone himself—if he had had the strength—he was sure that he would have heard Peter's voice.

NOVEMBER 12, 1951

1

Jim Curran woke up at eight o'clock on Monday morning, and although the remembrance of the woman's body in the back of his car was clear in his mind as he awoke, he felt relaxed, calm, and somehow pleased with himself. His mind was very sharp, he knew exactly what he had to do next. The body was perfectly safe in the locked car with the blanket over it; and even if the woman was missed, there was no way to trace the murder to him. The only person he remembered seeing was a man they had passed on the way to his car, and that man—although he had passed next to them, on the same side of the street—had barely looked in their direction; besides, it had been too dark to see anyone's features closely. There was a remote possibility that he could have known the woman—but even if that were true it would not matter—he didn't know Curran, and the town was probably filled with strange men of average height and nondescript coloring like himself. He visualized a possible headline in the paper: "Missing girl last seen with stranger," and smiled. He had nothing to worry about. He had only to dispose of the body, and he would have to wait until dark for that.

When he had had his breakfast, he cleaned up his small house with great thoroughness. The impatience and the nervousness of the day before had disappeared, and he found himself enjoying the process of creating order in his house. When he had finished cleaning, he washed his face and hands again, and put on a clean shirt. He had had the forethought, before he had put the body in the car, to strip to his underwear, and the shorts and shirt would, of course, have to be disposed of, too. But neither the disposal of the body or of the underwear caused him any uneasiness. He had his plan worked out in every detail. He went downtown a little after eleven o'clock, parked his car on Washington Street, locked it, tested every door, and then put a nickel in the meter. He had placed an open bottle of Air-Wick on the floor in the front of the car; just in case. He had not bothered to look under the blanket covering the body.

Filled with a sense of satisfied well-being, and a genuine feeling of accomplishment—as if he had done something, and done it well, that had required doing for a long time—he decided to take a walk, replenish his supply of liquor, and have some lunch. He had driven into town in a spirit of bravado, reacting with pleasure to the idea of being a murderer (he repeated the word softly to himself) at large, but he warned himself not to carry it too far. It might be wiser to buy some food that he could eat in the car, drive out to some isolated place, and wait for darkness.

When he returned to the car with the sandwiches and the bottle, he had one second of real panic. A policeman was standing by the car parked in front of his, writing out a ticket. His own car was perfectly safe: there were more than thirty minutes on the meter still, but the presence of the policeman gave him more of a thrill than he had bargained for. He decided not to get into his car while the policeman was that close, and walked across the street, keeping his eye on the car. In order not to seem conspicuous, he walked into the Hall of Ethnology, looked briefly at some Indian exhibits displayed in the first room—petroglyphs, whatever they might be—and then, although he was alone in the room, looked cautiously out of the window. The policeman walked past his car, glanced at it, and then turned back up the street. Jim watched him for a few seconds, walked hurriedly to the door, opened it, glanced up and down the street, and started across towards his car. Halfway there, he had another idea, turned back, and walked into the bank where he cashed a check for two hundred dollars. He then walked to the car, unlocked it, got in, and drove up Washington Street towards the Federal Building, turned left around the loop, and started out the Taos highway.

⌐

It was not until almost five o'clock that he drove back into town. The Sangre de Cristo mountains were already blending into the darkening sky, and he felt a stirring in his blood as he realized that in about one-half hour it would be dark. He would be glad to get it over with. He checked his plans mentally as he drove slowly up Canyon Road and parked the car by his house. The lights were already on in the Simms' house, and as he got out of the car and locked it, Richard Simms came out of the studio door and smiled at him.

"Hello, Mr. Curran."

Jim made a gesture with his hand, took the key from the door of the car, and stepped away from it in Richard's direction. "Hello, Mr. Simms," he said. "How are you?"

"Fine. I saw you drive in and I wanted to ask you what had happened to your dog. I haven't seen it around."

Jim's eyes narrowed and he felt the muscles in his face tightening. "My dog?" he asked quickly. "I don't know. She just disappeared. Why?"

Richard's face took on a puzzled look. "I'm sorry to hear that," he said. "My wife and I finally gave up the idea of keeping a dog in this part of town...because of the poisoning that's been going on around here. I hope nothing like that happened to your dog. Have you advertised for her?"

Why did he want to know so much? Jim searched his face for a sign of suspicion, but found no trace of it, although he seemed a little less friendly than he had been when they had last spoken to each other. He shrugged his shoulders, took a package of cigarettes from his pocket, offered them to Richard, who refused. He lighted one for himself, returned the pack to his pocket, blew out a small cloud of smoke, and laughed. "She wasn't much of a dog," he said casually. "I don't…I hope nothing happened like poisoning, but, well…I don't exactly miss her. She kind of adopted me in the first place, but she was a nuisance."

Richard's look then—unmistakably questioning and judging—lasted a little too long for comfort. "I'm glad you don't miss her," he said slowly. "And I suppose you've seen the story in the paper about the dog, haven't you?"

"No." Jim shook his head and looked away. Had Richard ever actually seen his dog? He was not sure, but unquestionably Mrs. Simms had seen it. He wondered what the story was and just how much the Simms' knew—or had guessed—by this time. "What was the story?" he forced himself to ask.

Richard's face paled before he answered. "It's the most sickening thing I've ever read," he said. "You'd better get the paper and read it for yourself. I only hope it wasn't your dog…but I mentioned it to you because the description fitted her. Wasn't she a small, brown and white hound?"

The back of Jim's neck began to sweat. He nodded quickly, wondering how he could get away. "I hope not, too," he said. "I'll get the paper, but I've got to go now…I've got a date in a few minutes."

Once more, Richard appraised him, and then turned away. "I still hope it wasn't your dog," he said over his shoulder before walking into the house.

Repressing the fear and nervousness caused by the conversation with his landlord, Jim went into his house, forced himself to finish his cigarette and take a quick drink before getting back into the car. There was no question in his mind that Simms was suspicious of him. He'd been a real fool to leave the damned dog up there! At least he'd had sense enough not to leave the girl's body. But the idea of going back to the place again disturbed him. Maybe his plan of disposing of the body down the well shaft piece by piece was not such a good one after all. Still, when they started drilling again it would dispose of it so thoroughly that it was worth trying. The only thing that would take any time would be having to cut it up in small enough pieces.

2

Marion Mercer just happened to be looking out of the window when the car passed her house. She watched the lights as they turned into the driveway beyond hers, leading to the place where the well was being drilled. It was not the well-driller's car, she was sure; she had heard them leave. It was partly curiosity and partly the fact that she had been unable to forget the dog, that made her decide to see what was going on over there. She took her flashlight and put on her coat and opened the door. She hesitated in the open doorway, went back into her room, and took the revolver from her bedside table. She looked into it to see that it was loaded, put on the safety catch, and went out of the house. She had never had to shoot the gun since she had owned it, but she was convinced that something funny was going on near that well; she would even shoot if necessary.

She thought of taking her car, and decided against it. Whoever it was, they would hear her, and if she actually turned into the driveway leading to the well-rig she would not be able to turn around and get out easily. Besides, she knew the land well, there was no fence between her property and the well site, and the moon was bright enough so that she would be able to see quite clearly from a distance.

She walked carefully and quietly, picking her way through the small trees. She did not need to use the flashlight, but still held it firmly in one hand, with her other hand clutching the gun in her pocket. She stopped at about one hundred yards' distance from the outline of the well-rig and held her breath. Illuminated in the moonlight was the figure of a man. He had an axe in his hand, and was standing over a pile of something on the ground. His back was to her, and he was staring at whatever it was on the earth before him. She would have been able to distinguish it if he had not been standing between her and it. She watched him, in complete silence (and with a wave of fear shuddering through her) and saw him raise the axe high in the air.

Just as it was about to fall, he stopped; his body stiffened, he let the axe down slowly until it hung by his side, and then turned and looked squarely in her direction. She felt sure—although she was now terrified—that he could not see her through the trees, but she did not dare to move. As she watched him, he seemed to hunch in her direction and peer through the night at her, and then suddenly, he dropped the axe, ran to his car (the motor was still running, the parking lights were on, it was headed in the direction of the road). The accelerator roared, and the car—with a great splattering of gravel and mud—raced down the driveway and out into the Old Pecos road. She continued to watch it, motionless, holding her breath, until the taillight winked over the hill in the direction of town, and disappeared.

She took a deep breath, admonished herself for being so afraid, and walked, trembling and defiant, to where he had stood only a moment before. In spite of the moonlight, she could hardly believe what she saw. She switched on the flashlight, swallowed hard, and looked again. She let out a faint cry, felt the chill take possession of her body, and then in sudden and complete panic, turned and ran towards her own house.

When she reached the house, she went in, locked the door behind her and stood, without turning on a light, behind the door, trying to control her breathing, and listened. She could not hear anything over the pounding of her heart. When she had regained her breath, she put down the flashlight, walked to each window and pulled down the shades, locked the other two doors, and then lighted a lamp in the kitchen where it would not shine out of any window giving on the road. Feeling her way back through the darkness, she got to the telephone, dialed "O," listened impatiently as it rang and rang, and when the operator answered, said—her voice was so low that she had to repeat it twice—"Get me the police! *Hurry!*"

3

JIM CURRAN DID NOT KNOW what had happened, but he had known in his bones that someone—someone he had not even seen—had seen him. The sudden access of terror that had taken possession of him had been overpowering. He had driven—at over sixty miles an hour—down the Pecos trail, barely making the bad turn before the Camino, then down the Camino and Canyon Road. He stopped on the road near his house, was about to get out of the car, and then changed his mind. The body, lying up there near the well site, had his fingerprints on it; so did the axe; the car tracks would be clearly visible on the damp dirt road. He had been a fool to think he could get away with dissecting the body and disposing of it, piece by piece, down the well. What had happened to his self-confidence and clarity? Still, it would have been the perfect way to destroy the evidence; he could still remember the way the bit had pounded the solid granite into a fine powdery mud.

Like a man waking from a dream, he knew in his heart that it was all over now; he had made too many mistakes, irrevocable ones. He was in full flight, but he could at least prolong what he was sure was the inevitable end. He shifted gears and drove slowly down Canyon Road to the Alameda, paused at the stop sign, and turned left. At the junction with U.S. 85, College Street, he stopped again, waited for the car to cross in front of him, and then watched it disappear around the bend, up the hill.

Impulsively, he followed the car, but near the city limits, he changed his mind again and turned right abruptly on the cut-off between the Las Vegas and Albuquerque highways. If he travelled south towards Albuquerque it would, somehow, be safer. He might even find a hiding place in Albuquerque; he had a picture in his mind of a big city, big enough to be safe.

He checked the gasoline gauge and congratulated himself for two things: that he had filled the car with gas that afternoon and that he had had sense enough to cash a check. The fact that he would probably have to abandon his checking account, as well as everything he had left in the house on Canyon Road did not distress him particularly, but only made him irritated with himself. He could just as easily have drawn out all his money and packed his car.

By seven forty-five, he came to the end of the Santa Fe mesa and started down the long hill. There was a car at some distance behind him, and when he had descended a few hundred yards, before the first wide turn, protected on the right and left by a metal guard-rail, he could see the glow of lights coming up the bend towards him. When he was almost at the turn—where the road veered deceptively to his left, he saw something in the road ahead of him, in his lane. It took him a few instants to realize that it was a rabbit, cowering, frightened and blinded by his lights, its eyes burning steadily in his direction.

He had a sudden, idiotic impulse of what amounted to terror...the rabbit, like himself, was trapped in the net of certain destruction; the idea of grinding it to death under the wheels of his car was horrible, unthinkable. He glanced at the left side of the road, saw the bright glow of the lights approaching from the south, and veered to the left. Just as he did so, the rabbit hopped to the left and stopped again, and the double headlights of two cars, one in each lane, rounded the turn in his path...

4

THE 12TH OF NOVEMBER ARRIVED, gray and forbidding, into the lives of Richard and Dorothy Simms. To Dorothy, about to leave her husband for the day, even the weather seemed almost too well suited to the mood which had overtaken them both since Richard's return from New York. In a few days' time, she had felt herself driven into an emotional impasse, frightening and confusing to her, and the prospects for the future were bleak. She recognized (it was clear enough now) that whatever was at the root of Richard's trouble, it was serious. She was unable, this morning, to chide him for feeling sorry for himself; she could not attempt any false cheer in an effort to lift him out of his depression. He was like a man gripped by a disease; an illness that was eating its way into the heart of their marriage, dragging her down relentlessly with him.

They both regretted the anger they had expressed the day before, but there was no apparent means by which they could dissipate its effects. The regret only served to increase the depth of Richard's gloom and discontent.

She left Santa Fe under the clouds of what looked like an impending storm in the mountains, and the overcast gray skies epitomized and gave form to the gloom that surrounded them both. She tried to find courage in the fact that she no longer met only a blank wall in her husband. He did not attempt, as he said goodbye to her, to hide his melancholy or to pretend that it did not exist. The pretense, at least, was gone. But the admission and the lack of pretense were not encouraging; they seemed more than anything an acceptance of defeat.

Her trip to Albuquerque was discouraging. Because of the weather, the land—that land which had always communicated a sense of space and freedom and limitlessness to her—was hard and unfriendly without its accustomed sun. The mountains to the north of town were hidden in mist and clouds—it was certainly snowing up there—and the land to the south of the great mesa stretched away from her as she drove, an endless enemy towards which she was travelling, leaving behind everything she wanted in life. How was it possible that her life had become so complicated and difficult? What was happening to their marriage? She could not stop loving her husband. She could not stop being concerned about him. She could not fight the natural demands of love. But now, it was as if her love for him was at fault. She had accepted their happiness and companionship, their entire life together, with such ease, such blindness...she had no preparation for this abyss...

Except for business (she obtained exclusive Santa Fe listings for some ranch property near Albuquerque; a minor feat that would please Mrs. Simms, at least) her expedition was a failure. Albuquerque, big, sprawling, and unattractive, increased her feeling of loneliness. With time to spare—to kill—because of her reluctant but firm decision to stay away all day, she had walked along the streets listlessly, had done a few errands, seen a dull movie, and eaten two meals alone. She hated to eat by herself in a restaurant; the very act of entering unaccompanied, being led to a table, ordering, and then eating silently, made her feel defensively conspicuous and unprotected. If anything should happen to herself and Dick...This day in Albuquerque was like a preview of her own future.

She started back, uncertain and afraid of what awaited her at home. She no longer felt that there was anything she could do for him or for herself except to go back and be there, to stick it out and to hope—in the same blind way that she had always taken them for granted—that something would happen.

Spurred on by a grim determination, she picked up speed as she started out of Bernalillo where she ran into an increase of traffic going north. She managed to get by most of the cars, and by the time she reached La Bajada Hill, she had passed everything going in her direction except one truck. Two or three cars coming from the north prevented her from passing it, and by the time it was grinding its way around the turn halfway up the hill, a string of cars had piled up behind her. The truck was going just fast enough to make passing dangerous, but finally, impatient and angry with being held back, she decided to take a chance. Her own lights and the lights from the truck flooded the road as she pulled out, across the yellow warning line, to the left of the truck and started around the turn. Just as she came abreast of the cab, the lights of a car coming from the north came into full view. The car was in the middle of the road, its lights were very close. There was nothing for her to do except to get by...

5

By early afternoon, Richard Simms began to hope that his
wife would return in time for supper. Her absence, much as he had
thought he desired it, had made no difference. Because of the serious-
ness of the words they had exchanged the day before, because of his
own feelings of regret that morning, he had not been able to think of
anything else all day. Reviewing their lives together: the things they
had done, the way they had lived, what they had felt for each other,
he began to realize that he was striking senselessly at the very thing
that had the most value for him in life. He walked to the window,
looking out over their land, at the physical results of their marriage: the
garden, the studio, the guest house; the things that had resulted from
their years together. They were not very much, but they represented
himself and Dorothy. What he could see and touch in and around
the house, the accumulation of their years together; these things were
themselves, their imprint.

He looked at his watch: nearly five o'clock. If she was going to return
in time for dinner, she would certainly be leaving now; she had said
that her appointment was for two o'clock in the afternoon. But she had
also said that she might stay down for dinner. He thought back to her
departure of the morning, and while he did not—even now—actively
regret her leaving, he had an odd and uncomfortable sensation of
foreboding about it. It had not been an unfriendly departure; but an

unhappy one; she had seemed to be embarking on a distant and final journey, not a simple trip of sixty-odd miles from which she would return that same evening. He shivered, rubbed his arms, and moved away from the window. There was something in his own thoughts, in the very air around him, something intangible that sent a chill through him...there was something *wrong*.

He walked into the living room, sat down, looked around the room and then got up again. There was something cheerless and unfriendly about the silent house now. He lighted a lamp, walked back into the kitchen and poured himself a drink, carried it back into the living room, and then went to the door, opened it, and picked up the paper. He glanced at the headlines and then walked impulsively to the telephone, looked up a number in the book, and dialed it. He ordered flowers more from a need to dispel something in the atmosphere of the room than for any other reason, and then sat down, took a swallow of his drink and opened up the paper.

A little while later, when he heard the car come into the driveway, he got up and walked to the door and went out. That would be Jim Curran, and he wanted to talk to him. He had no good reason, really, for what he was thinking, but his intuition was so strong that he was unable to resist it...

6

THE CONVERSATION WITH CURRAN HAD not proved anything to him, but it had strengthened his conviction—which he knew was entirely unfounded—that it was Curran's dog he had read about in the paper. The conversation also did something else. He remembered that Dorothy's word for Curran had been "inhuman" and now, after talking to him, it began to seem especially appropriate. What was it about that man? What was that indefinable sensation of evil that Richard had felt about him...and why was it that such a person as Curran should be involved in their lives just at this particular time?

Automatically, his reason informed him that he was not being logical; Curran had nothing to do with them at all, he was just one more in a series of tenants. Impatiently, he brushed these things aside. Perhaps it did not make sense, perhaps there were no *reasons,* but what he felt was irresistible...the feeling that he had had earlier that something was wrong had only been intensified when Curran had arrived and when he had gone out to talk to him. There was something about the man that threatened them. He was sure of it.

∻

Dorothy did not come back for dinner. She had not come back by nine o'clock, and Richard had finally given up. It was just after nine-thirty, as he sat in the living-room staring at the flowers which had not brought any life into the room, that the telephone rang. He was so filled, by that time, with a premonition of imminent disaster that he was unable to answer it immediately. On the third ring, he picked up the receiver...

7

STEPHEN WILLIAMS ARRIVED IN SANTA Fe in time for a late lunch. His dream of the Southwest, the place to which he was going to escape from the monotonous routine of his job and his wife, had fallen apart steadily as he had penetrated into this bare and lonely land. From Clines Corners to Santa Fe on U.S. 285, he had seen practically nothing to indicate that man had ever settled in the bleak, ugly, moon-like landscape. Santa Fe was an additional disappointment to him: the adobe buildings, narrow streets with Spanish names, and, above all, the people—what were they? Indians? Spanish? Mexican?—made him feel as if he had crossed a frontier into a foreign land, a land in which he did not feel at home, and in which nothing attracted him. There were a lot of white people, of course, but the atmosphere and the flavor of the place did not belong to them.

After lunch at a cafe on the Plaza (there was even a menu in Spanish as well as in English) he found the post office and picked up the letter from Marjorie. He read it quickly and stuck it into his pocket, but he could not get it out of his mind. He was ashamed with his anger when he had been unable to reach her by telephone, and the fact that she had wanted to welcome him with a letter on his arrival here, touched him more than he wanted to admit to himself.

Loneliness, although he had never known it before in his life, had been one of the strongest influences in Stephen Williams' life. He had struggled against it since his childhood, had married to avoid it, had kept a job he hated because the idea of looking for another job—the dismal, lonely process of searching for a niche among strangers—had frightened him. Why on earth, then, had he come out here? What had ever happened to make him believe that a trip to such a place as this could hold any promise for him?

Walking aimlessly along the streets of the town, he felt even more lost than he had the day before. What was he going to do? If he went back, he would have to submit to Marjorie's triumph (he could imagine her crowing over him); and if he stayed? To stay was already an intolerable idea, and yet he had to come to some decision now; he had, at least, to find some place for the night. He put the decision off blindly, and walked impulsively into a movie theatre. He came into the middle of the feature—he did not even know the name of it—and it did not take his mind off himself and his problem. Sitting in the dark, his feeling of being alone in the world deepened inside him. He would have to do something about it.

When the movie was over, he went into the first bar he saw. He stood at the counter, ordered a beer, and looked around him. The place was dirty, and the only other people in it were a group of dark-skinned Mexicans, two men and a woman seated in a booth, rattling away at each other in Spanish and laughing loudly. In any other place, in any other town, it was the kind of group that he might, conceivably, have joined, or who might have asked him to join them. But these were people that he could not even talk to and as they glanced at him from time to time he began to feel that their laughter was at his expense. He ordered straight whiskey and a beer chaser, drank that, and then ordered another. The last drink made him feel a little better, and he walked out of the bar with a contemptuous glance at the people in the booth.

Although it was not very late, he was hungry again, the thought of food was the only comforting thing that came to his mind, and—in spite of not having liked his lunch—he went back to the same place on the Plaza. It was the only anchor he had in the town, the only place he knew.

During dinner he decided that he could not stay here. Albuquerque, he knew from the map, was bigger. Probably there'd be more white people there, too. If he left around seven he could get there about eight-thirty, and the thought of not having to spend the night in Santa Fe gave him a slight lift.

By the time he had finished his dinner, he was feeling better. The idea that there might be something waiting for him—just what, he did not know, although he had a vision of something warm, friendly, welcoming—made him want to get there in a hurry.

He drove fast on the way out of town and did not have to slow down until he came up behind a New York car just at the beginning of what looked like a long hill. He had to stay behind it as it went around a turn, and he pulled up close, as if to push it ahead. When he saw a free, unobstructed stretch in the road ahead—there was a turn to the left, but he had enough room, particularly going downhill—he pressed hard on his horn, pulled out, and accelerated. He was going so fast that he had to put his brake on as he came to the curve, and then he let up on them again; one of the secrets of good driving, one that a lot of people didn't know, was to accelerate around a curve. He put his foot back on the gas and started around. When he saw the car just ahead of him and the lights of the upcoming cars almost blinding him, he jammed his foot on the brake again, but he was too close...

8

Caroline Pratt, Tom Foster, Henry and Mabel Franklin, Robert and Mary Hume and their children, had all gone to the Jemez Indian Pueblo and all for different reasons. With the exception of Robert and Mary, none of them were there specifically because they wanted to see an Indian dance, and the Humes were there mostly out of a sense of duty: Toby and Emily should see at least one real Indian dance while they were in the Pueblo country.

Of all the spectators, and there were not very many, Henry Franklin enjoyed the experience the most. He had determined to go, mostly as a means of forcing his wife to do something she had not suggested herself; it was a way of keeping a precarious hold of his newfound and uncomfortable domination of Mabel. The dance supported his ego in an unexpectedly pleasant way, although he did not mention it to Mabel. He noticed with satisfaction that all of the women seemed to have subservient roles to the men in the dance, and that among the Indians who were not dancing, it was the men who sat around while the women carried food, cleaned the houses, chopped the wood, baked the bread...did all the work. Exactly as it should be.

Mabel Franklin was also aware of these things, but to her they were an indication of how far modern woman had come on the road to liberation from slavery, and it strengthened her determination not to let her husband continue to lord it over her. She was recovering rather rapidly from the shock of Henry's outburst of masculinity in Kansas City. It was high time, she decided, to put him in his place again.

Caroline Pratt, walking through the pueblo during one of the pauses in the dancing, watched the Indian women with envy. There was nothing she would have wanted more than to be able to serve Tom Foster in some way. She bitterly regretted her deficiencies as a cook and housekeeper; had she been able to make a home for him, he might really be convinced of her affection. Make a home for him? They hadn't had the time for anything yet...if she could just hold on to him a little longer, there would be time for everything. To be able to walk with him, with his arm through hers; to have him not despise her but actually accept her in a friendly way, was already a great deal; enough to give her cause to hope for more. And the fact of their togetherness, their physical closeness, in public (even if it was pretty much an Indian public) was certainly something—like an announcement of their mutual existence. She was willing to accept what he gave her; she was even very grateful.

Tom sensed her happiness and gratitude and was moved by them. He could not help but like her, and he admired the way in which she had given herself completely over to him. He had wanted to come here in order to avoid the constant intimacy which was unavoidable when they were alone together, but she had been so happy all day that he was ashamed. He glanced at her as they walked, looking at the body he had come to know so intimately in the little time since they had met, and then moved closer to her and tightened his hand on her arm. He would have liked to go to bed with her right then and there; there was something about her that made him sexually insatiable; he wondered if he would ever get enough of her.

Toby Hume thought the dance was awful. The Indians looked to him just like the ones in the museum he had been taken to see, except that these were not stuffed. The one thing that had interested him during the whole, interminable afternoon had been one little Indian boy who had been running around—no one paid him the slightest attention—in a dirty shirt and no pants. He had even stopped right in the middle of the Plaza and relieved himself in front of everyone. Toby had looked quickly at Emily, but she had become suddenly ladylike and was pretending not to notice.

Robert and Mary Hume had a good afternoon. There was no one thing that made it a special occasion, but the intensity of the dancing, the continuous monotonous rhythms of the drum, the dancers' feet, and the chorus; the costumes and the general air of festivity and celebration which filled the village, communicated itself to them both. Since the day before when they had driven into New Mexico, their trip had ceased to be a chore...they were really on a vacation at last. For the first time in almost a month, they were not having to make plans about what they would have to see next, how many miles they would have to drive the following day.

Although neither of them knew very much about Indian rituals, the symbols—the basic, everlasting symbols of nature—corn, pelts, feathers, branches of trees—things that had importance and value in the maintenance of physical life, were obvious enough. They felt the spirit of thanks and rejoicing in the ceremony, and it was rather wonderful, Mary thought, to have a religion in which one danced to the honor of one's God.

9

NONE OF THE THREE CARS following Dorothy Simms up La Bajada Hill was there by the direct intention of the occupants. The Illinois Cadillac would have been in Santa Fe long before if Mrs. Franklin had not decided that it was time to assert her will. When Henry said, as they left the dance, "Well, I'm looking forward to a good dinner at the hotel," Mabel smiled at him, shook her head, and said: "I think we'll try some Spanish food in Bernalillo, dear. I saw a sign for a place on the way down." She took the keys from his hand and got into the driver's seat of the car. Henry had hesitated for a moment...a decisive moment, he knew. If he gave in now, there would be no going back. He opened his mouth to speak, but one look at the determined profile of his wife sitting in the car, and his mouth snapped shut. He walked around the car, avoiding her eyes, and got in beside her. He was embarrassed, and hoped that no one had seen them, but he was secretly relieved after the strain of self-assertion. He just was not cut out to rule anyone. "I think that's a good idea," he said meekly, when he had closed the door of the car.

The Hume family had even less reason to be in that particular place at that time. They were anxious to get back to Santa Fe and get the children to bed. It had been a long day. But after a flat tire on Route 44, and the long wait while they fixed it at San Ysidro, the children were clamoring for food and Mary decided they'd better go into Bernalillo and eat.

Tom and Carrie had stopped at the first bar on U.S. 85 for a drink and the drink had turned out to be five martinis each. During all the time they had been drinking, they had not talked very much, and he had stared at her hungrily, ordering additional drinks to prolong the anticipation of the moment when he would be in bed with her again. She had started to talk to him, to tell him again how much she was in love with him, but he silenced her by reaching for her leg under the table; the sheer weight of his desire was overpowering, he wasn't even listening to the words she said.

When he had paid the bill, they walked unsteadily to the car, and to her surprise he handed her the keys. "You better drive," he said thickly. In the car, he smiled to himself, ran his hands over her body, kissed her, and then said: "Let's get home, baby. Let's get home and go to bed."

She had not driven two miles when he was sound asleep, with his head on her shoulder. She let his head down into her lap, careful not to wake him. She was pretty tight, but she had never felt any happier in her life.

At the foot of La Bajada Hill she came up behind a Pontiac station wagon with an Ohio license. There were at least two cars and a truck ahead of it, and she decided not to try to pass them. Much as she wanted him, she could wait; to have him sleeping against her this way gave her a special possessive satisfaction. Nothing, no one, had ever belonged to her so much.

10

ALL DAY MONDAY, PETER WELLS had been unaccountably happy. His morbid, self-accusatory mood of the past few days had lifted as suddenly as it had come on him. Kelly had awakened him very early, licking rather mournfully at his face, and Peter had laughed at him, gotten out of bed, dressed quickly, and taken him out—it was not yet dawn in Garden City—to exercise. Kelly, delighted, and shuddering as much with joy as with cold, ran around the court, sniffing voluptuously at the various fragrant corners of the buildings, the trees, the automobile tires. To Peter's amusement, he made a careful olfactory search of the office—where the woman had been so reluctant to have him—and after an apparently serious decision, lifted his left leg just at the front door.

After a quick breakfast at an all-night truck stop just outside of the town, they started to drive fast. With any luck at all, Peter thought he should be able to make Albuquerque that night. He was no longer concerned with the whys and wherefores of his journey; he was only anxious to get there. His feelings about destiny, fate, and the mysterious forces which he had felt had been driving him along embarrassed him as he thought back to them. He had succumbed, naively, to a depression brought about by his conversations with his father about life and death, and while what his father had said still made sense to him, his worry and his depressing reactions seemed ridiculous.

He arrived in Santa Fe late in the afternoon, late enough so that he decided to have a drink and dinner there before going on to Albuquerque. As he had driven into the town, his feeling of elation and well-being had increased; there was something about the vastness of the countryside that made him feel expansive...here, there was enough space for everything. He thought, as he was having his dinner, that he might even stay here for the night, but his desire to get ahead, to end this journey, to get settled and back to work, pushed him on. He could get to Albuquerque in an hour or so, and if the weather held, he should be able to make Hollywood by Wednesday.

He left Santa Fe a little after seven, heading south on U.S. 85, and the car—as if it, too, was responding to his wish to get ahead—seemed to want to go faster; he found himself tearing along through the night at over seventy miles an hour. He did not slow down until he saw the taillights of a car ahead of him, about twenty miles south of the city. He would have passed it, but it started down a hill ahead of him, picked up speed unaccountably, and he dropped behind, letting the car brake itself down the hill. The car in front disappeared around a curve to the left, reappeared for an instant as Peter started around the curve behind it, and then went out of sight once more. As he came around the turn, putting on his brakes, he heard the horn and saw the lights of a car behind him. He slowed down still more as it came up close and watched it tear past him. He shook his head; there was just enough room ahead so that the man could probably pass safely—there were lights coming up around the turn—but he was appalled at the speed and recklessness of the driver.

As he watched it disappear around the turn, he put his foot on the brake. The movement was completely instinctive, he was not going very fast by that time, but he had sensed something...The sensation (it had produced an oddly chilling ripple along his spine) had been very strong, even alarming. The car ahead of him had barely disappeared when he thought he heard something. He rounded the turn, jammed on his brakes and came to a full stop. He had heard something all right…the road was a jumble of cars, lights, wreckage. He looked quickly around, saw a wide shoulder on the left side of the road, drove across to it and got out of his car…

11

Order, which had ceased to exist until the sudden, unexpected arrival of a State Police car on a routine highway patrol, had come slowly, with monotonous, routine efficiency, out of the chaos of the accident back into the lives of the people involved. Bodies were extricated from the wreckage, wreckers and ambulances arrived, cars were moved, a single lane was cleared through the tangle of the accident, and through traffic was pushed relentlessly on its way.

Twenty miles south of the scene of the accident, in the corridor of the hospital outside of the emergency room, the combined smells of blood, sweat, medicine, cigar smoke (from the cigar of one of the policemen), and the sickeningly sweet odor of burnt flesh mingled with the subtler odors of fear and death.

Reality, the fundamental, basic reality of life, had been imposed upon everyone involved in the accident for at least a short time. The dreams, illusions and enchantments, the superficial aims and purposes, desires and wishes, of the victims and the spectators were stripped away by the shock, leaving only the human essentials. The veneer of civilization that passes for human dignity had—for a time—ceased to exist.

For the doctor, supervisor, nurses, orderlies, ambulance drivers, and even the police, the aim and the purpose—as much because of habit as for any other reason—was not only to preserve life, but to restore order and security, to efface the accident by removing all its traces.

With the debris cleared from the road, the night, the land and the hill remained; indifferent to what had taken place, ready for the next time. Except for the people directly involved, who would continue to reverberate to the consequences of the accident until such time as their wounds were healed and their habitual life reestablished, the accident became in the course of the night just one more event to be recorded in the reports of the Safety Council, reported in the newspapers, added to the columns of the statisticians.

12

P ETER W ELLS STAYED AT THE scene of the accident for a long time.
He lifted, or helped to lift, the bodies of James Curran, Dorothy
Simms, Henry Franklin, and Stephen Williams from their cars. He
was sickened by the smells of blood and burning flesh, the cries and
moans of the people; terrified by the deathly unconsciousness of Dorothy Simms; repulsed by the whimpers from Stephen Williams, and
infuriated with Mabel Franklin. When there was nothing more for
him to do—he reported to the police and agreed to stay in Albuquerque for as long as they might need him—he walked, shakily and
disconsolately, back to his car. He felt drained of any emotions, and
was completely appalled by what he had experienced.

Why had it had to happen? Why to those people? It could not, in
his mind, be resolved—as it would be for the police with their facts and
reports—by finding out who had caused it. There was something more
than any human action involved. Why had Dorothy Simms tried to pass
that truck then? Why had Stephen Williams passed him? What series
of coincidences, what acts of fate, had selected this group of people?
What was it that had protected him?

The warning—and his feeling of alarm was unmistakably that—had
stopped him just in time. He had felt the approach of death—even if
he had not known at the moment what it was—reaching out for him,
like a huge hand with fingers outspread, for all of them. Had it been just

for him, then, or had it come too late for the others? Either it had not been quite big enough to get them all, or else it had not been intended to reach them...yet.

The aim of life is death, his father had said. The aim? He could see no purpose in this kind of dying; only an end, brought on, somehow, by the people themselves, as if the urge to die, to destroy life, had momentarily become more powerful than any other instinct in them.

He looked at the dirt and the blood on his hands. Was life—and the drying blood, infinitely precious to the bodies from which it had run out, was the essence of life—so cheap, inexpensive and worthless, that it could be wasted in this way? What had these people lived for—some of them would certainly die—what had life meant to them? What were they dying for now? What had any of them achieved or acquired or fought for during their lives? Had any of it been worth anything to them?

He took the bottle of water, which he always carried for Kelly, from the back seat of the car, poured some of it onto his hands, and then wiped them with his handkerchief. A fresh trickle of blood—he must have scratched himself—ran a little way down his palm, and he blotted it with the handkerchief. Then he put the bottle back, opened the front door of the car and got in behind the wheel. Kelly made a whining sound, came over to him, and pushed his nose into his side. He probably needed to get out...but not here; not in the middle of all this.

He drove slowly down the hill, through the lane which the wreckers had cleared. He was numbed and exhausted, but the uselessness of the destruction, the lack of logic and reason in it, continued to torment his mind and sicken his worn feelings. The gift of life, which (although he had never felt it in just this way) had such enormous, irreplaceable value, seemed almost worthless. This same scene, this same kind of violent death, was being repeated constantly, daily, hourly, all over the earth.

He could understand, somehow, that nature required death of every living organism. It demanded its quota through sickness, disease, old age, manifestations of violence, volcanoes, floods, storms...but in all of these things there was a curious logic; creation and destruction were nature's prerogatives, they could not be questioned. But what made no sense to him, what robbed life of any apparent purpose and design, was man's own war against man. Not only armies of men fighting each other, but the so-called accidents, the murders, the suicides...

At another whine from Kelly, he pulled off to the side of the road and stopped the car to let him out. Untouched by anything that had happened that night, boundlessly happy to smell and snort with pleasure, to relieve himself copiously on a fence post, the dog was the personification of vital, healthy life. Watching him, it occurred to Peter that he should be eternally thankful that he, himself, had been spared. It would have been so easy to have been just one car ahead.

And yet, he did not feel thankful or even glad to be alive. He was puzzled and disturbed in the very roots of his being. He got back in the car, called Kelly, and started down the road again. Much as he hated the idea, he would find himself a place to stay in Albuquerque; as soon as he knew that the police no longer needed him, he would continue on his way to California, he would go on living in his own small sphere, he would forget what he had seen tonight...He *would* do these things; there was probably nothing in the world that could stop him. But of what value were they? Of what importance? To whom could they possibly matter? Did such actions, finally, constitute *living?* It hardly seemed so.

On the outskirts of Albuquerque, he glanced at his watch in the light of a street lamp. He had intended to telephone home that night, but it was too late now. He would call in the morning.

13

LONG BEFORE THEY HAD EVER met, the mutual destiny of Mabel and Henry Franklin had been decided for them. The need to dominate, direct, possess, and triumph over at least one other human being forever was as much a part of Mabel's character as the color of her hair or the shape of her nose. Dedicated as she was to the preservation of her own individual power, her immediate reaction to the successive impacts of the cars which had struck the Cadillac, on the driver's side and then from the rear, was one of outrage. Through the car, which represented her to the world, symbolizing power, wealth, and position, she had been attacked personally.

She was not injured, and she could not—immediately—understand what had happened to her husband. He had, unaccountably, slumped over the steering wheel and remained there motionless and silent. The interior of the car did not appear to be damaged; except for the crack in the window of the left front door, no glass was broken, even. What could be the matter with him?

She had decided, after dinner in Bernalillo, to let Henry drive back to Santa Fe. Knowing, as she suggested it, that he did not want to drive, the suggestion was only a consolidation of her triumph; his submissive acquiescence to her will was a final substantiation of her resumption of power after his unforgivable and inexplicable self-assertion.

Henry's behavior now was as peculiar and as mystifying as his outburst in Kansas City. She took his shoulders in her two hands, lifted him back off the wheel, shook him fiercely, and said in a loud voice: "Henry! What's the matter with you?"

In the same way that Henry Franklin had feared life, and because of that had sought out, under the convincing (to him) disguise of love, the protection of a woman whom he had long since come to fear and hate, he was also mortally afraid of death. The unknown and the unpredictable had hung, precariously, over him from the time of his birth. At the moment when he first realized the accident was inevitable and that there was nothing at all that he could do to prevent it, his terror had been so great that nature—as if to reach out and protect him from an emotion that was unendurable—had taken a hand. Henry had had a heart attack. As he had lain against the steering wheel, gasping for breath, he had succumbed to his own death. The only struggle left inside him was a physical one, like the reaction of a chicken after its head has been severed. He no longer felt anything, nor did he think. Death, that permanent threat to his existence, had already marked him.

As his head and shoulders were thrust back against the seat of the car; as he heard Mabel's strident voice; as he looked into her infuriated and hysterical eyes, he was no longer afraid of anything. He knew that he was going to die, and the fear of dying had completely disappeared. It was not painful, it did not even seem dangerous. It offered him what he had longed for all his life: oblivion and an escape from the deadly routine of his existence with his wife. He gave her a long and terrible look; his eyes bored straight into her, and Mabel, also for the first time in her life, understood. He was getting away from her forever; he did not want to live. With a cry of terror and resentment, she struck the seat of the car with her clenched fists and burst into hysterical sobbing.

In spite of threats, imprecations, offers of money, and finally pleas, Mabel was unable to get any special attention for her husband. Like the others, she was forced to wait for the arrival of the ambulance which did not get Henry to the hospital until after nine o'clock. She did not regain her composure until he was safely installed in a bed on a ward; again, in spite of every effort she had made, she had been defeated. There were no private rooms. But the waiting, the intensity of her feelings, the effort, the fury...none of these things were of any avail. Henry, stubborn and obstinate to the end, had apparently stayed alive just long enough to give her as much trouble as possible. He died, very peacefully, before eleven o'clock, and Mabel had to be put to bed in his bed (after they had moved it to a woman's ward) and treated for shock and hysteria. As she succumbed to the powerful effects of the drug, she felt herself sinking into a life-long abyss to which there would never be any end. She was old now; powerless and friendless, betrayed and destroyed by the death of her husband.

14

JAMES CURRAN FOUGHT VERY HARD for his life. From the moment
he had first seen the rabbit and known, absolutely, that he could not
kill it, he had seen the end coming and had struggled against it with his
entire being. As he had sideswiped the first car, turned and struck the
guard-rail, bounced off and struck the Cadillac and then over-turned
and hit the guard-rail again, he had maneuvered his car with absolute
concentration and determination. Unable to move, having to wait until he was finally extricated by three men from the burning wreckage
of his own car which had exploded into flame as he overturned, he
had endured a fantastic agony of pain. His compulsive battle against
life, which had led him to every violent means of attack against it,
including torture and murder, had finally turned against himself.

The suffering he endured before he was given a sedative in the
hospital finally became almost exquisite. The sense of ecstasy and the
resulting peace he had felt with the dog and the woman he had killed,
reached a peak for him. The very agony brought him, at long last, to
terms with his own existence, an existence which he had detested and
against which he had rebelled, eternally. Convinced of his own imminent death, he felt the assurance of a final victory taking place. Life,
the enemy he had endured for so many years, was defeated at last. It
was not a question of wanting to live or wanting to die. The increasing
waves of pain, like the messengers of fate, assured him continually

that this was at last the end. His first moment of real terror came when the effect of the sedative began to wear off. Instead of disappearing into death, he had come back—impossibly and unaccountably—to life itself.

15

CAROLINE PRATT HAD STOPPED THE car by instinct when she had seen the lights of the southbound cars, and immediately afterwards, the sound of the first crash. Tom, asleep, with his head in her lap, came to slowly after the sudden stop, opened his eyes and yawned. "What's the matter?"

She put her hand on his head, holding it down. "Don't look," she said quickly. "There's been an accident ahead of us."

He pushed her hand away, sat up, rubbed his eyes, and peered ahead through the night. Before he could see clearly through the jumble of lights, Carrie had begun to back the car and he turned to her in astonishment. "What are you doing?"

"Isn't there a back way to Santa Fe? Through Madrid?" As she said this she was already shifting into first and beginning to turn.

He watched her silently for a moment: "Don't you think we ought to help?"

She shook her head, completed the turn, and started south: "I can't Tom. I can't get involved with anything like that."

His astonishment, verging on anger, increased. "You can't get *involved?*" He didn't seem to understand her very well, he was still hazy from the drink and the sleep.

"I couldn't stand it," she answered. "Please try to understand me. I can't stand the sight of blood."

"What if you'd been in that accident and someone had just turned around and driven away?"

She glanced at him quickly, but did not slow down. "Please," she said urgently. "Let's not talk about it now. Tom. *Please.*"

They drove back to the junction of U.S. 85 and Route 44 in complete silence. Although his mind was still thick with alcohol, he felt stunned into silence by the way they had driven away. In the face of what might have happened to the people involved in the accident, it was incomprehensible and unnatural for them to be driving away without having made any attempt to do anything about them.

As she slowed down to make the turn, he gripped her arm. "Carrie, we have to go back. We have to do something. Call the police or get an ambulance or *something...*"

How could she explain to him? How could she tell him so that he would understand and forgive her? She could feel the coldness in his hand and his voice and she knew she would have to dissipate it. Except that she had felt compelled to get away, she did not really understand what she was doing. The suddenness of it, the shock, the threat that had seemed to her implicit in those few seconds of disaster on the road had all combined to drive her away. She had done it as much out of protection for them both as for any other reason; protection from what she did not quite know, but the accident had in some way epitomized the fury and the hostility of the outside world, as if it had made an attack on herself and Tom.

She completed the turn, drove a few hundred feet, stopped the car, and looked at him. "You're angry with me, aren't you?"

He sighed. "Not exactly angry, Carrie. I just don't understand you. To drive away like that when..." he paused and looked at her. In spite of what he had said about going back, he knew that it was too late now. "Somebody's life might have depended on us, Carrie, don't you see?"

Her lower lip trembled. "I'll go back then, Tom."

"It's too late now." He turned away from her and shrugged his shoulders.

The tears came of themselves and she covered her face with her hands. "I always do the wrong thing," she muttered. "I don't know what's the matter with me. I've never been happy before in my life, Tom, and I couldn't stand the idea of getting mixed up with..." she wiped her eyes with the back of her hand, "...well maybe with death. I had to get away, Tom. I couldn't help it. I know it's awful. You're right to be mad."

"Don't worry about it," he said. "I think I understand. Why don't you let me drive home?"

She nodded, opened the door and got obediently out of the car and walked around it while he moved over in the seat. Again they drove in silence, until suddenly—and for no apparent reason—she began to cry again. He listened to the sound of her crying, gripped the wheel a little more tightly, and continued to drive in silence.

16

It was not until the few seconds between the time when Dorothy Simms knew that she was going to collide with the car coming directly at her and the actual collision, that her self-confidence and her acceptance of life failed her completely. Much as they had been attacked by her own sense of failure and inadequacy in relation to her husband, they had not, until this moment, collapsed. But following the flash of fear that had shot through her, she saw her life in an entirely different perspective.

As she felt herself being lifted from the car, lifted later into an ambulance, and was still later aware—dimly—that she was in a hospital somewhere, being taken care of, urged to live, she knew that her life was hanging by a thread, a thread which had almost been severed in the collision. In the hospital bed, it lay beside her—an unfinished tapestry on which she had been working blindly all her life, taking stitch after stitch without ever having seen the entire pattern before. Now, the continuous thread of herself, which had been woven day by day, week by week, and year by year, hung loosely, threatened by the scissors of death. It seemed to her that it was she herself who had tried to cut it and failed, and the decision still lay before her, was still in her hands.

It was not until, coming from some deep abyss of darkness, Richard's face wavered into focus before her and she became gradually aware of his actual presence: the feel of his hands, the sound of his voice, the look on his face, that something in her began to struggle. She felt pain then; pain, despair, hope, and love simultaneously. She had re-entered herself, come back across death itself. Whatever had had to be decided was over. Feeling herself drifting slowly back into blackness again, she made an enormous effort to speak and to move, but she was incapable of warding off unconsciousness.

Before his face disappeared and she went completely under again, a hard, furious determination had crystallized in her. She was going to battle for her life.

17

THE BODY OF HIS WIFE—FOR it was hardly more than a body now—lay immobile under the hospital blankets, with only one arm and her head exposed. The actual injury to her head had not been serious, but the loss of blood had weakened her to such an extent that her skin was transparent.

Sitting by the bed, Richard Simms was equally motionless. From the time he had been brought into the ward—he had hardly recognized her at first—he had stopped feeling anything. The fear that she might die, his feelings of guilt about the way in which he had let her leave him that morning; the way he had excluded her, had vanished. He was unable to remove his eyes from the bottle of plasma and the long rubber tube that lead from it to the needle which they had taped to her arm. Everything depended on the trickle of life that was entering her through the transparent tube.

If he had not, in a sense, driven her away from him; if he had not let her go alone to Albuquerque; if he had not been responsible for her state of mind, she would have come home earlier...this would not have happened.

In her presence, watching a fight for life and death that was out of his hands, it was no longer a question of who was to blame or why it had happened. The only important thing was that she must, somehow, be made to live. With his hands clenched together and his eyes on the diminishing level of liquid in the bottle, Richard concentrated his entire being into what amounted to a prayer for her survival. It was not a prayer to God, nor was it a prayer for forgiveness, but a prayer for survival and the continuance of their lives.

He understood in his heart that the happiness, work, companion-ship, arguments, trials, depressions, separations, and ecstasies they had weathered together were the fundament and the experience out of which they had, together, acquired reality and meaning. They were indissolubly what they were together, not apart. The time: the moments, days, weeks, years they had expended with each other had created *them*. He was praying as much for his own life as for hers. He did not ask for anything more than the chance to conclude—in its own proper tempo—what they had begun. He knew now that he would not be able to withstand this sudden, violent, severance. If she did die—and he was forced to accept that possibility—he would also be destroyed.

If she did die...his hands tightened together and he looked away from the bottle and the tube, turning his head to look at her face, and his feelings came back into him with a rush of anger against himself for what he was thinking. If she did die...

The force of the emotion broke out in his body and he moved, with-out getting up from the chair, towards her. With his hands touching her arm, his head very close to hers, he said: "You are not going to die."

It did not matter if it was the plasma that had suddenly taken effect; it did not matter what had caused it. What mattered was that Dorothy Simms betrayed death at that moment. As if his will to live had managed to break through to her, she moved her lips, struggled feebly with her arm and made a grimace of pain. The feeling of hope that surged up in Richard brought the tears to his eyes. Fate and nature which had combined, unpredictably, to attack him through his wife, were giving him another chance.

18

WHAT THE HUME FAMILY BROUGHT into the hospital was fear. Fear of blood, fear of what might have happened if they had been in one of the other cars, fear of the violence they had seen, fear of infection from the cuts on the children's faces...fear of death.

To Mary Hume, the accident was like the opening of a door into the unpredictable and the unknown. The circle of safety and security in which she and her family had always lived was shattered by this one shocking blow, and the outside world, a world that existed in the newspapers and on the radio, a world of strangers, enveloped all of them. She clung to her children, sitting in the back seat on the way to the hospital, not so much to comfort them as to try and recreate the illusory web of complacence that had, up to now, always existed for her. But the fear was not so easily defeated and spread itself, infecting her husband and her children as well.

The fear did not begin to subside until they were in the hospital where the children's faces were washed and they were given injections against tetanus (far more painful than anything that had happened to them up to then) and told, rather peremptorily, to go home. They left the hospital at ten-thirty, ashamed of having been there at all; the bright lights of the emergency room, the smells, the bodies on the stretchers had made them self-conscious and embarrassed, as if something more serious should have happened to them.

On their way back to Santa Fe, they drove past the scene of the accident, where only two cars and the tire-marks on the asphalt remained as evidence. The children, still reacting to the shock and to the presence of fear in their parents, were gripped by their own imaginations; Emily, fingering the cut on her lower lip, wondered if she would be scarred for life; Toby, with a scratch on his forehead and a swollen, blackening eye, prepared himself to lose the eye itself.

It was not until his mother was putting him to bed, and he said: "Can't we go home tomorrow?" that the fear cracked and a feeling of relief broke over all of them. Even Mary laughed, a little hysterically. The idea of their own home, secure, comfortable, belonging to them alone, dissipated the effects of the accident, bringing them all closer together. The outside world, the world of roads and cars and other people, the world that had threatened and struck at them, retreated a little.

When Robert and Mary went to bed, they made love—by unspoken, mutual agreement—with a kind of fury that more than equalled the force of the fear they had felt earlier. Something primitive was aroused in an attempt to obliterate their experience, for even if they had not been directly involved (neither of them had been injured) they had been inside the periphery of death's reach that night.

When her husband had gone to sleep, Mary lay awake beside him, in the grip of an alarm that she could not defeat. The idea of death refused to retreat from her mind now; what she had learned, what she could not forget, what would threaten her for the rest of her life, was that death…the personal death of herself and her family was inevitable and unavoidable. It would remain, in the same way that it now seemed to hover over her, like an extra presence in her family, waiting patiently and tirelessly for a victim.

19

ALTHOUGH HE HAD THOUGHT, AT least for a moment, that he was certain to be killed, when he knew that he was alive, was not—miraculously enough—even seriously injured, Stephen Williams did not feel any better. The accident had not been his fault. It had been the fault of the woman who had tried to pass the truck coming up the hill and of the car ahead of him that had been going so fast. Of course, he'd been driving pretty fast himself and if he had been less frightened, he might have stopped his car in time...

He felt that the accident had been a deliberate act against him; that the world, once more, was striking at him viciously. Why? What had he done to deserve this? Why was it that his life seemed destined for calamity? Everything had failed him; he was alone in a forbidding, friendless land, in a hospital where they did not take him very seriously—how could they know, really, after so superficial an examination, that he was not on the brink of death?—where he had nothing, where no one cared about him.

Weakened by the shock, the fear and the pain, he began to cry. If there was only someone or something in the world...

He thought of the apartment in New York, saw it clearly in his mind, saw Marjorie's face, and what had been so repellent and distasteful to him so recently reached out and beckoned to him. What was he doing here? If he had not left, senselessly, this would never have happened to him.

For a moment his tears redoubled and then he sat up in bed, wiped his eyes, and looked around for a nurse. There must be a telephone somewhere in the hospital. If he could just talk to her—maybe she would even be able to fly out—everything would be all right. He knew that she would take care of him, see that he got to a good doctor, nurse him. Just the thought of her voice on the telephone comforted him a little. And she did love him. Her letter proved that. He hadn't been very fair to her, he guessed, even if she had deserved being left alone for a while.

20

It was almost two a.m. on Tuesday, the 13th of November, when Marjorie Williams heard the telephone ringing. When she had hung up, having heard Steve's voice, having been assured that he was—probably—all right, she shivered, but it was more from pleasure than from cold. She was worried about him…yes. But most of all, she knew that he needed her, and wanted her to come to him. She had told him she would fly out, and she had known from his tone of voice, although he had protested faintly, that that was what he had wanted.

Busily composing in her head, she picked up the telephone again. She would have to send a telegram to her office, she would have to get a ticket on the first plane, she would have to pack. She wouldn't get any more sleep that night, but it did not matter in the least. Already, in her mind, he was back in the apartment, lying in bed, a bandage around his head and perhaps on his arm, smiling at her as she brought him a tray. Everything was going to be all right again…

21

THE TRUCK-DRIVER AND THE POLICEMAN were the last to leave La Bajada Hill. For the truck-driver, it meant another day lost, accident reports, interviews with insurance company investigators, trouble with the company probably, a possible black mark against him, failure to meet his schedule and his quota...a real headache. And all because the woman in the Mercury had tried to pass him. People were God-damned fools.

For the policeman, it was one more accident in an unending series, distinguished only by the number of cars involved. Everyone had been identified, finally; all the reports were made up; it could have been worse. He looked at his watch as he drove the truck-driver back towards town. He still had one hour on duty and he wondered what else would happen that night to keep him from getting home on time.

22

"I WOULD HAVE CALLED YOU earlier," Doris Hart said, when she had given him a rapid resume of what had happened, "but Dr. Fenton didn't want me to, and then," she gave the doctor a meaningful look, "he told me to call you and just left. Almost an hour ago. Not that it's up to me to judge…"

Doctor Morales raised his hand a very little, smiled at her, and said: "Shall we go up to see the patients, Mrs. Hart? I know that you and Dr. Fenton have done everything for them and you must be very tired, but I would appreciate it if you would come along with me."

In the elevator, he looked at her again with that same gentle smile. "Dr. Fenton is very tired, very overworked," he said. "He takes it all so much to heart…and now with his boy in the war…" he shook his head and sighed, motioning her out of the elevator as it stopped.

When they came downstairs again, he sat down at the desk in the emergency room, looked over the accident reports, and decided he would have to stay the night. Mrs. Franklin would probably give some sort of trouble before the night was over; the Williams man might be difficult; but it was because of Mrs. Simms and Curran that he had decided to stay. Except for the serious loss of blood, Mrs. Simms looked as if she would come through. He was not at all sure about Curran.

He got up from the chair at the desk. "I think I'll go to my office and lie down," he said. "Have me called, of course, if anything comes up, and in any case…" he looked at his watch, "I'd better have a look at Mrs. Simms and that Mr. Curran in an hour or so. What about you? Can't anyone relieve you for a while, Mrs. Hart?"

She smiled defensively. "I'll be perfectly all right, Dr. Morales. After all, it's my job to stay on duty."

He looked at her before starting towards the door. "You are very faithful, Mrs. Hart," he said. "There are not so many of us who are so…" that same smile again, "devoted to our duty. Still, try to get a nap. It's been a difficult evening for you."

Dr. Fenton, Mrs. Hart, the nurses, the supervisors, the orderlies, the interns, all the personalities that went to make up the staff of the hospital…Dr. Morales thought about them one by one as he lay on the couch in his office. In their way, they were all doing their best; they were all making an effort. It was not always, in fact it was hardly ever, good enough; and the mistakes they sometimes made were often the difference between life and death. Still, it was already a great deal. For most of them, he knew, it was a thankless, underpaid job; a career that had been selected for any one of a great number of reasons: because of some misguided feeling of wanting to help (the impulse was rarely one of genuine unselfishness); because of a compulsion to deal with the sick and the dying. It didn't matter. The amount of suffering and labor that had gone into the building of the hospital, the number of lives that had been saved, repaired, helped…it was more than enough, and at the same time it could never be sufficient. There would never be an end to the struggle, the demands, the work.

He glanced at his watch again and closed his eyes. He was very tired and tomorrow would be another hard day. But he was very glad, as he had been so many times in his life, that he was a doctor.

23

Back at home, Dr. Fenton could not sleep. He wondered how long he would continue to be able to bear his own existence. There was no catching up, no reward, ever. For every child brought into the world, for every life wrested from death, for every successful operation, there was an equivalent failure, almost always for some stupid reason. What was the use of any of it?

He pictured Morales—probably at the hospital now—going from bed to bed, smiling that infuriating smile of his, while all the time, behind his mask, he would be making criticisms and judgments about the cases; noting his—Fenton's—failures, wooing the hospital staff with his winning ways. It was bad enough to have to be on duty so often, but to have, in addition, to compete with the oily manners of someone who was only a damned Mexican!

He turned over in his bed and buried his face in the pillow. If it wasn't for his age, for the money, he'd quit the whole thing, but it was too late for that now.

24

Every trace of the accident had been washed away from the emergency room. Doris Hart sat at her desk, the desk where Dr. Morales had so recently sat for a moment, straightened the papers, lighted a cigarette, and looked at the clock. Her night was half over.

She could not get the image of Dr. Morales out of her mind. Whenever he came into the hospital, something seemed to happen. Tonight, for instance, as soon as she had seen him, she had known everything would be all right. He brought an atmosphere of competence and certainty with him; it made her feel safe and relieved of an enormous burden of responsibility. Just the way he smiled at her was enough to make her feel that she did not have to worry any more. She contrasted him, briefly and favorably, with the other doctors in the hospital and with Dr. Cramwell. If any of them had his understanding, his patience, his dedication...

She wondered what it would be like to be married to a man like that, and the thought of marriage made her think of Donald. Except for a little while every evening, she would not see him again until Saturday and Sunday. She pictured herself getting home: the dirty dishes on the kitchen table, perhaps a note from him. And the bedroom with the unmade bed and his pajamas lying on the chair.

What was it that Dr. Cramwell had written? "Psychological problems?" "Primeval female sexual manifestations?" It was all a lot of nonsense. And why was she spending ten hard-earned dollars an hour to go to him? The truth of it was very simple, suddenly, and it was ridiculous that she had not seen it before. She had wanted someone to talk to, to eat with, to sleep with, and when she and Donald had gravitated towards each other, it had seemed good enough for both of them. What else, after all, was marriage?

What had taken her to Cramwell in the first place? Had she expected a miraculous movie romance? As for neuroses, compulsions and all the rest of it...big words for little problems. What, finally, was so bad about her marriage? Donald was good enough company when they were together; he had never minded that she wasn't beautiful, he was considerate in many ways even if he didn't make the bed or wash the dishes in the morning.

She thought of her husband with curious, unexpected tenderness. If she stopped going to Dr. Cramwell, he'd be able to afford a new suit, and she might, eventually, be able to buy a television set.

NOVEMBER 18, 1951

1

SITTING IN THE TRAIN BESIDE his wife, Stephen Williams was embarrassed and unhappy. They would be back in New York in a few hours now, back on Seventeenth Street, back in the life which he had tried to escape so blindly such a short time before. Nothing had changed for either of them in that time except that they had spent all their savings. All they had now was the insurance money from the car.

He looked at Marjorie, who gave him a bright, encouraging smile, and then looked out of the window of the train at the Hudson River. She had taken good care of him, had dealt with the insurance people, the police and the hospital, bought the tickets back...everything. She had not blamed him, there had been no recriminations...yet.

He felt her hand on his, and then he heard her voice. "It will be good to be back home again, dear," she said. "And it's so wonderful that you're really all right. In a week you won't know that anything happened."

He saw the apartment in his mind: the double bed, the dirty bathroom, the dust, the grime on the window sills. He saw himself looking for a job. He wished, guiltily, that he had been seriously injured, had lost a leg, or been blinded. But she was right...nothing had happened. He forced himself to smile at her, and swallowed hard. "That's right," he said. "And it will be good to be home."

She smiled comfortably, and then it came, as he knew it would: "Running away like that," she said happily. "Just like a little boy."

⌒

The pain had seemed to be unendingly unendurable. He had felt it all week even through the heavy doses of sedatives he had been given. It was not until Saturday, the 17th, through the half-delirium of the drugs, that he conceived the idea that he was being punished and that there was only one way out, one escape. He demanded to see the police; there was something he had to tell them. They would not take him seriously at first, but he had caused such an uproar on the ward that the nurse had sent for the doctor—the Spanish one— who had finally sent for the police.

Although he made his actual confession—haltingly, but in great detail—to the policeman, he was mostly aware of the grave, penetrating look on the face of Dr. Morales, standing at the foot of the bed, listening without comment. When he had finished, the doctor and the policeman exchanged a look and started for the door. Jim Curran heard the conversation, or part of it. "I guess he did it all right. How bad is he?" No reply from the doctor, but Curran could imagine the gesture he had made. "Can you save him?" There was a long pause before the doctor said, slowly: "I can try. I can't guarantee anything."

The doctor returned a little later. He smiled at Curran, sat down in a chair beside the bed, and the smile disappeared. "You don't have very much to live for, do you?"

Jim did not reply, but only stared at him fixedly.

"Would you like to see a priest?"

He shook his head.

The pain, temporarily relieved after the confession, started up again with renewed intensity. It did not really stop until just a few minutes before he died.

There were traces of Henry everywhere. Mabel had worked automatically, mechanically for three days, getting his clothes together, sorting his papers, writing notes, acknowledging cards and flowers; it was almost over now. Pausing, as she passed the bedroom window overlooking the lake, she looked out at the cold blue water. She could remember the way Henry had liked to sit there, in that particular window, lifting his eyes occasionally to look out. Even when the clothes had been sold or given away, when every trace of him had been obliterated, he would still be here to plague her through her memories.

The coldness of the water seemed to surround her. He had been such a little, uninteresting, unimaginative man; a man she had had to take care of all her life. Without her he would never have accomplished anything; would never have made any money, never have had an apartment like this; never have had a Cadillac. She remembered, it was hardly ever out of her mind, the look he had given her in the car after the accident. There was no doubt about it, he had wanted to die.

She turned away from the window with the tears—tears of anger and bitterness—leaping to her eyes. How had he dared to do this to her, to leave her like this? What was she going to do?

"Darling, I love you so much."

She said the words—as she had said them so many times in the last few days—more to reassure herself than to make a declaration to him. She knew, not with her mind but only with her instincts, the way he defended himself against her affection and wriggled in the net of sex and money that she had wound around him. The words, automatic and compulsive, forced him into a corner where he would have to say something, make some reply.

He moved away from her, turning in the bed at the sound of the words, and finally he said, quelling his own resistance, "I know you do, Carrie," and then, reluctantly and dutifully, he kissed her. "Good night, dear."

She took him in her arms as he kissed her and she did not let him go. "You never say you love me, Tom. Never." He almost stopped breathing for a moment. He had a sudden impulse to tell her that he did not love her, that he wanted to be left alone, that he wanted to go away, and he knew that whatever he said at this moment would be decisive; that this was the moment in which he would have to accept or reject her. The money in the wallet in his trousers hanging on the chair, the car, the promise of security for as long as he would want it... all the possibilities loomed up before him like spectres, luring him to accept her. And after a while, his mind argued, she would calm down, her demands would cease.

"Of course I love you, Carrie. I just don't talk much, that's all. You know that don't you?"

He heard his own words, felt the grateful acceptance in her body, and shuddered inwardly at the lie. He saw the pattern ahead of him, the travelling, the love-making, the spending of money, and at the end of it, inevitably, the break-up; the day would come—as surely as death itself—when he would not be able to go on with this.

Feeling her hands again, rousing him hungrily, picking at his body insistently, he smothered a sigh and responded slowly waiting for the moment when he would be caught up in physical passion again. After all, it was not so high a price, and it would not—at least he knew that much—have to last forever. The blood began to surge through his body then and he kissed her viciously, punishing her and himself with the bittersweet violence of his desire: automatic, animal-like, and irresistible.

Dick had been wonderful all week. And as she had felt herself coming back to life, her self-confidence renewed by his constant, strengthening presence, she had known that the accident had shocked him out of his gloom and depression. She had *known* that everything was all right again.

Even so, as they drove into the yard and stopped the car, she felt a spasm of fear. Now that she was almost well again—now that they were back, faced with the same life they had had before, with nothing essentially changed—what was going to happen? Would the effects of the shock wear off, letting him back into the emotional abyss from which it had—at least temporarily—released him? If he had, in some way, found himself—themselves—only because of the accident, what guarantee was there that the effect would last? She got out of the car carefully as he held the door open for her and held her arm, and she was unable to repress a faint sigh.

He looked at her, alarmed. "What's the matter, darling? Do you feel all right?"

She was touched, very deeply, by the look on his face, the concern in his voice, and she smiled and shook her head. "No, it's all right. I'm just a little unsteady, that's all."

When she walked into the living room, everything was as she had last seen it; everything except one thing—the drooping, dead flowers in the vase on the table in front of the window. He was standing beside her, and followed her eyes as she stared at them for a moment. "I'd better throw those out, I guess," he said.

She turned her head to look at him. "Where did they come from, Dick?"

His face reddened and he looked away from her. "Oh," he said casually, "I bought them last Monday. I'd sort of thought you might get home for dinner that night."

"Last Monday? You mean the day of the...the day I went to Albuquerque?"

He looked at her and nodded, and she sat down very suddenly.

He knew what she thought at that moment, and he knew that it was both true and untrue. The accident had not altered or solved anything, but the shock—and as he saw it again, the scar on her forehead made the original shock echo through him once more—had rearranged something inside him. He took the flowers into the kitchen and out the back door and threw them in the trash can. As he stood in the open doorway and looked at the guest house, he was reminded of Jim Curran. What curious and sinister fate had led him to this house, to the hideous crimes he had committed, and finally to the almost unbelievable coincidence of running into Dorothy on the hill?

There was no answer to any of that...any more than there was an answer to the inscrutable inner workings which had led them through this whole experience in which the accident seemed only the final culmination in a pattern which had been set at the beginning of his own depression.

He closed the door and walked back into the living-room where Dorothy was still sitting. They were still the same people, they were alive, they were together; the same happiness and torment lay ahead of them. No, nothing had changed, but the dismal cloud through which they had made their way blindly, had come to an end.

He put his hand on her shoulder and looked out of the window at the beginning sunset. How beautifully the day was dying, and at the same moment, how inevitably it was bringing them closer to their own end. The intermixture of sadness and joy he felt gripped at his heart; whatever man's destiny or his role in the world, in whatever way such questions might harass and torment him, he was profoundly and inextricably involved in some great, eternal process. Life, too, was inevitable.

⌣

The house was warm, the smell of the roast in the oven trickled through into the living-room, and Mary Hume lighted the lamps one by one. Bob was sitting in his study, getting ready to go back to work the next day, the children were still outside, playing. She wondered why they had ever decided to go away from here in the first place. If Bob hadn't had to give up his summer vacation that year; if the children had not been in a progressive school that did not disapprove too much of skipping a month of the school year; if she herself had not been fed up with the daily routine of housework and cooking, they would never have gone away.

She went back into the kitchen, looked at the roast, and decided it was time to call the children. All week, as they had been on their way home; even after they had arrived, and during the unpacking, the house-cleaning, she had remembered the night of the accident, still fearing it, still aghast at the chance that had, miraculously, placed them just one car back. But tonight, for the first time, the memory did not frighten her any more. With the sounds, the smells, the familiarity of the house, the sense of herself and her family at last back in the place where they belonged, there was nothing for her to fear any more. Whatever had almost happened to them, had not happened. Life was resumed. They were safe.

It was all over now. Although the sun was shining this morning, it had snowed on the fresh earth over his father's body the night before, so that the mound was indistinguishable from the other graves.

Because he had been held up by bad weather, (the plane had been grounded in Kansas City) and had not arrived until the 14th, he had not been there to see his father die. He had been only a few hours too late. But he had known from the look on his face, how his father had died; he had not needed Mrs. Jones' reassurances.

And now what? Standing in the fresh snow, brilliant in the morning sunlight, he went over in his mind, the time since he had left here, only ten days before. His destination, in spite of the direction in which he had started, had been here all the time. The journey, a journey that from the beginning had been made under the shadow of death, was over; another voyage was about to start. He knew that he would go out again—back to Albuquerque where he had left his car and where he would have to see the police, and from there on to California—but this time there was a difference. This time he was taking with him the final inheritance of his father, going out—with that added equipment—to the next beginning of his own life.

He walked slowly back to the house through the winter sunlight and the bare trees. In only a few months' time, the snow would have disappeared, to be replaced by leaves and blossoms, rain, heat, productivity, growth. There was no doubt about himself in his mind now; the seeds of his discontent, affirmed by death, sown in the winter soil of his being, had already taken root. There was nothing, any longer, to hold him back—to keep him from embarking on his own final journey through life. He paused to look back at the cemetery for the last time. It was the house of the dead, but he had come out of it enriched by the legacy of his father's life. The big tree, stricken by age, had fallen; the shadow it had cast, protective and sometimes dark, now gave way to the sky, the wind, the rain and the sunlight...and the smaller tree it had shaded for so long.

AFTERWORD

By Alexandra Carbone, Managing Editor of
The Fritz Peters Collection

Documentarian of *On the Fritz*

WHY FRITZ? WHY NOW?

Because stories are not book reports. They are concentrated potions of experience. A quality story induces catharsis and understanding—a way to get more life out of life, to gain a wider view. Like Fritz Peters' *Boyhood with Gurdjieff,* our point of departure.

When we read the memoir years ago, we wanted to see Fritz mow lawns and make trouble on the big screen. Seeking out his other works, we discovered deeply personal stories about compelling times and places. The complex characters and paradoxical truths jump off the page and walk with the reader. We found classics – ahead of their time and falling out of print – so we embarked on a mission at Vanitas Vanitatum to republish Fritz Peters' books, to make a documentary about him, and to adapt his books into movies. What you hold in your hands is the first step.

Life And Work

The themes seem disparate, but they coalesce in one person. Mental illness. Homosexuality. Spirituality. Military service. Death drive.

Nonconformism. The war of the sexes. The self and society. Work. Fritz wrote about them because he knew them; in fact, could not escape them, had something he had to say about them, something to get off his chest. The books are highly personal, highly autobiographical. Multiple friends of his reported that "He only wrote when he had a book in him," and when he did the writing would come out in a mad rush, "sometimes in only a couple weeks."

Fritz lived from 1913-1979. Born in Wisconsin, he spent much of his turbulent youth in France, interacting with remarkable people operating at a frontier of human experience. People like his mentor and father figure, G.I. Gurdjieff, and his aunt, Margaret Anderson—plus the gaggle of avant-garde greats in her milieu. Fritz learned that words and thoughts were a path to social standing and self-respect. "He was brilliant, talented. He hung out with e.e. cummings and D.H. Lawrence. He enjoyed the fame he got, but I think he wanted to be a big star," said his daughter, Katharine Rivers.

It is difficult to define a person, even in hindsight, since people are developing stories. But by midlife, Fritz's best writing was behind him. His memoirs *Boyhood with Gurdjieff (1964)*, and *Gurdjieff Remembered (1965)*, are the exception. His literary career after *The Descent (1952)* mostly amounted to rejected manuscripts and burned bridges. In the mid-1960s, a reader at Farrar Straus scrawled, "I doubt that the manuscript will get anywhere—it is so obviously [close to/or] psychotic. The poor bastard has had (and has given others) an awful life. I am not hopeful that anything will result."

Succumbing To His Demons

"He had a death wish, he was drinking himself to death," said Fritz's friend, psychologist Barbara Vacarr, of his last decade of life. Cirrhosis was noted on his death certificate. At the close of World War II, his mentor, mystic and healer G. I. Gurdjieff, recognized the delicacy of Fritz's condition and recommended that he drink, but "consciously"...

> He insisted that I had such a need, but that it was periodic, and predicted that if I gauged the need properly I would go through periods where I would drink—or would need to drink—a good deal, and also sometimes through long periods when I would not need to drink at all; in fact, at such times, I would find that liquor might even be harmful for me.[1]

Gurdjieff implies that alcohol was a way to modulate Fritz's erratic moods, and probably anesthetize painful memories, but finding the prescribed balance proved perilous.

Mental illness has a nature and nurture component, both at play in Fritz's development. His childhood amounted to mitigated orphanhood due to his parents' divorce and his mother's nervous breakdowns. His mother remarried multiple times, selecting husbands who were not safe or did not want Fritz and his brother Tom present. Fritz preferred the care of Margaret Anderson, his maternal aunt, and her partner Jane Heap—largely so he could live at Gurdjieff's Institute. However, there were skeletons in that closet. This graphic episode that Fritz recounted in 1978 occurred when he was 11 years old. His disconnected, almost blasé attitude about it makes one wonder what other horrors he experienced:

> The final so-called disaster occurred when Jane [Heap], in a fit of anger...struck me with a board from a crate with nails in it.

1 Fritz Peters, *Gurdjieff Remembered* (Los Angeles: Hirsch Giovanni Publishing, 2021), 88.

Jane lost that one (or I won it, depending on how you look at it) because although the nails went all the way into my back and I was bleeding, I did not break down, cry, or otherwise participate in the scene. Jane was more than contrite, fell to her knees, hugged me, and begged for my forgiveness. I think that was the first time that my born 'rage to live' turned into active hatred. I told her that I would not only not forgive her—it was 'not my province' was one of the things that I said—but I told her that I would get even. I regret, in the long run, to have to admit that I did. On the same compulsive, unconscious, dreary level.[2]

His first novel, *The World Next Door (1949)*, shows how "succumbing to one's demons" in this manner, can be an oversimplification. As the novel unfolds in vivid stream-of-consciousness, we see that severe mental illness is not a sick spell that occurs in the context of a healthy mind, akin to a head cold. Instead, it is a state of confusion that overtakes a person who is a tenuous arrangement of wholeness; so, wholeness cannot be maintained over an extended stretch of life, with all its inherent hardships. Fritz explores the connection between alcohol and mental illness in this striking passage:

Only the liquor, a thin hot stream inside me, dripped like fuel to the last ember of warmth and light between my ribs, and fought the darkness. But there is another light beginning now: a light that does not warm, but reveals and distorts. In this light, pallor becomes sickness, and sickness, death. As the darkness itself had spread like the moving blotch of blood upon bright cloth, so this light penetrated the darkness.[3]

2 Fritz Peters, *Balanced Man* (London: Wildwood House, 1978), 62.

3 Fritz Peters, *The World Next Door* (Los Angeles: Hirsch Giovanni Publishing, 2021), 10.

When Fritz lost control of his mental state, on an extreme of what was then called manic depression, there would be no "Fritz" there to manage the alcohol, or moods, or work, or parenting, or other relationships. He would not know he was so compromised, and often neither would those closest to him. *Fig. 1* summarizes the periods of instability during Fritz's most productive decade of writing, much of which became fuel for his fiction. He recuperated in a mental hospital after his breakdown in 1958, during which he stared into the sun and claimed to be the second coming, just like the protagonist in *The World Next Door (see Fig 2)*. Forced to admit Fritz would never be a safe caretaker to their children, Jean Peters initiated divorce proceedings.

Fritz's ability to inhabit healthy and imbalanced states and communicate them to readers is one of his most illuminating transmissions—one for which he paid dearly. It would be an understatement to say that Fritz was a difficult person to live with and love. Though he was rarely single, his relationships were volatile and tended to end in explosions, if not mental breakdowns. This is perhaps why relationships—the ways in which they are doomed and the reasons they are inevitable—are what Fritz found most inspiring to write about. He distilled relationships into the heartbreaking truth that is the lifeblood of literature.

The World Next Door

The World Next Door is about a mental patient's relationship with himself, his medical staff, and his family. It examines everyone's interests and self-interest, as they scrap for dominance in the bureaucracy of a VA mental ward. Though highly autobiographical, it would be naive to take David Mitchell's words entirely at face value—he was, after all, suffering from paranoid delusions. Conversely, David Mitchell did not leave the VA Hospital against medical advice, whereas Fritz's former wife reports that he did *(see Fig. 1)*. Still, the novel speaks unflinchingly about how it feels to go through electroshock and other crude techniques of early psychiatry, about cruelty from overburdened attendants, about a post-war government institution that cared for some of its veterans (white, straight) better than others (black, gay).

In *The World Next Door*, the protagonist is conflicted about his homosexual inclinations. He claims not to prefer the company of men—he does not, therefore, identify as homosexual. However, he asserts the naturalness of his homosexual relationship: "I was in love with him, that's all."[4] Societal context makes this stance understandable, yet revolutionary. This is because mental illness, discrimination, and homosexuality were linked in the context of a VA mental ward in the late 40s, much more deeply than today's reader might expect.

At the dawn of World War II, the U.S. military planned to cull any recruits at high risk for mental illness—prone to "shellshock," and costly disability payments. Psychiatry as a discipline was in its infancy, so the military added rounds of psychiatric testing to the physical screening process. After World War I, "The U.S. Government spent more than a billion dollars to treat mental casualties, and it was widely recognized that the government had a responsibility to avoid a huge loss of men and money in the next war."[5]

In 1941, the category of "Homosexual proclivities" was specifically identified as a form of mental illness incompatible with military

---

4 Peters, *The World Next Door*, 190.

5 Naoko Wake, "The Military, Psychiatry, and 'Unfit' Soldiers, 1939-1942," *Journal of the History of Medicine and Allied Sciences* 62, no. 4 (January 4, 2007): 466, https://doi.org/10.1093/jhmas/jrm002.

Fig. 1

His periods of disturbance (or, as we referred to them, his "manic"
periods) are repetitive and cyclic. As far as I have been able to
determine, after talking to his mother,(his former wife and a very
close friend of his, the following disturbed periods occurred:

1945   two hospitalizations in Army hospital in France

1947   committed to Lyons VA Hospital in N.J. for 3 months, released
       "against medical advice".

1950   suicide attempt and subsequent hospitalization in Clinton, N.Y.,
       after manic period of 3-4 months.

1953   automobile accident and hospitalizationfollowing manic period
       lasting from February to October.

1954   severe automobile accident after manic period of 1-2 months,
       around early summer.

1955   beginning period in May that decreased following our marriage
       in June.

1956   brief, but intense period following birth of our daughter
       in April, and another brief and not too intense period in
       August-September.

1957   June to November period, very intense in August then in October.

1958   December to February 9th commitment. Acute.

Fig. 2

Then, on January 17th, we moved. That morning he was completely
irrational and unreasonable. Any differing of even trivial opinion
caused a vinlent reaction from him. He took off his glasses and
"looked into the sun"---which is indicative of the degree of his
disturbance. (As described in World Next Door, in fact this was
just like the book). His talking was incessant and highly erratic,
but, as always, maintaining a certain logic, i.e., he would, after
many and lengthy digressions, always return to his original point.
During this time he spoke of his being the second coming of Christ,
of going to the sun, etc.

Excerpts From a letter from Fritz's wife, Jean R. Peters to his Psychologist, Dr. St. Pierre,
at the VA Hospital in Topeka Kansas, in 1958

(Fig. 1) We see how Fritz struggled with instability even in his most successful decade of
writing. Elements from his novels are present, such as the suicide attempt in *Finistère
(1951)*, and the car crash in *The Descent (1952)*.

(Fig. 2) *The World Next Door (1949)* is more directly autobiographical, as his wife Jean
attested in further notes about his 1958 breakdown.

service by the advisory board to the military psychiatrists running the screening process. Homosexual behavior was deemed a form of sexual deviancy and a pre-psychotic state.[6] Many recruits with homosexual proclivities desired to join the war effort, however, and managed to avoid detection.

At the end of World War II, the U.S. Military hunted down and dishonorably discharged these homosexual soldiers. Gay servicemen found guilty of sodomy were incarcerated, as it was illegal, and lesbian soldiers were also targeted. A dishonorable discharge rendered these soldiers ineligible for benefits, and they suffered sometimes serious indignities in the process. At worst, they were held in impromptu brigs, in prisoner-of-war conditions, possibly sexually assaulted, even, by their own captors.[7] This phenomenon is echoed in *The World Next Door* when David Mitchell has an experience of being sexually coerced by an attendant in the VA hospital. For those homosexual soldiers lucky enough to be stationed where the U.S. Army ejected them under less inhumane conditions, the outcome was still damaging. A diagnosis would be placed on the gay soldier's discharge papers which could out them as homosexual.

If a diagnosis was listed on the discharge papers, the soldiers would be associated with a mental illness that sounded severe. "Psychotic personality" was one such label.[8] Anyone looking at their records could see the reason for their discharge—such as potential employers who requested military records for job applications. Homosexuals who managed to be hired were not secure in their offices, either.

6 Wake, "The Military, Psychiatry, and 'Unfit' Soldiers, 1939-1942," 476.

7 For first-hand accounts of this see *Coming Out Under Fire*, directed by Arthur Dong (1994; New York: Deep Focus Productions, Inc).

8 Wake, "The Military, Psychiatry, and 'Unfit' Soldiers, 1939-1942," 485.

Thousands of homosexual employees were purged from Federal positions during the Lavender Scare of McCarthyism, under discriminatory practices which persisted in the following decades.[9]

It is difficult to know how these policies affected Fritz during his short stint in the military, since he was justifiably mentally ill enough to be hospitalized and was honorably discharged. This context explains, however, why the medical staff was aware of David Mitchell's gay relationship in *The World Next Door*, and why the flirtation with the gay General was such a delicate matter. It explains why it was so difficult for Fritz and doctors to separate his sexuality from his mental illness. It also explains the stakes of going straight, and how confusing the situation must have been for a man with homosexual leanings, and manic depression, who was also attracted to women. A post-war reader would know this background, and perceive the hidden currents it creates in the storyline.

On the psychiatric side, as Fritz describes in *The World Next Door*, homosexuals tended to be well-behaved patients and many doctors treated them sympathetically; doctors had bigger problems on a mental ward. However, sympathy has its limits in the context of the pathologization of one's sexuality. Homosexuals of the time had difficulty navigating their mental health problems, especially if they refused to renounce their sexuality. Ed Field had such an experience with a doctor "who immediately decided that my homosexuality was at the root of all my miseries, and set out to change me."[10]

9 Suyin Haynes, "You've Probably Heard of the Red Scare, but the Lesser-Known, Anti-Gay 'Lavender Scare' Is Rarely Taught in Schools," *TIME* magazine, December 22, 2020, https://time.com/5922679/lavender-scare-history/.

10 Edward Field, afterword to *Finistère*, by Fritz Peters (Vancouver: Arsenal Pulp Press, 2006), 333-34.

Homosexuality would not be completely de-pathologized, removed from the Diagnostic Statistician's Manual (along with any loophole that enabled billing insurance for conversion therapy), until "ego-dystonic homosexuality" was removed in 1987.[11] This was after years of gay activism and vitriolic national debates. It would be three more decades before homosexuals earned an uncloseted place in the military, in 2011. Accordingly, Fritz's first-hand account of attitudes towards homosexuality, and the realities of homosexual soldiers on the VA mental ward, in post-war America, is compelling reportage relevant to both U.S. and Queer history.

The World Next Door impressed the medical community in 1949 and was carried in psychiatric libraries. They valued it because it was a unique first-hand account of what a severely ill patient experiences on a mental ward. Timely and bold, it also struck a nerve with post-war readers. "Not so much composed as forced out of the writer by the need to put down a terrible experience while still raw and quivering from its impact," wrote Antonia White, in *New Statesman*. With its experimental treatment of such gritty subject matter, Peters' autobiographical novel was critically well-received on the literary front and Fritz was lauded as a young writer to watch.

Finistère

"I loved *Finistère* because it was a beautiful love story. It showed Fritz's tenderness and the connection at the place where you could see his soul," said Barbara Vacarr.

Finistère, published only two years after *The World Next Door*, is a

---

11 Jack Drescher, "Out of DSM: Depathologizing Homosexuality," *Behavioral Sciences (Basel)* 5, no. 4 (December 4, 2015), Page 565, https://www.ncbi.nlm.nih.gov/pmc/articles/PMC4695779/.

coming-of-age, coming-out story about a teen's love affair with the tennis coach at his French boarding school. It is Fritz Peters' most successful book, still relevant today as a landmark novel of queer literature. So much ground has been won for queer rights over the past century, and so many aspects of gender have been redefined, that the current mood is to be reflective about the past while envisioning the future. *Finistère*'s themes of confusion, isolation, and self-destruction in the face of intolerance are, sadly, still applicable to queer teens today. But *Finistère* also celebrates love's ability to blossom where it is required, and it portrays love as an instinctive tropism toward healing and hope. It is thus a pioneering gay paean as much as it is a classic romance relevant to anyone who loves.

Finistère would not be art if it did not ask difficult questions and reveal uncomfortable truths. Today's readers are, hopefully, dismayed that the lovers in *Finistère* are so far apart in age. Michel is in his late 20s, and Matthew is only a teen. Upon opening the book to read, this writer was concerned the material might be handled inappropriately. Closing the book, those concerns were allayed. *Finistère*, with all its controversial aspects, provides valuable insight into the field of human experience.

It is perhaps unavoidable to compare *Finistère* to Nabokov's *Lolita*. *Lolita* is also a classic, adapted to film amid controversy. Readers find its age gap scandalous. However, Humbert Humbert, the narrator of *Lolita*, has a predilection for young ladies and premeditatively targets girls without remorse. He marries Lolita's mother to get closer to the object of his desire. Humbert is, simply put, a pedophile. On the contrary, Michel is a gay man who is uncomfortable with older/younger affairs, even though they were accepted by his peers in 1920s Paris. Michel broke with his long-term lover when the latter engaged in an encounter with an adolescent, the last straw after multiple infidelities. Heartbroken and disgusted, Michel accepts a teaching position that his father arranges. Michel is relieved to escape the excesses of Paris and has abandoned all hope for love. Suppressing his sexual impulses entirely—"vows of chastity, purity, reform"[12]— seems the best course of action. Matthew, though younger, initiates and directs the affair. Such details mitigate Michel's questionable behavior as much as possible. Many readers will likely react with moral disgust anyway, condemning Michel, opining that as the superior, Michel should have drawn a line—should not have engaged in any physical encounter with a student. Michel could have waited, they might say, if the two really loved each other. That perspective is valid.

However, relationships like Matthew and Michel's happen, and they happen for a reason. *Finistère* faces this reality. Why did it happen in this case? Why was it doomed? Does that mean such relationships are always doomed? Would Matthew have survived to adulthood with nobody to love him? If Michel had loved Matthew better, would their affair still have ended in tragedy? Was it possible for Michel to love Matthew better? What family and societal contexts contributed to the outcome? How would you feel if you read it as a teenager? Would you feel differently if you read it as a parent? Have you ever done anything unwise for love? Saying Michel should have drawn a line is like saying Othello should have ignored Iago. Pondering controversial situations in stories develops wisdom and compassion, fostering better decisions in the real world. That has always been the utility of tragedy.

Finistère feels too closely observed to be invented, but due to the covert nature of the relationship, it is unclear to whom it refers. Even the dedication to the novel is an enigma: "For A.P.S. and L.S.B.S 1900-1950." Enigma invites conjecture. It is the only dedication Fritz

12 Fritz Peters, *Finistère*, (Los Angeles: Hirsch Giovanni Publishing, 2021), 146.

writes that does not use full names. A person born in 1900 would be thirteen years older than Fritz (born Arthur Peters), roughly the age gap in the novel. A person who died in 1950 would have passed while Fritz was writing *Finistère*. Fritz attended boarding school in France for short periods of time, though he never graduated high school nor worked as a teacher.

When Fritz wrote *Finistère* he was in his late thirties and married to *Harper's Bazaar* fiction editor, Mary Lou Aswell. Fritz dedicated *The World Next Door* to Mary Lou, "without whom this book would not have been written." Aswell also had an interest in mental illness; she edited a book titled *The World Within (1947)*, shortly before meeting Fritz, which is a collection of "fiction illuminating the neuroses of our time." She fostered the careers of many homosexual writers in *Bazaar*'s pages, including Truman Capote. Ed Field, (Fritz's friend, gay poet and World War II veteran) reported that what Fritz wrote depended on the relationship he was in at the time, so it seems that Mary Lou was Fritz's most effective muse.

Aswell would go on to partner with sculptor Agnes Sims, her first same-sex lover, and Fritz dedicated his next novel, *The Descent*, to Agnes. The two women moved to Santa Fe, where their household was openly possible. One of the most affecting dynamics in *Finistère* is the impossibility for same-sex relationships to endure in a culture that is so intolerant of them. Although the current fashion bends toward feel-good LGBTQ stories, it is also important to understand the necessity of societal support to provide a framework for lasting relationships. In *Finistère* the "problem" was not the homosexuality, it was the intolerance. It is this perspective that made *Finistère* so pioneering. Threatened by Matthew's naivete, Michel remarks, "I suppose there's no reason why you should be able to understand that your happiness is something the world would think of as ugly and horrible and unnatural. But they do and I guess you'll learn soon enough."[13]

The *New York Times* review echoed this sentiment, saying "So far as this reviewer recalls, this is the best novel he has ever read on the theme of homosexuality (Proust excepted) and its tragic consequences in a world made up of 'selfish, ruthless, cruel, egocentric people.'"[14] Ed Field agreed: "*Finistère* is a marvelous book. It was the first gay novel I read, the rest were pulp."

The Descent

During the breakup of his marriage to Mary Lou, at the close of 1950, Fritz stood on the side of the highway interviewing motorists in upstate New York. He was working on his next novel, *The Descent*. If *Finistère* is a novel about why homosexual relationships cannot work, *The Descent* is a novel about why heterosexual relationships cannot work. We see couples poisoned by gender norms; the desire to dominate and be dominated poisoning Henry and Mabel, the cycle of lust and shame poisoning Caroline and Tom, the projections of male inadequacy poisoning Richard and Dorothy.

At the time Fritz operated in society as a heterosexual, but he always had male lovers. Fritz writes female characters remarkably well for a male writer, inhabiting them in a manner that only someone who has been an object of male desire can. He has an objective, almost anthropological eye to gender relations. Doris Hart, the hospital admin from *The Descent*, exemplifies this when she casts off the desire for validation from her patronizing, patriarchal psychologist. "What

13 Peters, *Finistère*, 155.

14 Herbert F. West, "Deep Water — And Black," *New York Times*, February 18, 1951, https://www.nytimes.com/1951/02/18/archives/deep-water-and-black.html.

was it that Dr. Cramwell had written? 'Psychological problems?' 'Primeval female sexual manifestations?' It was all a lot of nonsense. And why was she spending ten hard-earned dollars an hour to go to him?"[15]

Doris Hart's reverie continues on a slightly different track, "She thought of her husband with curious unexpected tenderness. If she stopped going to Dr. Cramwell, he'd be able to afford a new suit. And she might, eventually, be able to afford a television set." *The Descent* is also a portrait of post-war America and its hyperactive consumer-conformism, playing out in intimate relationships. This conformism was itself a veneer over societal divisions and war trauma—exemplified by the character of Jim Curran, the troubled war veteran. How can veterans relate to those who stayed home, and vice versa? How can men and women bridge the gender gap? Another return to normalcy. Do we all realize how normal it is to feel unfulfilled? What is the American Dream's answer to that? Where are we all going, so fast?

A tightly written suspense novel with a *Twilight Zone* feel, *The Descent* was well-received. However, Fritz could not know the turn his life was about to take. He would not publish again for twelve years. After finishing *The Descent*, Fritz fell into a long-term relationship with a man for the first time, Santa Fe-based painter Cady Wells. Fritz thought Cady was "the one," but it ended in volatile fights:

> Although Cady was enraptured with Fritz, his friends found Peters threatening and hateful, and he was a deeply disturbed man (he apparently once tried to kill Cady with a knife).

15 Fritz Peters, *The Descent* (Los Angeles: Hirsch Giovanni Publishing, 2021), 255.

Another of Peters' lovers, the painter William Brown, explained that each time Peters had a homosexual love affair he would rebound from it by marrying.[16]

Cady died soon after their split, of a heart attack, and Fritz headed into family life, marrying Jean. As *The Descent* foretold, and as already discussed, family life was not a good fit. After their divorce, Fritz moved to New York and finally found a stable relationship, by Fritz's standards, with painter Lloyd Goff. He seemed more at peace living as a gay man, according to his daughter. He sent money home for the children and kept in contact via frequent letters, phone calls, gifts, and occasional visits. He finally attempted writing again. His U.K. publisher, Victor Gollancz, encouraged him to write memoirs. Fritz published *Boyhood with Gurdjieff* in 1964, for which Henry Miller wrote the preface, saying "I regard it as something on a par with *Alice in Wonderland*, a real treasure of our literature."[17] Although it was a critical success followed by a sequel, *Gurdjieff Remembered* (1965), in terms of sales the memoirs found only a niche. *The World Next Door* was recorded for French radio and there were references, in Fritz's letters to Farrar Straus, to film deals that never solidified. He attempted writing novels again, and the rejections hit hard. He harangued Farrar Straus to republish his earlier novels or else revert the rights to him. Fritz was soon short on cash, began drinking more and more heavily and took on a seedy appearance. At the start of the 70s, Fritz headed back to Santa Fe, began a new novel, and published a final essay about Gurdjieff.

16 Lois P. Rudnick, "Under the Skin of New Mexico: The Life, Times, and Art of Cady Wells," in *Cady Wells and Southwestern Modernism*, ed. Lois P. Rudnick (Santa Fe: Museum of New Mexico Press, 2009), 71.

17 Henry Miller, preface to *Boyhood with Gurdjieff*, by Fritz Peters (Santa Barbara: Capra Press, 1980), Page ii.

Although Gurdjieff had died some 30 years earlier, Fritz spent his last days remembering the man and what they had meant to each other.

Gurdjieff — Father Figure And Guru

Gurdjieff had a powerful personality and a magnetic aura; it was easy for him to attract seekers to learn the esoteric wisdom he had accumulated. A mainstay of the philosophy at his *Institute for the Harmonious Development of Man* was that people go through life "asleep," so precious few develop themselves anywhere near their capacity. This is due to a failure to "do the work"—people lack the knowledge and focus to develop their various "centers." The "centers" are the Intellectual, Emotional, and Physical modes of being. These centers operate individually and together, creating new processes, requiring many types of "work" to exercise them all. Gurdjieff even called his teachings, "The Work." Confronting the real world, and all the obstacles one must overcome to finish a job, was one way to "wake up." This was chop-wood-carry-water spirituality, involving tasks like cooking, gardening, roofing, lawnmowing. Music and dance held a special role in the curriculum. Gurdjieff also employed flamboyant tricks, like pranks, to incite friction between people, launching them headfirst into healing crises. Dealing with the "unpleasant manifestations of others" leads to self-awareness and growth. Therefore, Gurdjieff appreciated Fritz's diligence, as much as his aptitude for mischief:

> Gurdjieff laughed, "What you not understand," he said, "is that not everyone can be troublemaker, like you. This important in life—is ingredient, like yeast for making bread. Without trouble, conflict, life become dead. People live in status quo, live only by habit, automatically, and without conscience. You good for Miss Madison. You irritate Miss Madison all time—more than

anyone else, which is why you get most reward. Without you, possibility for Miss Madison's conscience fall asleep.[18]

Putting Gurdjieff's practices in parable form is what Fritz achieves in *Boyhood with Gurdjeff*, in the direct style of Gurdjieff's teaching. As Gurdjieff's personal assistant, Fritz had an intimate view of the goings-on in the Institute. Gurdjieff appreciated Fritz's interest in philosophy and psychology, saying that Fritz was a "trash can" for Gurdjieff to "dump" his teaching into. What probably made Fritz so empty is that he had been abandoned by his family. He needed a trustworthy adult who could direct his curiosity and his stubborn streak. Fritz would never shake Gurdjieff's influence and would always work to digest it – Gurdjieff's ideas pervade Fritz's writing. Though Fritz read voraciously, he never finished high school nor attended college. Gurdjieff's Institute was his education, the stories he walked with and measured against. Michael Vacarr, Fritz's friend explained:

> Fritz said Gurdjieff saved his life. He was the only adult who made sense to him. Could Gurdjieff have saved his brother's life? I don't know. There was something Fritz brought to the situation with Gurdjieff that allowed Fritz to benefit from it. And Gurdjieff didn't let Fritz get lost in feeling sorry for himself.

Shortly before his death in 1949, Gurdjieff enacted an impactful prank-teaching, when he made an announcement at a gathering of students that Fritz attended. As Fritz recounts it, Gurdjieff said:

18 Fritz Peters, *Boyhood with Gurdjieff* (Los Angeles: Hirsch Giovanni Publishing, 2021), 170.

'In life is only necessary for man to find one person to whom can give accumulation of learning in life. When find such receptacle, then is possible die.' He smiled, benevolently, and went on: 'So now two good things happen for me. I finish work and I also find one person to whom can give results my life's work.' He raised his arm again, started to move it, this time with a finger extended and pointing, around the room, and then stopped when his finger was pointing directly at me. There was an enormous silence in the room and Gurdjieff and I looked at each other fixedly, but, even so, I was aware that one or two of the others had turned to look in my direction. The tension in the atmosphere did not lessen until Gurdjieff dropped his arm, turned, and left the room.[19]

Fritz would struggle with the mantle of chosen successor for the rest of his life. Gurdjieff's motivations for announcing this were mysterious, and Fritz thought of a few explanations. First, it might be "actually true." Second, it might be intended to "expose" Fritz's "massive ego" to himself—this was the preferred explanation of many Gurdjieff followers. Third, perhaps it was "a huge joke on the devout followers."

There is a special irony in selecting a person with a Messiah Complex to be one's "true successor." It is even possible Gurdjieff was making a joke at his own expense. Whatever the case, Fritz was "moved, confused, and perplexed" by the event.[20] Fritz would spend the rest of his days causing fuss and friction at Gurdjieff meetings and claiming to be the true successor, whether he truly believed it or not.

19 Peters, *Gurdjieff Remembered*, 90-91.

20 Peters, *Gurdjieff Remembered*, 93.

Why Fritz?

Fritz was more human than most. With internal and external experiences so extreme, he encountered the range of human experience in a way most people do not. There has always been a link between manic depression and creativity, perhaps because it is difficult to communicate peak experiences without resorting to art. In person Fritz could be charming, present, helpful, and funny—also irascible, inappropriate, inebriated, and exhausting. All of that is in his writing.

Given Fritz's extreme states, it is surprising that the real power of his writing is its startling clarity; the bullseyes of emotional truth he finds. "The shadows are the first to go," is the first line of *The World Next Door*—Fritz claimed e. e. cummings said it was "the best first sentence in the history of the English language."[21] Fritz's writing is true, and clear, and evocative; also, readable. Fritz desired "always to be known as a readable writer rather than a great artist."[22] There is something of Gurdjieff's teachings and character in the pragmatism, the immediacy, the uncompromising search for truth and self, that is at the heart of it.

But the biggest tragedy of mental instability, which Fritz captures in *The World Next Door*, is being unable to understand, or control, the way one hurts people. "Seeing ourselves how others see us," as Gurdjieff would put it—is a challenge for everyone, but especially for those with a tenuous grasp on "self." Even in his healthiest and happiest moments, Fritz spent his life in this exile. He wrote to us from the electroshock table, from the queer underground, from

21 Jane Madeline Gold, *Down from Above, Up from Below* (Rhinebeck: Epigraph Books, 2021), 25.

22 Richard H. Costa, "Author Pens Tale of Route 20," *Utica Observer-Dispatch*, December 10, 1950.

puberty, from the side of the road, from a marriage on its last leg, from the rubble of World War II, from Gurdjieff's intentional community. Fritz went there and reported back—that was his gift.

FRITZ PETERS

1913 – 1979

Born in Madison, Wisconsin, Arthur Anderson "Fritz" Peters was the author of both novels and memoirs, which touched on themes of spirituality, mental illness, homosexuality, self and society, always through the lens of an unrelenting individuality and nonconformism.

Peters' most successful novel was *Finistère*, published in 1951, which sold over 350,000 copies and was an influential and unapologetic work of early gay literature. Due to instability in his family life, Peters spent his childhood between Europe and the United States, often nurtured by those adults who were able and willing to assist.

Central to his upbringing was his aunt Margaret Anderson and her partner Jane Heap, creators of *The Little Review* literary magazine, along with other members of their circle, such as Gertrude Stein. Most notably, the esoteric teacher Georges Gurdjieff interacted closely with Fritz from an early age and was hugely influential in Peters' life and literature. *Boyhood with Gurdjieff*, Peters' most popular memoir, paints these figures and their projects in a thoughtful and intimate light.

About The Publisher

VANITAS VANITATUM
PUBLISHING
LOS ANGELES

Vanitas Vanitatum Publishing is the literary wing of Vanitas Vanitatum Entertainment – an L.A. based production company built on instinct, courage, and craft. It was founded in 2025 by Giovanni J. Guidotti, CEO of Giovanni Eco Chic Beauty.

The Fritz Peters Collection was originally republished in 2024 by Hirsch Giovanni Entertainment + Publishing, which was founded by Guidotti and Hollywood industry veteran David M. Hirsch.

www.ingramcontent.com/pod-product-compliance
Lightning Source LLC
Chambersburg PA
CBHW061654190726
48289CB00006B/1874